To Ken
— R. D. Hammond

THE FFLATLANDS

A Novel By

R. D. HAMMOND

ArcheBooks Publishing

THE PFLATLANDS

A Novel By

R. D. HAMMOND

Copyright 2006 by R. D. Hammond

ISBN: 1-59507-130-X

ArcheBooks Publishing Incorporated
www.archebooks.com

9101 W. Sahara Ave.
Suite 105-112
Las Vegas, NV 89117

All rights reserved, including the right to reproduce this book or portions thereof in any form whatsoever. For information about this book, please contact ArcheBooks at publisher@ArcheBooks.com.

This book is entirely a work of fiction. The names, characters, places, and incidents depicted herein are either products of the author's imagination or are used fictitiously. Any resemblance to actual events or locales or persons, living or dead, is entirely coincidental.

Hardcover First Edition: 2006

DEDICATION

To Sarah and Nikol (real-life toughwomen),
Doug and Jeff (real-life magicians),
and Thalia and Calliope (real-life muses)

THE PFLATLANDS

R. D. Hammond

PROLOGUE

Before Babylon, before the cavemen, even before the Earth as we know it was formed, a perfect realm came into being in a fiery and wondrous spectacle. This was a place where gods and goddesses cavorted with mortals on a daily basis...a place where chivalric knights and mystical wizards thwarted evil without fail...a place where tales of epic battles sprang from the excited lips of bards...a Golden World where life, as its inhabitants knew it, was heroic and pure beyond the capacity to describe.

This is obviously not where our story takes place.

Down and slightly to the left of this planet, however, lies an astronomical improbability. Blatantly spitting in the face of physics with its rectangular orbit, defiantly refusing to form a sphere like all the other good little planets, this abomination to common sense proves anything is possible by being everything that isn't.

These are the Pflatlands.

The Pflatlands are, not surprisingly, pflat.

The Pflatlands

The story of their creation still provokes bewildered stares throughout the known universe. It is a curious phenomenon among people of the Golden World to dedicate every accomplishment—even the most mundane—to their gods. On a typical day, getting out of bed took three hours and two types of prayer mats. Then, exhausted by their hardy morning of waking up, Golden Worlders would go right into the proper incantations for an afternoon nap. Purifying themselves for lunch involved animal sacrifices and incense. For the sake of brevity, we won't even get into the adventure that going to the bathroom was.

The cosmic problems with this are not the societal complexity, but the aftereffects on the Golden World's heavens. When enough people worship one idea in a certain way, an appropriate deity comes into being. And when you have everyone on the planet worshiping everything in sight, the problem is immediately evident.

The Golden World had too many gods.

But what does one do when the infinite heavens just aren't enough to house your coworkers? After lengthy deliberation, the eldest and chief deities came up with a brilliant plan. Gathering all the most uselessly specialized immortals, they announced a rash of "promotions" had broken out. As a reward for their colleagues' hard work, each was charged with creating his or her own world. Some succeeded admirably. Some failed miserably. But either way, they were gone, and the ruling pantheon finally had enough room to breathe. The people of the Golden World could continue their complex rituals. Their associated masters and mistresses could smile upon them when they avoided a crack in the pavement, or combed their hair, or whatever. The problem was solved without a hitch.

Well, almost without a hitch.

Two of the rejected deities, Barl and Despor—Gods of Beer and Recreational Sports, respectively—had barely gotten out of the starting gates before they were too winded to continue. Still, having made it this far, they took a moment to enjoy some of Barl's finer work. Around the seventh bottle of fermented nectar, they came up with the wonderful idea of the Pflatlands.

By the time the Golden Pantheon realized what was going on, Barl and Despor had synthesized a world skewed by drunken stupor right in the Golden World's backyard.

Alarmed by what this would do to their property value, the Pantheon dispatched Lumina, Goddess of Reason. She desperately propped up mistakes with whatever science was handy...but every time she would fix something, it would break something else in Barl and Despor's spaghetti-logic rules of existence, or the two would break something while trying to help, or something would just go flat out haywire of its own accord. In one final, desperate lunge for normalcy, Lumina summoned all her powers, took up her pen, opened a blank book, and wrote. She wrote until her fingers were sore, and her rear end numb, and with the slamming of its cover[*], she announced a new order for the turbulent world.

The book was called "The Rules".

She presented her new work to Barl and Despor, who were just waking up with an appropriately epic hangover. After their stomachs had settled, all three decided it might be best if they keep out of trouble for a while...say, several eons. Thus, Barl and Despor hid themselves as only a god can, and Lumina returned home to report the problem solved.

What she hadn't reported—not in the book, not to the Golden World tribunal, not even to Barl and Despor—was "The Rules" was a complete and utter hack job. Lumina had never, in her eternal and unaging life, seen a disaster as large in scale as the Pflatlands. She was so flustered when she took up her pen, she had no idea what was coming out the tip. Sure, there were bits and pieces she could recall—something about orcs, and a paragraph about the underworld and the speed of light, which may or may not have been related—but she was so pressed to come up with something that she couldn't think twice, let alone revise.

As the years passed, wars were fought, and people died, and odd, unexplainable phenomenon took place—but it was all well within the specifications of "The Handbook", which was written much earlier than

---

[*] The book's. Just so we're clear.

The Pflatlands

"The Rules", and much more carefully. Yet, as she poured herself into her original duties once more, Lumina couldn't get rid of one little twitch around her all-knowing eyes. There was something, somewhere, that she should have done, like some sort of Great Cosmic Coffeepot that she had forgotten to turn off. She consoled herself that, if she couldn't remember what it was, the mortals living by her work needn't concern themselves.

Nevertheless, the nagging feeling remained.

R. D. Hammond

CHAPTER 1

In the beginning was the First Dark Age, when no one ruled.

Then there were the elves. The elves ruled for a while, until they didn't anymore.

After that, mankind took over.

Most races agree it's been downhill ever since.

In the distant past of the Pflatlands, the expansive Elvin Empire was forever partitioned into two separate lands: the High and Lower Kingdom. It should be noted that these names are not necessarily representative of quality; while the Lower Kingdom was busy perfecting blank verse poetry, the High Kingdom was enjoying the fine artistic stylings of a Second Dark Age, which mostly involved hitting things with very large cudgels. These names find their origins in the ancient mapping methods of the Pflatlands, which placed the High Kingdom in the north and the Lower Kingdom to the south. Today, we know this to be laughable. The High Kingdom clearly lies in the west, not the north. Unfortunately, this is just the sort of thinking that persists in the uneducated mind, like rumors that the world is round.

The Pflatlands

But we digress.

The anomaly that schizmed a once mighty empire in two is easy to describe, but impossible to comprehend. One evening, the Emperor went to bed, content with life, pleased with his station, perhaps planning to raise taxes or proclaim an increase in his pay. The next morning, he found a giant forest smack in the middle of his empire. The birth of the Argury Woods was literally that quick. No one could explain where it had come from, but it was nevertheless there—and just as suddenly, the Reagent placed in the North Empire (technically the west) to oversee matters distant from the throne in the South Empire (technically the east) was on his own to rule half the world. Undaunted, the Reagent did what anyone in his situation would do. He went mad with power, arming himself with an Inquisition and a reign of terror. Under the resulting anarchy, the High Kingdom degenerated into the Second Dark Age. Knowledge of this would have disturbed the Emperor greatly, if any messengers could've gotten through the forest without being eaten.

And the forest's sudden appearance was only the tip of the iceberg. After Argury sprang up, another bizarre event took place; the native Pflatlanders of the South (east) and North (west), who previously spoke a unified tongue, were suddenly speaking two entirely new and incomprehensible languages. There was, and still is, confusion over Old Pflatlandic's division into Higher Common and Lower Common. No one has ever questioned the source. In one day, Argury had irrevocably changed the course of society, elves and Pflatlanders alike.

But enough of the external manifestations. What about the internal?

It's difficult to say, since a lot of people that go deep into Argury have an unfortunate tendency to not come back out. The woods are lush, dark, and most certainly not natural. Attempts to map the outskirts have met with success, but these maps can't possibly claim to know the real Argury. The jungle holds its most dear secrets deep in its center, secrets which might not drive a man insane, but certainly give him a number of neuroses and perhaps a phobia of some sort. Its most fantastic creations lie where time and space distort such that it would never conform to a sheet of paper. This isn't to say everything wild in the woods is hidden from the public eye, however. Evolution has not only derailed in Argury, but caused spectacular flaming carnage with two other trains and a bovine life form. Snakes grow wings. Dogs grow scales. Plants grow legs—each other's legs. With "normal" in Argury being a wholly subjective term, Mother Nature could get away with significantly more than she did anywhere else, and she took full liberties. It was typical in Argury for Nature to violently seize a particular animal and inflict all sorts of strange evolutionary mutations, until it had tentacles, two heads, specked eyes, nightvision, and opposable thumbs...within the first year.

Even still, the inspired lunacy of Argury biology is nothing compared to Argury civilization. You may be asking: Who would be crazy enough to live where reality could, on any given day, call in sick, without so much as twenty-four hours of advance notice?

First of all, stop talking to yourself.

Secondly, the answer is perfectly obvious: The fae.

Let's dispel some stereotypes first, so we can work from a proper and mature standpoint. A faerie is not innocent, nor is he or she inclined to frolic. Furthermore, they only prance for tourists—which isn't very often, given Argury's aforementioned reputation for swallowing up travelers and not giving them back. Perhaps the lost humans find a shapely dryad or nice hunk of satyr to frolic with and don't want to come back. Perhaps they have a boulder dropped on their head by an angry spriggan[*]. Who knows? Either way, they're never heard from again. But back to the fae: When they learned of the new forest, they flocked to it. And not just small percentages, either. All the fae were represented: sprites, pixies, spriggans, bogies...even the exotic eastern fae, the djinns, the kitsunes, and the kappas...none could resist exploring. It was a fierce attraction that made perfect sense. Chaos breeds more chaos. Some of these migrants would recede back into their homelands, disappointed. Some returned mourning the high cost a new and hostile environment could extract. Some simply found what they were looking for and had no more reason to stay. But by and large, many remained,

---

[*] This isn't necessarily saying there's any other kind of spriggan.

The Pflatlands

and the shift in population density was not lost among the two Kingdoms. Argury was soon known by a second name: the "Faerie Forest."

But as much attention as the fae receive, it's worth mentioning they're not alone. Deep in the woods lives another race, the Kar. Quiet and gentle, distrustful but not unfriendly, these humanoid people are a subject of curiosity for a variety of reasons. But we won't burden you with further details, for it's already growing late in the morning—and it's high time all sleepers were awakened.

•

It was another typical day in the Argury Woods. The typical sun shone hard against the typical jungle canopy, its warm, red rays falling on a typical hut and simmering in dazzling patterns through leaf-covered windows onto a typical branch floor. The chitter and buzz of insect and bird filled the ears of a Kar suspended in a typical vine hammock, which swung gently back and forth in response to his movement.

As was typical for this Kar, Dahn Kluklahn, he rolled over and pulled a hide blanket over his head—much to the chagrin of the young woman leaning against his front door. She crossed her arms and silently counted backwards from twenty. Fair warning, she thought.

"Kunlah!" she called sweetly, but loudly. "Cheh'renoh! You've slept enough today, brother."

"Cheh'kulu, Shoh," Dahn grumbled faintly. "Come in. Make yourself at home."

"Don't be like that! You've been sleeping well into midsun, like you always do! Now get out of bed, lazy!"

Another muffled grumble came from under the blanket. Shoh decided she had heard enough. She padded to the other side of the room, effortlessly scaled the inside wall, and reached towards the hammock's knot with two fingers. Within moments, Dahn was plummeting towards the ground. He shrieked, landing with a soft thump on the wooden floor below. The blanket fluttered lazily over his head.

"That was awful of you." He rubbed his half-open eyes.

"I know." Shoh grinned and leapt to the floor, landing with a soft whisper of air and nothing more. "But it worked."

"I would've gotten up eventually!"

"That's what you said the last three days! I'm worried about you. You've been sleeping far too much lately."

Dahn smacked his lips and reached for a flaxen wrap, fastening it around his lower body while he staggered towards consciousness. He was young—maybe 19 or 20 years—and hardly stood out in a crowd. Still, he possessed a slightly squared jaw, brown hair which reached his shoulders, and clear, expressive eyes. About halfway between five and six feet, he was small of stature and thin, though healthy. His ears poked out of his hair, their fur silken and grey. They matched the cat-like tail extending from the base of his spine. All in all, Dahn was just an average Kar.

"I need a comb," he complained.

"Yes. Yes, you do," Shoh confirmed, playfully picking at his matted ears.

Whereas Dahn was merely average, Shoh was unquestionably a beauty, her appearance considered exotic even among her own race. Her lips were fuller, her nose was slightly hooked, and her hair was a flaming crimson, but it was her eyes which remained her most noticeable feature, two all-capturing pools of green. Villagers whispered that fae blood ran in Shoh's veins. It was entirely plausible, since she and Dahn weren't related by birth. It was also the most likely explanation for the bobcat points of her ears and tail.

Dahn shuffled across the sturdy floor to his tiny, partitioned washroom. He leaned over a stone basin on the wall and tugged a cord, letting stored rainwater in. He rubbed his face and ears vigorously and combed the tangles from his hair and fur.

"What excitement do you have planned for today?" Shoh asked, taking the hammock and scaling the wall again. Holding fast with fingers and claws, she tied a square knot with one hand, suspending the hammock once more.

"I'm not sure," he replied blankly, wincing as the bone comb worked out knots. "I'll need food at some point. I might go for a walk."

"Again?" She slipped to the ground, adjusting her leaf halter-top

The Pflatlands

and ankle-length loincloth. "You've been doing that a lot lately, too. What's wrong?"

"Nothing." He checked, one final time, that his hair and ears were properly aligned, then draped his tail over the back of his wrap. "At least, I don't think it's anything."

"You don't think so? I think you'd know if there was something wrong with you."

"You're right. I'm going to go get my mail."

"Already done."

Shoh retrieved a bundle from outside and lobbed it to him. He bowed in thanks and began sorting it into piles.

"Let's see what we have here. Junk, junk, junk...Hmm! I might already be a winner."

"Of what?"

"Doesn't say, I have to order something first." He threw it on the junk pile and continued sorting. "More junk, junk, letter from parents, junk—"

"Hey!" Shoh fetched the letter from the growing pile. "This isn't junk!"

"Are you sure?" he asked through gritted teeth.

"You really should think about talking to them, you know. Maybe things will be different this time."

"You're right, I should." He paused. "There, done."

He reached to snatch the letter out of Shoh's hand. She drew it back with a slight scowl.

"Just take it with you?" she pleaded. "If you're sure you won't like what they have to say, you don't have to read it—but at least keep it. It's a start, right?"

Dahn's eyes shifted, he struggled internally, and finally, he relented.

"Alright." He tucked it into the belt of his wrap as Shoh beamed a smile. "But no promises on reading it. I've had enough drama to last me a lifetime."

"Thanks." She kissed her brother gently on the cheek. "And who knows? You might smooth over your differences one day."

"I doubt it very much, but thank you. I'm going out now."

"Alright. Have fun out there! You look like you could use it."

"I'll try." He gave his little sister one last hug.

Dahn's hut was built on the wide branch of a mighty Argury juabon, a mile-diameter tower of wood and leaf, unmovable by storm, tool, or creature. The house was small and modest, with brick walls, treated hides for roofing, leaves for insulation, and a curtain of spotted fur on the door. The massive tree trunk formed a fourth wall, and the branch underneath served as the floor. It was the only hut on the branch, almost directly underneath another equally wide tree limb and only minutes away from the marketplace. Dahn didn't mind the noise, though he was annoyed when the higher branch blocked his rainwater collectors. He didn't mind the solitude, either. He always had an easier time relaxing alone.

He strolled along the empty pathway, admiring the kaleidoscopic canopy of the forest. The sun glinted through the greens and blues in random patterns, sparkling on the ground beneath his feet. He soon reached one of the suspension bridges which led to the marketplace. He gripped it tightly as he stepped onto it, claws clacking on the smoothly carved bone. Like every day when he crossed that bridge, he told himself not to look down. Like every day, he did anyway, seeing a tangle of vines and branches and darkness he always imagined himself plunging into. He shuddered and swallowed, gripped the vines tighter, and hurried across.

"Apples! Apples for sale! Fresh from the guarnas and hand selected by sprite farmers!"

"Cheh'kulu, dremohl! Try one of our juabon staves? Shaped with adamantium chisels mere minutes after falling from the..."

"Wines for sale! Imported Elvish wines from the desertlands!"

The Kar marketplace was built on interlocking, intricately carved plates made from discarded juabon wood; supported by a network of vines, treetops, and living branches, it had been set into place a long time ago and showed no indications of going anywhere anytime soon. Dahn crisscrossed through the maze of booths, tuning out the cries and advertisements of salesmen. He rounded a corner and arrived at his destination, a square stone counter encasing stocks of fruits, vegetables, and

The Pflatlands

meats packed in preserving salts. There was a new woman working the stand today. She was a bit taller than him, her hips flaring smoothly into a slight hourglass figure. Her fur dress clung nicely to her curves. The inside of Dahn's ears reddened.

"Good day, friend," she purred softly. "May I help you?"

"Hih. Te beh Kluklahn, Dahn. I'm here to pick up my order. You must be new here."

"And you must be very observant. I suppose the next thing you'll say is how you would've noticed me before."

"Toh, toh." Dahn shook his head with a sheepish laugh. "I don't flirt with the workers. Their job is difficult enough."

"Then you're a darling apple. Your wife must be very lucky."

"Me?" Dahn blinked. "Wife?"

"Oh, I'm sorry! Wives?"

"Toh!" he peeped. "I haven't had success with one woman, let alone many."

"Really?" She flipped her tail lazily while she packed bundles of food into a large sack. "You seem sweet, though. And you're just the right age for it."

"I've been told so. I don't know. I haven't found the right girl, I guess."

"I've found it's more about the right time than the right person." She finished her packing. "Here's to hoping you find time and person soon, hmm?"

"Here's to hoping," Dahn smiled back, taking the sack from her. Caught unprepared for the weight, he struggled with it briefly, but managed to get it over his shoulder. "Thank you for your help."

"Not a problem, dremohl. Will you be coming to the stage? There's a performance of Kuntar the Long-Tailed today."

"That sounds nice, but—"

Dahn trailed off, noticing the booths had stopped their chatter. It didn't take long to find the source. An older, wrinkled Kar was shuffling slowly down the path, hollow eyes on the ground. He wore a familiar ash grey robe and black collar and held a closed sack limply in one hand. His hair, or what was left of it, was cut very close to his head.

The fur of his ears was beginning to thin as well, exposing the pink skin underneath. Behind him, the short, amputated stub of what was once an orange tail occasionally twitched. Kars slid to the side and shunned him as he passed, some signing themselves. He made eye contact with no one. None attempted to approach him. He turned a corner and was gone again. Business resumed as normal, warily at first, then gradually more energetic.

"Huh?" Dahn jumped in surprise, feeling a hand on his shoulder.

"I said, are you alright?" The attendant looked concerned.

"Oh, yes. It's just—I always feel sorry for the slave caste. I suppose I shouldn't."

"Your sympathy is admirable, but you're right. They're slaves for a reason, friend."

"Te qehnah. I know. Why was he—you know—"

"Mm. He spent thirty years as a Groundswalker. Something changed inside him, I guess, and he turned himself in. The chief knew right away what had happened. He could tell he had lost everything just by looking into his eyes."

Dahn nodded mutely.

"I hear the druids gave him something to dull the pain during the cutting," she continued. "You know, to go easy on him. They were trying to show other Groundswalkers that we're not unmerciful."

"I can't believe someone would doom themselves to either that...or Infernus." Dahn shook his head. "It's not like Lady Green asks much of us."

"No one knows why he chose to be a Groundswalker. I don't even think he does. Such is the madness of Narr." She turned her head far to the left and spat on the ground. "It's a shame Tremelor didn't take him while he was young. At least he's saved his soul for the next life."

"Hi. I hope Lady Green gives him peace soon." Dahn coughed. "I'm sorry, that was kind of depressing. I should get these things home."

"Oh, it's just life, friend. It's neither avoidable nor should be avoided. You will take care? I hope I'll see you again."

"I hope so as well." He shifted his sack to the other shoulder. "Take care."

The Pflatlands

Dahn traversed the haphazard booths once more, crossed the little bone bridge, and returned home. While putting away his food, all he could think of was the slave's hollow eyes. The rationeer said their chief could tell he had lost everything. Even Dahn could see that, and he was certainly no member of the chieftain caste. Yet, no matter how illogical the slave's sins were, he couldn't feel anything but pity for him. He supposed the grocer was right. The Groundswalkers, who chose to follow the path of Narr, deserved no pity. After all, they would show no pity to victims of their mad designs. But the slave had looked genuinely hurt, and he seemed to have learned the proper amount of humility. Was it really his fault he fell prey to an evil beyond any Kar? He had come back of his own accord, hadn't he? Was it fair to make him live the scant rest of his life as a slave?

Shaking off that line of thought, Dahn fetched a few yellows* from his ration supply, peeling and devouring one for brunch. He kept the other on hand for a snack, absently lobbing it into the air and catching it. He meandered leisurely out his door and down the branch, away from the hustle and bustle of the marketplace. He had thought enough for one day, and it was already giving him a headache. He just wanted to walk and enjoy the scenery.

---

*Like oranges, except—well, *you* know.

R. D. Hammond

CHAPTER 7

There is a little town in the Pflats.

This is not surprising in and of itself. Latest figures indicate 63.9% of the inhabited western Pflatlands is small towns. The remaining 36.1% are enormous cities which devote a significant portion of themselves towards recreating the small town they were founded on. No one really buys this act. Even in a world made by two drunken rabble-rousers and an overstressed, bookish matriarch, a cyclops cannot be a sprite. It just doesn't work that way.

Despite this, cities insist on small-town facades as a fashionable trend. More and more often, High Kingdom Highwaymen are ripping up perfectly good concrete and replacing it with unkempt, barely visible roads, complete with rocks handcrafted at just the right size to lodge in your mount's hoof and send you to the blacksmith's. (A blacksmith which, we might add, can be found nearby, under a quaint sign with a remarkable amount of E's in inappropriate places.) One could argue that this can all be avoided by use of a flat-footed mount—and one usually

The Pflatlands

does, assuming one works for the city government. You must keep in mind, however, that the only viable alternative to a hoofed mount in the High Kingdom is what's commonly called a "hopper". Hoppers are viable for travel the same way a flamberge is viable for surgery. Sure, it technically works, but you're likely to lose an arm or foot or other important bit in the process.

Returning to the point, the idea of bringing small towns to big cities is fairly ludicrous. Still, the tourism arm of the Merchants' Guild trots out data every year in support, compiled from figures provided by in-depth reports funded by—you guessed it—the Merchants' Guild. It's a scam of epic proportions, one that would make even Crystal the Needle, Queen of the Thieves' Guild, blush. But it continues, and the great cities of the High Kingdom declare, "Look at my pretty, pretty wings! Surely, I am one of the fae! Also, please ignore my gigantic, solitary eye." And everyone shakes their heads in disbelief, except for the tourists, who will happily spend their silver at any shop along the road. Tourists would throw silver directly at rocks if they thought they[*] had historical significance. In fact, Grand Vicar Ocelot of the Merchants' Guild is probably rolling out this scheme as we speak—assuming the Needle doesn't beat him to it.

So, when we say that there is a little town in the Pflats, we mean an actual little town. The town of East Dunsbar is not particularly remarkable. It has nothing special to offer in services. Most major guilds, even the all-pervasive Fighters' Guild, go unrepresented. (Both the rangers and merchants have satellite offices, though, since there's always a need to procure food and then sell it at unreasonable prices.) The local hostel's most significant boast is a Class B Run-Down Lodging License, which is still fairly mediocre, as the town couldn't put together a flophouse good enough for a Class A License. The local restaurants are all indistinguishable, offering the local specialty, Boiled Whatever Happened to Be Slow of Foot This Morning. As with nearly every location in the Pflatlands, there's a House of Yoseph's next door (Motto: "Eat at Yoseph's, Someone Has To"), but that's hardly worth mentioning.

---

[*] The rocks. Just so we're clear.

Truth be told, East Dunsbar is a phenomenally, staggeringly, overwhelmingly nominal town.

Nominal, that is, until you factor in the Argury Woods next door.

Argury is what fuels East Dunsbar's booming tourist economy, because heaven knows it's not the local culture. Things happen in East Dunsbar. Odd things. People will disappear for indeterminate amounts of time. Strange lights play in the forest. Voices are heard. Stories are whispered. Rumors are spread. Not a single one of them are nearly as interesting as the truth.

With this in mind, we find a girl in her late teens, soon to finish—possibly without any prior warning—the process of maturation into an adult. She is 5'4" and has straight brown hair cropped close to her jawline. She possesses a round face, slightly enlarged lips, and a pair of light grey eyes framed by round-rimmed glasses. She is wearing a white one-piece tunic, suede leather pants, black hiking boots, and a gold ring with a large ruby. A shortbow is slung across her body. She is riding a brown horse in the Argury Woods. Her turn-ons are long walks in the forest by herself. Her turn-offs are stupid people, annoying people, and people in general.

In a moment, she will swear in a manner most unbecoming of a young lady. It is there that our tale really begins.

•

"Son—of—a—bitch!"

Sarah put extra emphasis on each word to make herself feel better. It didn't work, so she followed with a crescendo of several more obscenities, climaxing in a conjecture about the goddess of forests' repute. Disgusted, she swung one leg over and out of the saddle and dropped to the earth below. She folded her map, continuing to rant at no one in particular.

"Do they even update these scragging things? No, better question. Do they even hire a translator? I mean, look. Look here. Look at these directions." She gestured wildly at a hastily scrawled note on the map. " 'Make with the turning of left at mighty tree.' What the hell does that even mean? Which tree? Do I just pick the mightiest looking one and hope for the best?"

Her horse, the only creature within earshot, offered no satisfactory explanation. With a frustrated sigh, she flung open her saddlebag and stuffed the map into it. She glared at the logo emblazoned on the saddle:

RENT-A-NAG™
A Division of Sweenie and Sons
"Our Prices are as Insane as Our Owners"

This is what she got for being cheap. Still, it's not like she could have afforded anything else. When you're running like a bat out of hell, little things like long term employment tend to get lost along the way.

She wasn't quite so naïve to think her exodus would be moment after moment of sheer, unadulterated pleasure...but then again, she hadn't expected to wind up in a dirthole like East Dunsbar, either. It boggled her mind that a huntress of her skill and pedigree had to bust her ass just to make ends meet. She wasn't particularly conceited. By no means did she think she deserved more than any other entry-level ranger—especially one perpetually lacking guild endorsement. But, for Jar'lin's sake, it's not like there were a glut of people working this end of the Kingdom! And besides, she was good at what she did. It started as a hobby, grew into a form of rebellion, and it was now an intricate part of her life.

And at the rate she was going, it would be part of her death.

It's all about competitive wages, she thought glumly. *Five years younger with comparable experience, and I still get two-thirds of what a man makes.*

It irritated her beyond measure, but at the same time, feeling sorry for herself wouldn't put food on her table. She extracted her metal canteen from the saddlebags, unscrewed the lid, and took a long drink of cool water. Replacing cap and then canteen, she paused to reflect on the scenery. Most rangers earned their paycheck by staying on the outskirts of Argury, away from the supposed wonderland inside. The environment was more open, the animals were easier to catch, and the backdrop was a lot more sane.

Sarah wasn't most rangers. She was a young, starving huntress currently having her fill of playing it safe. Stabbing her boot defiantly into a stirrup, she swung her weight back over her horse.

"Let's go," she said simply, snapping the reigns.

The horse came to attention and began a slow but even trot, the only pace of which it was seemingly capable. At the first perceivable weakness in forest density, Sarah veered left, off the path and into the deeper woods.

•

Tree branches creaked and swayed as Dahn ran across their length, light-footed and sure. Springing gracefully into the air, he caught a tree trunk with his arms and swung around to his next perch. He descended the sloping arm of that tree to the next, stepping carefully without benefit of claws. He recognized the brittle, flaked bark of an ironwood. His claws would be absolutely useless.

Pausing to take in a breath, Dahn sunk to all fours, then dangled his legs on either side of the branch. He leaned back and closed his eyes slightly, the junction between branch and trunk keeping him well balanced and safe.

He exhaled and opened his eyes.

This is where his walks always ended. This was why he couldn't tell Shoh where he went. He wasn't ambling aimlessly, as his little sister had thought; it was the view from this very spot that he came for. He always felt a pang of guilt for this perch out in the middle of nowhere, with the jungle floor spread so lushly beneath him. Blues and purples abounded among the growing plant life, dotted with the swirled oranges and yellows of dry and dying grass. Bouquets of exotic petals burst forth in brilliant splotches, some spiked with nasty appendages like thorns or spines (or in extreme cases, teeth), but all breathtakingly sublime in their own way. Still, there was no telling which plants would stay put and which would get up and walk, possibly after their next meal, which might possibly be him. It was, quite literally, a jungle out there. Fortunately for Dahn, the most dangerous creatures traveled by land.

Another reason this is madness, he thought.

In spite of all this, he still couldn't turn away from the beautiful waves of grass and vines, his imagination stirred by the occasional ripple or unearthly sound. He idly dreamed of what might be out there. Death, probably. Monsters, certainly. But no one, absolutely no one, knew for sure. Maybe it was because no one was stupid enough to go out there, but still…a Kar can dream, can't he? And Dahn had dreams, slipping off into his favorite, where he wandered the world as an adventurer and scholar. He would see everything there was to see, learn everything there was to know, experience things for which there were no words—and in the end, he would return a revered hero.

But, just as the chieftain in his daydream slipped a medal around his neck to thunderous applause, he was shaken back to reality by a harsh jolt. The sudden impact against the tree sent Dahn reeling around the branch, legs and arms locking as he hung upside down. His fur bristled in panic, and he snapped his head around wildly, searching for the source. Shortly after, the second blast hit, shuddering the ironwood down to its roots. He wouldn't need a third. With a hiss and a twist of his hips, he righted himself.

"Jar'lin above," he groaned. "A gnarling!"

•

Sarah leaned and held a low branch aside as her old horse nudged its way into the deep woods. It wandered lazily along a path that was entirely unclear, and she didn't see any reason to stop it. Goddesses know she wasn't having any luck finding adventure. Maybe the animal would.

Wandering off the beaten path didn't particularly bother her, either. She glanced at the sky through small breaks in the trees, smiling briefly at the afternoon sun. Astronomy was never one of her favorite subjects, but she knew enough. The sun rose in the east and set in the west, and the Golden Star was always in the southern night sky. As long as Sarah could see the heavens, she was never lost. It was just another in a long line of advantages her upbringing afforded her.

Education really is the key, she thought. Experience is no substitute for a stimulating academic environment.

Sarah scratched her nose and ducked under a vine.

Of course, there was also something to be said for experience, and she was currently lacking it. It seemed so simple on paper. The Argury Woods were the most talked-about location in the High Kingdom. You come here, you wait around, the excitement eventually comes to you. That was the theory, anyway. Right now, the excitement seemed content to lounge elsewhere on a sofa in its underwear.

Sarah's hand brushed a curvy green vine out of the way as the horse clopped under it. The vine slithered noiselessly up from the branch as she passed, a single bulbous eye opening at the tip. It curiously watched her slip away.

That was the most irritating thing about this whole trip—the sheer lack of adventure. Adventure was, in Sarah's esteemed opinion, how most adventurers were supposed to spend their time, and there was a particular lack in this area that she couldn't understand. There was a possibility that the "Faerie Forest" was exaggerated superstition, but she didn't really buy that. Up until three hundred years ago, the entire High Kingdom was convinced an absurd system of geological plates caused earthquakes. Only when one of the underground battles between the dwarves and the orcs went awry* were the age-old legends proven as mythological fact.

A musical titter went unheard by Sarah's ears. Lights were glowing gently in the tall grass behind her. Tiny, amused voices were lost amidst the faint wind whistling through the trees.

Sarah's mind was drifting. She was pondering how much a dwarf could make exporting adventure to East Dunsbar when she was startled

---

*In the year 244 of the Epoch of the Third Kingdom, dwarven engineer Thuddbeard Fumblefingers accidentally rotated his blueprints 90 degrees to the right without realizing it. The resulting maiden voyage of his drilltank burst into the pantry of the High King's summer home. The history books record Thuddbeard as saying, and here we are quoting directly, "Oops."

The Pflatlands

by a loud, echoing crunch. She spun in the saddle to find the source...and immediately caught a whipping branch to the face. Cursing lowly, she righted her glasses, pushed the branch aside, and peered into the forest depths. She couldn't really see anything except trees and, beyond that, more trees—some of which were, through some trick of distance and her myopia, curling into shapes normally reserved for obtuse works of modern art. Still, she knew what she heard. It was definitely real, and it definitely wasn't normal. In fact, the only relieving thing about it was that it didn't come from nearby.

She wasn't going to let a little detail like that stop her from investigating.

•

By the seventh hit, Dahn realized ironwood beats gnarling in nature's game of rock-paper-scissors. No longer fearing for his life, he resigned himself to a lazy stretch over the tree's highest limb. His grey tail dangled below him, curling and flicking.

"Stuck in a tree?"

The high, tinkling voice roused him from half-slumber. He rubbed his numbed back and found the owner hovering nearby—a four-inch tall sprite, with gossamer wings, silver-white hair, ruby eyes, and not a stitch of clothing.

"I suppose so," Dahn yawned, scratching the back of his neck. He leaned back over the thick limb. His head vibrated with the hits below. "You wouldn't happen to know what position it is, would you?"

"Last I checked, it was midsun. It's been some time since."

The Kar smoothed his frizzed hair back into place. The din below continued.

"Jar'lin above, he's persistent."

"He'll keep at it for a while," the sprite giggled.

They did that a lot. Personally, Dahn found it annoying, but as long as she kept hovering at eye level...

"Well, I need to do something. Any suggestions?"

She daintily put her fingers to her chin, deep in thought. Dahn immediately regretted asking. Sprites usually needed at least five minutes to remember their own name, let alone come up with ideas.

"We could drop a rock on it!" she proclaimed proudly.

He was genuinely impressed. This one was clearly a great mind of her century.

"It's ramming its head into an ironwood. Repeatedly. I doubt it would notice a boulder bouncing off its skull."

"True," she nodded, disappointed.

They lapsed into silence. The rhythmic pounding was vaguely irritating Dahn.

"Do you think I can outrun it?" he proposed.

"It might be worth a try," she hummed, still tapping her chin. "Don't slip, or you'll be killed in a horribly messy way!"

He peered at her.

"How can you be so…jolly about that?"

"Well, you have to look at the bright side of everything."

The gnarling slammed into the tree with renewed vigor. The branch shuddered violently.

"Bright side? Where's the bright side to being killed?"

"There isn't. That's why you have to make it sound jolly! Silly goose."

She slapped his nose flirtatiously. He stared at her, dumbfounded.

The beast slammed its dense skull into the tree one more time. With a crack and a groan, Dahn's perch shook in an alarming manner. Something was wrong. He wobbled to maintain his balance.

"What in the name of Lady Green was that?"

"Oh!" The faerie smacked her forehead. "That's right! I came up here to warn you, this old tree has probably rotted by now."

"Rot?" He started violently. "You couldn't have told me this earlier?"

"Well, you know how it is! I'd forget my own head if it wasn't attached…"

He gave the rupture in the trunk's bark a pained glance. Ironwoods still had the consistency of mature oak when rotted, but the persistent beast had broken through nonetheless. It hunched low and pawed the

The Pflatlands

ground, readying a tremendous follow-up. The Kar leapt to his feet and crouched alertly in one swift motion. His tail perked into the air behind him.

"Right. What was the bright side to being mutilated again?"

"Er." The sprite bit her lip. "I think we decided there wasn't one, actually."

The gnarling charged and leapt, slinging all its weight forward. With a mighty crash, the bark split and the trunk toppled. The Kar sprung to the tree beside it, beginning his escape.

•

Sarah frowned as she picked her way through the woods. Just as she was on their cusp, the sounds had stopped.

And another thing—where are all the fae? Her train of thought rumbled along, even while searching. Where are the hovering sprites? Where are the airy and mysterious nymphs? Where are the beautiful dryads with their weeping willow bodies? Where are the hunky, shirtless satyrs with taut biceps and rippling six-packs and huge—

A crash interrupted her internal monologue, and she glanced upwards in time to see an ironwood rapidly approaching. She vacated just as quickly, diving off her horse and into the bushes before the tree smashed her flat. From inside the vegetation, she exhaled a large sigh of relief. Ironwood was an active ingredient in Vorpal Clubs[*]; getting hit by an entire tree would have been far from pleasant. As soon as it came, however, her relief dissolved into panic. She had left her horse behind.

She frantically clawed her way out of the bushes. That horse was the only thing between her and a long walk over treacherous and uncharted land, but more importantly, that horse wasn't insured by the renter. Once her vision was finally unobstructed by pointy leaves, Sarah came face to face with an absolute scene of…her horse, calmly standing an inch away from where the tree had fallen. It clearly indicated its joy at seeing her again, after all of fifteen seconds, by licking her ear. Sarah

---

[*] A cheaper alternative to the Vorpal Sword, for the adventurer on a budget.

yelped in surprise and leaned her head to one side, shrugging a shoulder to dry her ear on her tunic. She scowled at the beast, who, in a display of overwhelming remorse, lowered its head and munched on the tall grass.

She circled her transportation, checking the rest of her equipment. The news was not good; her quiver had been jarred loose from its saddle attachment due to her hasty exit. She rested her face in her palm and groaned. The Sweenie and Sons salesman assured her that modular saddle attachments were the future of hunting, and she had paid five extra silver as a result. The quiver was probably squashed flat now. That limited her combat options to the dagger in her ankle sheath and the poisoned mini-arrow she kept in her left boot for emergencies. She reached for the latter, pulled, and found the back half of the arrow in her hand. Fantastic.

She climbed onto the downed tree, pulled off her boot, and shook it. As the other end of the arrow bounced free, she dropped the boot and fumbled for the airborne item, catching it before it could sink into grass. She opened her fingers with a sigh of relief. The protective cover was still unbroken, a smooth metal snap made of adamantium and aluminum. The covers were technically disposable, but she always recycled hers. Batches of twenty were worth a silver, and besides, it was the right thing to do.

She threw away the useless half of the arrow and looked critically at the remainder. Her day was now officially ruined. Taking the canteen from her saddlebag, she wet her lips with a quick swig. The brief respite provided a moment of reflection, and she felt vaguely guilty that, when she told her parents she was going out to hunt last week, she failed to mention she wouldn't ever be coming back. Only vaguely, of course. It passed soon enough.

•

Dahn leapt from tree to tree, the sprite buzzing cheerfully alongside him.

"...And it's situations like this that make you realize how important friends are, you know?"

The Pflatlands

The Kar shook his head as he swung through the treetops on a vine, the gnarling in hot pursuit. In transit, he somehow switched from clinging with hands to clinging with legs, then caught a low branch with both arms and swung acrobatically to a higher perch.

"Why—" he panted. "Are you bringing this up—right now—"

"I like to think I'm a good judge of character. I can tell who'll make a good friend. And I think we'll get along just fine!"

Dahn sprang up the branches like a staircase. He sank into the dense tree leaves high above.

"Don't take this the wrong way," he hissed as quietly as possible, "but I need all the concentration I can get right now."

"Oh, right." She nodded with a hushed whisper. "Sorry."

The confused gnarling turned its armor-plated head this way and that, searching for the hidden feline. Dahn's stomach knotted a little tighter as he looked out. Somehow, he had lead the beast right into one of Argury's rare clearings. The grass was far shorter, the trees were sparser, and the sky was mostly visible. Gnarlings weren't known for their keen eyesight, but even a molebat could spot him at fifty paces out here. The sprite's presence wasn't helping, either. He huddled closer into his camouflage, praying the beast was either too stupid or too blind to notice her bright glow through the leaves.

•

The second and third crash startled Sarah. That was the sound of bone on wood, not wood on forest floor. Something out there had knocked that ironwood to the ground. If it had toppled a tree that mighty and was still going at it, it could only be the insanely stubborn gnarling—more specifically, a gnarling that had treed its prey. The multiple crashes confused her, though. What in the world was agile enough to escape being treed by a gnarling multiple times?

She hesitated, then shook her head. Both prey and adventure had been delivered in a neat little package. It was now or never. She sprung to her feet to give chase, then grimaced deeply. Something sharp was poking painfully through her black leather boots. When she realized what it was, a flash of epiphany struck. She reached to yank it out of her shoe, fingering the point and smiling. It was crude and unorthodox, but it just might do the trick.

•

The sprite and Kar watched the gnarling sniff around the surrounding flora. The wavy leaves of a fern parted at its probing, giving way to three wriggling, foot-long worms. One didn't squirm quite fast enough, and the gnarling tore into it greedily, leaving only a split sheet of leathery skin behind. Dahn shot a worried glance at the faerie, who missed it completely.

"My name is Torethial Q Spritely! But you can call me Tor. What's yours?"

"Dahn. Now, shhhh!"

They silently watched the beast sniff.

"Something's weird about this," Tor complained. "He's being way too persistent."

The gnarling perked its ears and charged. Tor shrieked in horror at the new thwack on the tree. Dahn sighed and regained as much footing as possible.

"Tor, you can fly. Right?"

"Oh." The sprite giggled, hovering safely in the air. "Silly me!"

"Would you mind doing something useful? Like, I don't know, getting me some help?"

"Will do! Try not to die while I'm gone!" She whistled tunelessly as she flitted away.

What happened next would never be all that clear to Dahn. He would remember watching Tor fly off. He would remember being startled by a rustle in the underbrush. He would definitely remember the impact of the gnarling's final blow. He knew the tree was falling, and he knew he needed to move—and fast.

But Dahn was young and inexperienced, and the second worst possible thing happened. He froze. And then, the worst possible thing happened. In his panic to act, he overcompensated on his next jump.

The Pflatlands

Unable to bear the particular combination of force and angle, his toe-claws popped free from the tree's surface.

He plummeted through empty space, branches ripping at his clothing, then his bare flesh. As he reflexively strained to land feet first, the thought of death was several miles away. Dying wouldn't be so bad, really. It generally took care of itself: a brief fall, a sudden stop, and that was that. What concerned him more was what would happen should he survive.

•

Sarah pulled the green and purple brush out of the way and gazed into the clearing. Sure enough, there was the ugly little beast—all three feet of it, with its armor-plated crocodile head and lap-dog body. Still, gnarlings could hold a lot in their stomach, which was located somewhere in its head. The jokes about thinking with its stomach wrote themselves. The fact that gnarlings liked to keep it full was less a laughing matter.

The grotesque creature perked and lurched into action, crashing headfirst into a specific tree. The wooden tower toppled thunderously to the ground, taking several smaller ones with it. Something fell from its heights, crashing through lower branches and landing in the bushes with a meaty thump. Little of this mattered to Sarah, who finally had her opening. While the gnarling was distracted, she notched the ironwood sliver she pulled from her boot and let fly. Despite the aerodynamic flaws, the chunk of wood sailed true enough to impale the soft hide of the creature's rump. With a squeal of pain, the gnarling stumbled off of its back legs and fell, its oversized head preventing quick recovery of balance. Sarah rushed it with a banshee cry, burying the uncovered arrowhead into its spine. Within seconds, the thing convulsed violently, and then, it was dead. She wiped the sweat from her brow and overlooked the results. It wasn't the choicest of kills, but the head plating would make decent armor, which meant sizable money from the Fighter's Guild. It would also shut a decisive amount of mouths.

A rustle interrupted her thoughts, and she whipped out her dagger, scanning the clearing. She half expected the gnarling's mate to come charging after her; which would certainly be an appropriate end to both her day and life. Fortunately, no grass spread to make way for tiny, frothing crocodiles. As far as she could tell, it was the same blue-green sea of tranquility as before. She relaxed and heard the rustle again, along with a low moan of distress. Now more curious than anything, she tracked the sound to the bushes. Whatever had fallen from the tree was still there, and it was apparently hurt.

She couldn't have possibly been prepared for what she found. Haphazardly spiked through the bushes like a nail through wood, he was easily the most startling creature she'd ever seen. Human except for a grey cat's tail and ears, he had shoulder length hair and a trim, thin figure. He was also noticeably nude. He stirred again with a groan, and Sarah realized he must have been knocked unconscious. She faltered. This was nowhere on the list of indigenous Argury species she had read about, and that was a pretty extensive list. He might be dangerous once awake. Still, compassion overruled caution, and she decided it couldn't hurt to help. Unknown or not, he was injured, and surely less of a threat because of it. Besides, she had a soft spot for wounded animals. Especially ones that looked like that.

Pushing the branches aside, she cradled the young man in her arms, gingerly extracting him from his predicament. He hung limp in her embrace, his tail dangling. No yelps of pain escaped him, no limbs were bending the wrong way, and he was breathing evenly. Sarah wasn't a healer, but she was pretty sure the worst he'd suffered were some deep bruises and being knocked goofy for a while. The smaller woman grinned, easily depositing him next to the dead gnarling. Whoever this guy was, he was more interesting than any satyr. If this didn't qualify as adventure, she didn't know what did.

•

With a groan, Dahn slowly became aware of himself, then the world around him. He felt something soft under his head and something warm

The Pflatlands

nearby. He had fallen, but he seemed to be alive. By all accounts, things like that shouldn't happen. If you're knocked out of a tree by a monster with a head three times the size of its body—most of it teeth and stomach—the forest floor should be redecorated with your innards within seconds. As far as he could tell, all his major organs were still in place. He had somehow escaped his fall without injury, though he was certainly dazed and shaken.

His gaze went from murky to fuzzy, then sharpened. He detected another presence and tried to spring to his feet, but his limbs stubbornly refused. The result was a fumble of hands above him and a weak whimper. He heard a voice calling but didn't understand the words. He lifted his head—much as it pained him to do so—and realized the other presence was a woman. She was about his height, thin at the waist, yet pear-shaped in figure. Her silky brown hair hung loosely over her cheeks, and her pretty eyes were framed by some sort of decorative eyepiece. A bow was slung across her body. Bizarrely, she had no ears or tail, nor signs of their removal. She was frowning in concern over him, saying something in a soothing tone. The language wasn't anything he had heard before.

Exhausted with the effort of staying upright, he fell back onto the soft prop she had placed under him. His head rolled to the side, and he saw the dead body of his tormentor next to a firepit. It all came together. There was only one possible explanation for all this, and it was as exciting as it was reasonable.

Lady Green had come down from the heavens to save him. Everything was going to be okay.

To say he was flattered would be a huge understatement. Dahn had never thought himself anything more than an average Kar; if anything, he considered himself well below average. Still, his Lady's judgment was not to be questioned, especially concerning the debt of his life. He turned his head back to marvel up at her. He had to admit, he hadn't expected the Goddess of the Forest to be so, well, clothed. Speaking of which, the night chill rippling through his spine informed him his own clothes were missing, most likely torn away in the fall. He blushed a little. It's not that the Kar weren't comfortable going nude, but Lady

Green had bothered to wear something, and quite a lot of it. Dahn felt like he had shown up for a formal gala in casual attire. He hoped she would forgive the extenuating circumstances.

She was smirking at him now, shaking her head slightly. She sweetly brushed his hair with her hand and examined his bruised forehead. Dahn felt his strength returning at her touch. He thought it best to properly thank her, before she judged him ungrateful. Bearing the suffering involved, he lifted his weighty arms, folding them into prayer.

"Cheh'drehlinohs Ihl Mahba," he murmured in reverence. "El Kahri bih del'Mahba."

She smiled, and the Kar smiled back, relieved. And then, to fully show his gratitude, he kissed her.

•

Sarah stood over the young creature as his eyes fluttered open. Well, he was awake now, and he didn't go immediately for her throat. That was a positive step forward.

"I guess you don't speak Common, huh?" She cocked her head with a wry smile as his head lolled. She watched him try to piece everything together, hazel eyes still misty from the fall. He was fun to look at, that was for sure. He looked to be about her age, too. Sarah idly wondered if he would start following her around and, more importantly, what she would say to the innkeepers. ("I know you don't allow pets, but he followed me home...")

He continued to stare blankly at his surroundings.

Enough sightseeing. The poor thing was probably hurt—maybe worse than she had thought—and scared. She leaned forward, shoving his hair out of the way and examining his forehead. The gesture was fairly futile, as anyone could see the large, brown bruise on it. It wasn't like examination would make it go away, nor that Sarah knew what to do once it was identified.

He moved. It was slow, deliberate, not at all threatening. He was folding his hands over his chest as if in prayer, quietly uttering a purring, rolling tongue. Sarah actually felt bad for him. He had no clue who she was. He probably thought she was going to kill him.

"Hey." She smiled in as friendly a manner as she could muster. "Hey! It's going to be alright! I'm not going to hurt y—"

At Sarah's smile, he smiled as well, seeming to relax. He then craned his neck forward, and before she knew what was happening, he was gently pressing a hand to her cheek and kissing her—softly, passionately, and reverently.

Her eyes went wide at her personal space being violated. Within seconds, Dahn was slammed into a tree and pinned there. Her dagger was quickly brought out of its holster and to his throat.

"Hurt or not," she growled, "try that again, and you're a dead feline."

Dahn didn't even blink, afraid he would be gurgling and rolling around with a chunk of his throat missing afterwards. Parts of him were awed by the goddess' power. Someone her size was theoretically incapable of strength of this magnitude. The rest of him busied itself with the more immediate task of panicking. He cleared his throat and tried talking his way out of the situation.

"Ah, kunlah," he began, as politely as possible. "Kushkla de'te bihnu—"

Sarah narrowed her eyes and pushed him into the tree harder. Dahn realized she didn't speak Kar. He was beginning to sense things were not quite as they seemed. Nevertheless, he had to think of something, and he was fast running out of options. He took a deep breath, and then, something clicked. Prayers to Lady Green were traditionally in Elvish, not Kar. He tried again.

«Thālōkhe,» he said shakily, hoping his rusty Elvish wouldn't suddenly vacate his brain. «I am sorry for offending you, Great Lady. Your people clearly do not understand you as well as we hope.»

It was Sarah's turn to be surprised. With a cautious glare, she released him and took a few steps back. Dahn sunk to a sitting position, rolling his eyes heavenwards in thanks. He still kept a wary eye on the woman, who seemed rather angry about something.

«Your people?» she spat back, disgusted. «You put your tongue in my mouth! You're lucky you're still breathing!»

Dahn's head swam. The druids in his village were going to have a conniption when they heard about this.

«But you saved me!»

«Well, I'm happy I could help.» She wiped her lips with the back of her hand. «But that doesn't mean you can waltz up and kiss me full on the mouth! Jar'lin, I don't even know you!»

He frowned. This was bordering on insulting.

«Milady.» His tail bristled slightly. «I assure you, it's a sign of utmost reverence. Surely you're familiar with it after all these years!»

«You want me to use this, don't you?» She extended her dagger threateningly.

«Ah. Thank you, no.» He quickly adopted a less angry stance.

Right at that moment, Tor returned, bobbing crookedly through the air and singing out a greeting.

With her nerves already on edge, Sarah reacted to the tiny, glowing thing speaking in tongues by flinging her dagger on a direct line with it.

Tor dove out of the way with a shriek, avoiding a skewering by mere centimeters. After some midair scrambling to get her wings beating again, she found herself clinging to a reed for dear life, the flexible plant swaying from her weight.

Sensing no further threat, Sarah crossed the clearing to check on the intruder, surprised to find a small, winged female chattering quietly in a musical language. Dahn could pick out alternations between requests for divine entreatment, expressions of distaste for being dead, and curses to whomever sent a screaming load of death into her flight path. He displayed his sympathy with a glare at the woman's back. This was completely uncharacteristic. Lady Green would never attack one of the fae.

«Does everyone in this goddamn forest sneak up on you from behind, or is it just you two?» Sarah shook her head angrily as she retrieved her dagger. She removed it with surprisingly little effort, considering it had embedded itself up to the hilt in a tree. Meanwhile, Tor opened her eyes and looked at Dahn. Without a word, she made it clear that she would appreciate someone making this obviously psychopathic

The Pflatlands

woman leave as soon as possible.

«Excuse me,» he interjected, in as reasonable a tone as he could muster. «We seem to have gotten off on the wrong foot here.»

«No kidding,» Sarah grumbled.

«Perhaps it would be best if we start over.» He tried to mask his rising anxiety. «I am Dahn, of the Kar tribe Kluklahn. And you are?»

«Sarah,» she replied, gesturing faintly to herself. Her anger seemed to have burned itself out, leaving the simmering ashes of irritation in its place. «And as much as I'd love to stay and chat—really, I mean that—if you're alright, I need to get this gnarling to the Ranger's Guild while it's still in decent shape, or I won't even have money for food this week. So you'll excuse me if I'm unwilling to exchange pleasantries.»

"...Or spit," she added under her breath.

«Well, I could always bring you something from my—» Dahn stopped at the word "hut." Now that the adrenaline had worn off, the wheels in his mind were rolling. If this woman wasn't Lady Green, then...

«That's...sweet. I guess. But I'm not a big fan of mice.» She hoisted the gnarling carcass with one hand and sheathed her dagger. «Look, I've got to get going. I'm sorry I almost killed your little friend over there, I really am. For future reference, humans usually don't kiss total strangers. And for Jar'lin's sake, get yourself some clothes.»

Dahn cringed, his form crumpling. Human. The word echoed through his head, sealing his fate.

•

After putting out her fire and grunting her partings, Sarah left through the woods, the dead beast slung over her shoulders. From a nearby toadstool, Tor shook out her wings, still trying to slow the rapid pulsing of her circulatory system.

"What in the Sulphur Pits was that all about?" she huffed.

Dahn did not reply. The sprite did her best impression of nodding sagely, then wiggled her hips flirtatiously.

"Well, if that's how you Kar thank people, you can thank me any time you want!"

"Weren't you supposed to get help?" He glared accusingly at her.

"Couldn't find any," she shrugged.

"I see." He rested his head in his hands. "I'm not surprised."

"We should probably get going before another one of those things shows up," she suggested, sensing his patience was wearing thin. "Gnarlings, I mean. Not humans. Although those aren't very nice either, Mr. Kluklahn—"

"Dahn," he corrected.

"Oh, so we're on a first name basis now!" She winked, shifting the conversation to small talk. "I live at an encampment nearby—there's all sorts of people there! Elves, satyrs, sprites, pixies...even a merman in the lake! Though the local water nymph is getting pretty annoyed with him. How about you?"

Silence.

"Hey, zombie-kitty!" She gently prodded his upper arm, giggling once more. "Where do you live?"

"Nowhere," he replied in a cracked tone.

"Nowhere? You must live somewhere! I mean, at the very least, you could point out the nearest—"

She noticed the trail of leaves leading to the crushed bushes next to the toppled tree. Reason finally penetrated the oblivious faerie's brain. She had never seen a Kar out of the trees before. There was a reason.

"You're—you're a Groundswalker now, aren't you?" She brought her tiny hand to her mouth in a gasp.

Dahn slowly nodded, then let out a choked sob. Tor flew to his shoulder and stroked his hair in deepest pity, trying to comfort the young creature as best she could. The tears began to fall as the truth finally and unmercifully seized him.

CHAPTER 7

Upon returning to East Dunsbar, Sarah made a quick stop by Rent-A-Nag™ to return her horse—along with a suggestion of what the salesman could do with it. After that, she made a beeline through the crowded streets of the Market District. People parted and gaped at the young girl carrying a hideous carcass on her back. She reveled in the attention, grinning fiercely as she strode down the cobbled road.

The local furrier was a bald and burly man named Walter, who possessed a comical handlebar mustache and forearms the size of leprechauns. As far as Rangers' Guilds went, his was slightly above Rat Infested Cellar in quality, but still well below Dingy Hole-in-the-Wall. To approximate the latter, Walter offered the finest selections in low quality, high-proof alcohol, freshly drawn each morning from his very own bathtub. Granite slabs were strewn throughout the Guild as chairs and tables, and torches cast dim, flickering light on the stone walls. Compounding the dungeon ambiance was the shop's location, an honest-to-Jar'lin cave. While the setup was unusual, the cavern was on a prime piece of real estate near the Market District's edge—and besides, upkeep costs on a cave were remarkably cheap. Most of Walter's patrons were crusty old men with serious alcohol problems, prone to harassing patrons who weren't crusty, old, and male. They all had an unhealthy obsession with people "paying dues"—and by "dues", they usually meant their bar tab. Those who didn't were doomed to a reputation as an arrogant punk. The thought that these punks might be working never seemed to occur to them.

A group of these so-called veterans were gathered around a table, howling at some obnoxiously obscene joke, when Sarah entered. One smacked his buddy in the arm and pointed, openly staring. The other man weighed punching him in the mouth against following his finger and decided the latter took less effort. The process continued around the table until the entire group was watching her. Sarah paid them no attention, heading right to the rough wood counter and proudly dropping her kill.

"One gnarling hide," she proclaimed. "One night old, pierced twice in the back and rump. Amateur preservation job, but the teeth are still intact. What'll you give me?"

Walter turned an appraising eye on the dead beast's hide, whistling lowly. He reached under the bar for a leather apron and tied it around his large torso.

"Looks good, gotta be worth at least five silver a tooth. That brings the total to…lessee' here." He did a few mental aerobics. "About 450. You kill this by yourself?"

"I got kind of lucky." She rubbed the glittering ring on her right hand with her thumb. The inlaid stone sparkled in the torchlight. "The thing was distracted by some poor native. I took it out while its back was turned."

"It's a fine job, distracted or not. Tell you what. Since it's in good condition, I'll throw in an extra 25 silver for the hide. Not much of a demand for gnarling skin, but I can turn a profit on it somehow."

"Actually, after all the trouble I went through, I'd like to make a trophy out of it. How about you keep the extra silver, we take eight teeth off the bill, and you make a necklace out of them?"

"Deal," Walter nodded. "I'll be right back."

The Pflatlands

He heaved the dead creature over his shoulders and struggled into the back. Sarah leaned against the bar with a sigh of relief. Four hundred and fifty silver! Even after expenses, it would be enough to live on—for the next few days, at least. She clenched her fist, pumping it in silent triumph.

"Hey, babe!" A white-haired man shouted across the bar, three decibel levels over what was needed to hear him from the Lower Kingdom. "You sure made a lot of money off that gnarling!"

"Yeah!" another chimed in. He was missing half his teeth and, as a direct result of time around his friend, most of his hearing. "Maybe now she can pay the man who killed it for her!"

They broke into atrocious peals of laughter. The only other occupant of the bar, wrapped in a light brown cloak and enjoying the least caustic beverage on the menu, slid further down his bench from them. He stuck his nose deeper into his broadsheet, which trumpeted:

HIGH KINGDOM HIT BY SCANDAL
High King Unappreciatively Vague, Refuses Comment

"I tell you what, honey," the first ranger belted out again. "You get your cute little ass in the back and get me some more ale, and I'll do the next job for half price!"

He lobbed his empty tankard at her to another burst of guffaws. It clanked a few feet away and rolled across the sandy floor, halting in front of Sarah's feet. Her eyes focused tightly on the men around the table. Picking it up, she stepped to their table, meditatively turning the tankard over in her hands. She bent at the waist, giving them the same plastic smile and flirtatious view as a bar wench.

"Excuse me, sirs," she said, in a giggling and high-pitched voiced. "I think you may have dropped this."

She held the tankard out for the first hunter, who reached with a leer and another obnoxious laugh. Suddenly, she yanked it out of his reach and squeezed—first with one hand, then with both, easily compacting it into a warm wad of imitation pewter. She opened her hand high in the air and let it hit the table with a loud thud.

"Your balls are next," she stated plainly.

The men weren't laughing anymore.

"So, the little witch has a Ring of Strength." The first ranger rose angrily. "I should've known you needed help to bring that gnarling down."

"Maybe we can get a little extra for it after we cut it off her, Stan." A second joined him.

"I killed that thing with half a poisoned arrow and no quiver," Sarah snapped back. "Top that, dragonbait."

"I wouldn't want to," Stan replied haughtily. "I'm smart enough to go prepared."

"Was I supposed to need help, or was I supposed to come prepared?" She folded her arms over her chest. "You've got a real problem making up your mind, you know that? Should I come back when you're less drunk? Oh, wait—that would mean you'd have to get off your lazy, ale-swigging ass for a change, wouldn't it?"

"Why, you little—"

Stan didn't get much farther than that, his face turning a bright, colorful shade. With a glance amongst themselves, the rest of the rangers rose to their feet. Sarah backed up a few paces, yanking her dagger out of her boot and mentally kicking herself. Not only was it four-on-one, but she was going to lose money for starting a brawl. One of these days, she was going to learn to keep her mouth shut.

Fortunately, the fight was over before it began. Stan had taken two and a half steps towards her before the cloaked man, who'd been previously nursing his ale substitute and remaining deathly quiet*, slipped one leg off his seat and slightly behind the ranger's. One forward roll and a cry of surprise later, Stan was on the ground, his left leg scissored tightly. The robed figure pulled, and there was a sickening crack from somewhere inside Stan's knee. He screamed in pain and hobbled up on one leg. The outsider stood and glared icily. With nervous looks and lowered heads, the drunken louts helped their friend out of the Guild. They didn't bother looking back.

---

*The two were most likely related.

The Pflatlands

Sarah arched an eyebrow, sheathing her knife. Underneath the brown sackcloth cloak, most of the man's brown skin was covered by a white, formalized cotton outfit. His hair was coarse and black, bound into a long braid and tied off by an ornamental yellow ribbon. His eyes were almost solid black, and he sported a short, bushy goatee over his chin and mouth. He was also twice as tall as her—and nearly twice as wide, as well.

"So." Sarah shook her head in wonderment. Well, she had wanted adventure. It'd certainly been an eventful couple of days. "Hunt much, or do you just come to the Ranger's Guild to break legs?"

The man regarded her coolly. His voice was a rich baritone. "I was under the impression it was customary to thank those who save you."

"If you try to kiss me," Sarah muttered, "I swear to Jar'lin, I'm putting a knife in your ribs."

It was her rescuer's turn to arch an eyebrow. Sarah waved it off.

"Never mind. Thanks. You may have saved that man's life."

"Or yours."

"I can handle myself."

"The strength of giants alone does not make one great," he intoned. "The strength of unicorns must accompany it."

Sarah stared at him.

"You're a monk, aren't you?"

The man bobbed his head in silence. She turned and hammered the bell on the counter. Walter dutifully returned, still stringing her necklace.

"I'm going to cut out early. Could you have the money delivered to my room?"

"Sure, but it'll cost you 10 extra silver."

"Make it seven."

"Eight."

"Done. What about the necklace?"

"One last tooth to string in. I haven't punctured it yet."

"I'll just take the necklace with seven and the spare."

"Whatever slays your dragon," Walter shrugged, handing over the requested items. Sarah tied the new jewelry around her neck and flipped the last tooth to the monk. He pulled it out of the air with a disturbingly effortless hand motion, giving it and then her a critical glance.

"Wise man once say, 'Gnarling tooth worth enough for free night at Inn.'" She grinned, adjusting the bow slung over her body. "Thanks again. Try not to snap anyone else's kneecaps."

He watched as she took a torch off the wall, disappearing into the blackness of the exit.

"A strange one, her," he commented. He pocketed the tooth in the folds of his cloak.

"Yeah, and mean as the animal she killed," Walter replied. "If she ever learns to trust anyone, she'll go far."

"And if she does not?"

"Then I hope she's got a small fortune for the Guild in her will," he shrugged.

"And if she does not have a fortune?" the monk pressed in disapproval.

"Then why the Infernus should I care what happens to her?" Walter snapped back. "Cripes, first I gotta knock out all these gnarling teeth, then you start spouting your philosophical crap at anyone who'll listen!"

Walter cursed and complained all the way to the back of the shop, where he disappeared into his workroom, slamming the door. The monk left a few pieces of silver on his table for the drink and departed. He also decided against leaving a tip.

•

The cool evening air took the edge of Sarah's temper as she returned her torch to the outside holder. For the love of all that was holy! Was it just her, or were people getting stupider by the minute these days? Every now and then, people like the monk bolstered her plummeting opinion of humanity—but for every person like him, there were four more like Stan, and that was just the humans. She didn't even want to consider other races. After all, she'd recently had a foreign tongue jammed between her teeth, and Jar'lin only knows where it'd been.

And after all this, I'll probably have to buy a new quiver, too. She laid one hand against the cave's cliffside. I honestly don't think this could get any worse.

Thunder boomed through the clouds overhead as the first drops of moisture fell from the heavens. Sarah would've kicked herself if she was flexible enough to do it.

•

The rain beat down hard on one particular Argury village, sending everyone scattering, flying, or creeping to their homes. True to Tor's descriptions, the local community was diverse. Huts and shelters stretched around the circular enclave, from the highest trees to the bottom of the lake. Fae and non-fae alike lived in relative harmony. There was always the occasional spriggan who decided to take up residence, but the noisy and belligerent creatures never stayed long, forging ever onwards in their incomprehensible quest to erect megalithic monuments. No one knew why spriggans did what they did. Anyone who asked usually received a boulder to the head.

Tor had found a place for Dahn in a pretty, though patchwork, dwelling on the edge of the small lake. The hut was all natural, made solely from the reeds and leaves of bigger, heartier plants—save for one large, humming spike of metal jammed through the roof. The inside was spacious enough, divided into two plain rooms, kitchen and bedroom. The former held Tor and the lady of the house, who were sharing a kettle of ginjin tea and chatting worriedly. The latter held Dahn, curled in a fetal position underneath a thick blanket. He wasn't asleep. In fact, he hadn't slept since the accident. He only rose from his apathy long enough to take offered food and drink before sinking right back under the covers.

The kitchen was sparsely decorated but warm and homey, consisting of a wooden counter, clay bowls and cups, a wood burning stove, a table, some chairs, and a wooden exit door on either side. Tor and her friend sat at opposite ends of the table, gently sipping tea from earthenware cups. The other woman was inescapably lovely, with golden skin, a shapely figure, and yellow hair tied above her head in a small ponytail.

She wore a completely sheer wrap of silk around her body. It was intended to be a nightshirt. A human would have thought she wound herself in plastic wrap. A male of just about any species most likely wouldn't have cared.

From her tabletop seat, Tor finally broke the brief silence, slurping loudly from her pintsized cup.

"I don't know how long he'll be like this. I mean, everything he knew is gone." The sprite waggled her fingers, and a small sparkle of energy popped from her fingertips. "Poof. Just like that."

"It's, like, totally unfair—y'know?" The blonde nymph pouted cutely and stuck her hands on her hips. "So he fell out of tree. So what? There's no reason to, what's the word, ostrich-eyes…"

"Seline? What do ostrich eyes have to do with anything?"

"No, no, no." She shook her head with a vague gesture. "It's, like, that one word. When you push someone away and totally ignore them and junk."

"I don't have the slightest idea what you mean."

"Well, anyway," Seline continued, "I would be totally bummed to go back after what he's been through!"

"He says if he goes back, they'll—they'll cut off his tail!" Tor looked horrified.

"Gag me! They want to chop off his tail for a single mistake?" Seline huffed. "Like, whatever. I'd just find somewhere else to live, if I were him."

"It's not that simple. He's got a younger sibling he took care of. And besides, Kars are very social creatures! He must feel awful about being alone in the world."

"Wow. That's totally uncool."

"Totally," Tor agreed. "I think his biggest problem right now is that he thinks he's completely worthless. He's probably afraid no one will show him love, or affection, or even friendship!"

"Oh! So the little cutie wants affection?" Seline brightened instantly, rising from her chair. "Like, you should've said so earlier!"

"I don't think he's in the mood, Seline," Tor warned.

"Yeah, I bet," she snorted in disbelief. "Kar are always, y'know, in the mood."

She stood in the bedroom doorway, throwing her hips seductively at the lump in the blanket. Tor sighed and turned back to her tea. Finding her thimble-sized cup empty, she dipped it into Seline's, refilling it while the nymph's attention was elsewhere.

●

A polite cough at the door roused Dahn. He rolled over as quickly as he could, which took just outside of four minutes. After being in the dim bedroom for so long, his eyes adjusted painfully to the bright light spilling from the kitchen. An amazingly curvy silhouette was highlighted by it, back arched seductively. The shadow reached slowly to her hair and pulled off her ponytail holder. With a practiced shake of her head, her hair fell down in rippling, golden waves.

Now that she had his full attention, Seline stepped to the bedridden Kar, fully extending her shapely legs. She bent slightly and batted her long eyelashes, placing her barely covered body tantalizing inches away.

"Can I get you anything to eat, friend?" she purred sultrily in Kar, flashing a sexy smile and winking impishly.

Dahn stared in disbelief, then shook his head mutely. Seline was undaunted, raising a smooth, tanned leg and setting it firmly on the edge of the bed. She ran her index finger lightly up its length.

"It's awfully cold outside." She brushed his hair away from his face. "Maybe you'd like someone to—y'know—help keep the bed warm?"

Dahn continued staring. Wonderful. This girl had all the subtlety of a fireball spell in an enclosed stone room. He rolled back over and curled up again, hoping that, if he ignored her long enough, she'd go away.

"Well, if you change your mind," Seline whispered hotly in his ear, "you know where to find me."

She slunk back to the kitchen, swaying her hips for all she was worth. Meanwhile, Dahn wondered if the merman's house would have been more comfortable. The fact that he couldn't breathe underwater was looking more and more like a plus.

Leaving the bedroom and Dahn's line of sight, Seline snatched her ponytail holder and tied her hair back up. She slumped in her chair crossly.

"I told you so," Tor commented, without looking up from her tea.

"That was totally bogus. The last time I visited a Kar village for spring break, one of them was, like, all over me!"

"It's going to take more than a pretty girl to snap him out of this. We need to think of something! Or he's just going to waste away!"

"Is there anyone else he knew before the fall?" Seline rubbed her chin thoughtfully. "Like, someone that isn't a Kar?"

"I don't know." Tor racked the entirety of her brain, which didn't take long. "I got a little information out of him, but not much."

"How about after the fall?"

"No—wait a second—yes! One person."

"Male or female?"

"Female. Mean as a bat out of Infernus, too. But they seemed to get along!"

"Really? How could you tell?"

"Well, she threw a dagger at me."

"Omigod! That's so awful!"

"Yeah. But she didn't throw a dagger at him!"

"So, she probably likes him!" Seline nodded in agreement. "Well, we should invite her over or something."

"It's not that easy, Seline."

"Why not?"

"She's human."

Seline groaned, now understanding their plight. She raised her teacup to her lips and was surprised when nothing came out. She peered into her now empty cup.

"Hey! What happened to my tea?"

Tor burped quietly.

The Pflatlands

The sprinkle became a thunderous shower before Sarah could leave the Market District. Cursing the weather, she sprinted back to the Happy Boar Inn. The rickety two-story building was tucked between the post office and the local tavern[*], and the quality of its exterior was barely exceeded by its interior. Out of breath and thoroughly soaked, Sarah wrung out her hair and clothes on a moth-eaten bearskin inside, then dripped her way to the front desk.

"May I help you?" A scrawny youngster dressed in a red cap, cloak, and a red vest with yellow buttons greeted her.

"Yeah, I've got a package coming for me later tonight. Could you keep it safe until morning?"

"Certainly, ma'am," the clerk smiled.

Sarah grimaced; she didn't fancy herself a "ma'am." She thanked him anyway and ascended the stairs, leather boots clomping on uneven wood. She had originally wanted a long, hot bath when she returned. Right now, she didn't want to look at any form of water for the rest of her life. She opened the door to her room and took the key off the inside nail, where it spent most of its time hanging. Sarah never locked her room while she was out. It was inconvenient to keep track of keys in the wild, and besides, she kept everything of value on her person.

Stepping inside and locking the door behind her, she drew the curtains, then slipped from her clothing in privacy. Taking a towel from the corner of the room, she blotted the water from her body, then her hair. She peered in the mirror at the matted mess on her head, running her fingers through it to no avail. It was going to stand straight up in the morning, no matter what she did. She just knew it.

She took the tunic hanging on the room's single chair, slipped it over her head, and fumbled her arms into the sleeves. It was extra large, the hem reaching her knees and the sleeves extending well past her hands—not tremendously warm, but comfy enough to sleep in. Her original outfit replaced the nightshirt on the chair. She placed her glasses on the wooden nightstand by her bed, and, finally, she put out the lantern. Snuggling into the soft feather mattress, she was soon

---

[*] "Bob's Beer-O-Rama."

slumbering peacefully, lulled into unconsciousness by the gentle sound of rain on ceramic tile.

It was not a habit of Sarah's to leave her windows unlocked, but living on the second story, she didn't think it necessary to lock them. In the dead of night, she slept right through the quiet creak of her shutters being pushed open.

From the outside.

•

You know all the stories where faeries steal innocent children and leave ugly creatures in their place? Take them with a huge grain of salt.

First of all, many of these stories are ridiculously sensationalized. Full of warped pride at being part of something so abnormal, the parents usually demand someone with a harp and half an ear for epic poetry write a ballad, right that instant, to warn others of their terrible fate. (Naturally, they want full details of who they are and what clan, tribe, or country they represent.) One wonders how the baby was plucked from the midst of such "loving" parents in the first place, which underscores the other problem with this vicious media distortion. Despite myths to the contrary, the average faerie has all the stealth of a box of aluminum cans falling down three flights of stairs.

We'll illustrate our point by looking at three races who have had the most fingers pointed at them: the sprites, the pixies, and the elves. First, having met Tor, you can understand why three to four of her closest kin would have a difficult time breaking into a nursery undetected, let alone carrying a horrible monster in and lugging the actual baby out. Furthermore, a child at six months would be more than capable of using a sprite for its rattle or, worse, its teething ring.

The pixies are even less enthusiastic about this sort of thing. Most of them are content to sit on mushrooms and sigh wistfully, composing odes to the object of their affection—who, in turn, are writing his or her own ode to someone else, and so on. Eventually, the pixies are going to establish a solid ring of odes. It's bound to happen. Perhaps they'll use it for long distance communication, like medieval minstrels. Maybe, one

The Pflatlands

day, they'll even invent the odeophone. But this is all beside the point; not only is kidnapping children a deplorable waste of ode-writing time, but pixie magic extends solely into the realm of sensory illusions. The worst they could do is cause the wee child to bawl its eyes out.

And the elves? Your average elf is as interested in a baby human as your average human is interested in a baby wolverine. They certainly wouldn't go out of their way to steal one, let alone bother a neighboring troll for a trolling to leave in its place.

Taking the next logical step, the nastier unseelie fae are also disinclined to pursue these endeavors. Take the bogey, for instance. The sprites' uglier and thoroughly less charismatic cousins not only have the same problems as their fairer kin, but they absolutely loathe children. Mothers are always making thinly veiled threats in the name of the "bogeyman," and who wants to justify that sort of prejudice? And the spriggans? Don't make us laugh! While they could get away with it, the spriggan-shaped hole in the wall would be a dead giveaway as to the culprit. Besides, spriggans have no need for a human child. The titanic rocks they work with are sufficient for throwing at people who annoy them[*], and there's no attraction to the child as a food source. Believe it or not, most spriggans are vegetarians. It's best not to let on that you know, though, unless you want a boulder upside your skull.

So, what's the answer? If someone is doing it—and the frequency of the stories certainly indicates someone is—who really steals human babies and leaves changelings in their places?

The surprising answer: the nymphs.

The painful truth is that the kidnappings are acts of mercy, not mischief. Sure, there's the rare occasion where a passing nymph will look in a window, and her heart will absolutely melt at the cutest widdle baby she ever saw—but for the most part, they're following their protective maternal instincts. It all works out in the end, anyway; the parents learn their lesson, the baby gets a new and caring mother, and the changeling gets a chance at a college education. The only missing detail is why nymphs would leave changelings in the baby's place. Why not just take

---

[*] Which is to say, everyone.

the Goff-damned thing and be on their way? While they don't take part in the crib raids, the dryads had originally suggested substitution of a baby troll or goblin (or even a hobgoblin, for variety), ensuring the prank's first sign would be a glass-shattering wail. Tongue was planted firmly in cheek the entire time. Nymphs being nymphs, the suggestion was taken seriously, and the tradition has stuck. To this day, dryads everywhere steadfastly deny their role. It's not a proud moment in their history.

You may be wondering where all this is going, and quite frankly, so are we. But the next time you hear someone complain about their child being swapped with a changeling, you'll know one of two things: Either they deserved it, or they're looking to blame someone over their own horrid little monster.

•

Wind and rain blew into the room, rustling the curtains. Sarah stirred slightly with a pained moan, then rolled over and pulled the blankets closer. Carefully, gingerly, Tor flitted into the room and landed on a bedpost. Seline followed seconds later, weightlessly riding the drafty winds. She was wrapped in a pure white linen, which could only be called "clothing" due to the sheer, random chance it happened to cover more private areas. The nymph closed the window, and both faeries held their breath. To their relief, Sarah kept right on sleeping.

Seline knelt next to the bed, murmured a quiet greeting, and brushed the human girl's forehead with her fingertips. A slight glow radiated between her hand and Sarah's forehead. Sarah's breathing deepened.

"So, she's completely out?" Tor buzzed in front of Sarah's unconscious face, examining Seline's handiwork.

"She should be totally zonked for another six hours or so," Seline replied in a hushed voice.

"Do you think she'll be angry?"

Seline looked heavenwards. The thought honestly hadn't occurred to her.

"I guess she might be a little ticked off, but she'll just have to, like, mellow out."

"Well, she already saved Dahn once. She won't mind doing it again, right?"

"Do you think he'll get along with her?" Seline mused.

"I don't see why not." Tor stroked the sleeping girl's cheek affectionately.

"Well, like, what does she have that I don't?" The nymph was the tiniest bit insulted. "She's a total stick from the waist up!"

"Maybe he doesn't like buxom women. I mean, he didn't go for us, right?"

The two giggled over Sarah's sleeping form. Suddenly, a key rattled in the lock outside. Their breaths caught in their throats. They weren't expecting company.

Seline scrambled for a hiding place, eventually squeezing under the bed on all fours. Tor did aerial figure eights in a blind panic before forcing open the clothes drawer with a few mighty tugs. She buried herself under a pair of white socks mere moments before the doorknob turned.

The door creaked painfully. Sarah continued her sound sleep, oblivious to everything. It stopped, held dramatically, then swung fully open to reveal two men. One had a bloated and wrinkled face, his cherry-colored cheeks and nose a sign of one cheap drink too many. He also had a distinct limp, a brace around one leg, and a short sword on his belt. His partner had hollow green eyes and a tangle of black curls sprouting above his head. A jagged scar ran down the outside of his eye, breaking at the eyelid before continuing down his cheek. A brown leather belt was wrapped around his waist, several wicked-looking tools hanging from hooks on it. That was all Seline and Tor could see from their hiding places, for the rest of him was covered by a black silk suit and a matching bandanna.

"Burning Infernus!" the older man cursed quietly. "Think you could make any more noise?"

"Relax," his partner sneered. "She's still asleep, isn't she?"

"You better hope so. For both our sakes."

They stalked into the room, closing the door behind them. The man in black flipped down the covers. With a flick of his hand, he produced a fine powder from a leather pouch on his belt. He blew it gently into Sarah's face.

"There. She'll sleep soundly for a few more hours—which is far more than I need." He traced a finger over her cheek in a way that would have made her shudder (and break it) if she were conscious. "Pretty. You sure you want her dead?"

"Positive," the other grimaced. "I want her Ring of Strength, too."

The assassin balked and pulled the covers back farther. The glinting gold ring was still on her right hand.

"Ring of Strength? You said nothing about magical aid! Your fee just doubled!"

"For Goff's sake!" Stan exclaimed. "I blew a small fortune bribing the clerk for the room key! Besides, she can't use it while she's asleep!"

"Fine." He drew his dagger and offered the hilt. "Slit her throat yourself. But don't blame me when the High Guard comes calling."

"You assassins really play hardball, don't you?"

"That's the way the Guild trains us. Pay the fee, or do it yourself."

"And what's to keep me from killing you and saying you did it?"

"Seven years of training under the most lethal killers in the Pflatlands. Try me."

The two locked eyes. The assassin didn't flinch.

"Fine, whatever." Stan shook his head in defeat. "Twice as much. I'll get the money somehow. Just get it done, and make it untraceable."

"Of course. The customer is always right." The assassin flipped his dagger upside down, catching the hilt in midair. Placing his hand on Sarah's forehead, he forced her head back, exposing her throat.

Heavy footsteps echoed down the hall.

The assassin's blade halted a hair above Sarah's jugular, and the two would-be killers exchanged angry glances. They weren't expecting company. The man in black sheathed his weapon and donned a pair of clawed knuckles, leaping high into the air and burying them in the ceiling. He pulled himself flat with impressive strength and hung there. The white-haired man cursed vigorously and stood beside the door frame, hiding in the shadows as best he could.

The Pflatlands

•

Groeke hesitantly approached the door, following the clerk's directions. Second floor, first room on the left—yes, this was definitely Sarah's. He figured now was as good a time as any for their first formal meeting. He had gone this far to find her. It was best to get it over with, and quickly.

He knocked on the door. No answer. She was probably asleep, or...

Alarm bells rung in the back of his head. After years of sharpening his instincts to a razor's edge, he could tell when something was out of place. This whole setup was not only out of place, but had packed its bags and left for a tropical location at least a week ago. He tried the doorknob, and the door swung open, unlocked. That was unusual. He knew Sarah was more careful than that.

As he stepped inside, everything in his immediate field of vision made sense. The dark, silent room was interrupted only by moonlight and Sarah's breath. She was lying on the bed in her nightshirt, in a deep and undisturbed slumber. Groeke was not fooled by the serene scene. He scanned for some sign, however subtle, that something was amiss. His hawk-like eyes caught a hint of movement in the open drawer on his left, and he squinted in confusion. Why were Sarah's socks glowing?

There was no time to ponder further, as the air suddenly shifted behind him. Someone was expecting company. He pivoted, and a shortsword swung by him with lethal force. Without hesitation, Groeke swung his arm upwards and under the sword's hilt, knocking it over his attacker's head. Wrapping the crook of his arm around the man's armpit and neck, Groeke lifted him high into the air, then slammed him, back first, against the ground. The sword slid across the floor and clanked harmlessly into the wall. The rush of air escaping his attacker's lungs confirmed that he was out cold. To Groeke's amazement, Sarah kept right on sleeping.

The monk stood and finally looked over his attacker, recognizing him immediately.

"Stan Chryzdolf. First, your leg is broken for your foolishness, then you are defeated with a single blow. Perhaps, one day, you will learn."

Something sharp bit painfully into his flesh. Grasping at his now-bleeding shoulder, he spun in place, only to catch a two-footed kick to the teeth.

"Hmpf. Is that why you're the World's Most Dangerous Monk?" the assassin taunted as he dropped to the ground. "You maim old men in squalid bars?"

"Old men should not attempt murder if they wish to stay unharmed." Groeke ripped the steel throwing star from his shoulder and pushed his fingers into specific pressure points. Despite the pain, he barely grimaced. "I do not believe I have the pleasure of knowing your name."

"Nor will you. How fortunate—the one and only Groeke Farkhis, right here before me. I can finally prove to the world that you're nothing but a fake."

"Quo'chi-ka is not fake," Groeke replied angrily, removing his hand. Most of the hemorrhaging was now under control. He raised both fists, ignoring his throbbing shoulder. "Or perhaps you would discover for yourself?"

"I don't plan on giving you an opportunity to show me."

The man in black charged with a flat-handed chop. Groeke raised an arm to block—which was exactly what the assassin wanted. He went low with an elbow to Groeke's stomach, then followed with a palm thrust under the chin, snapping the monk's mouth closed. Groeke backpedaled and hit the wall, temporarily stunned. He clutched his shoulder and glared at the assassin, who blew air across his palm as if blowing smoke from a gun barrel.

"What's the matter, grappler?" the assassin taunted. "Your precious fighting style not real enough?"

With a fierce growl, Groeke curled his fists together and exploded from the wall. His blow smashed solidly into the assassin's chest, knocking him flat.

"The most fatal mistake of any fight," he observed stoically to his downed foe, "is to think it is over before it has begun."

The assassin sprung to his feet with a snarl and snapped out his weapon, lunging forward. Groeke caught his wrist, and the two strug-

The Pflatlands

gled violently in close quarters—the assassin trying to force the shiv into Groeke's chest, the monk trying to force it away.

Abruptly, both men stiffened with a look of genuine astonishment.

"I'll take this," Seline said pointedly, removing the knife from the assassin's hand.

Their eyes rolled into the back of their heads, and they fell to the ground in a heap, sleeping soundly. A-rustle-in-the-sock-drawer-later, Tor was hovering beside the blonde knockout.

"Whew! Took you long enough!"

"I had to wait for an opening. It would have, like, totally grossed me out if they killed each other right in front of me."

"Did you hear who they were?"

"Not really. I was too busy thinking of how to get out of here. Did you?"

"I couldn't hear a thing under that sock!"

The nymph stooped over the assassin's unconscious form, groping through his clothing.

"What are you doing?" Tor shot her a mildly disgusted look.

"He might have something I need!"

"Seline, that may be important to you, but you should wait until he's conscious before you—oh." Tor blushed slightly. "Oh! You're looting him!"

"Well, duh! What did you think I meant?"

"Never mind. Just hurry up!"

"Okay, okay!"

The only objects Seline had the slightest clue how to use were the sleeping powder, a few shuriken, and a portable rope and grapple. She took the sleeping powder and blew a minute amount in the assassin's face.

"Now what are you doing?" Tor asked edgily.

"Hello? We can't have this dweeb waking up before the other guy. He'll kill him while he's asleep! That would be totally uncool!"

"Oh." The thought, like so many before, hadn't occurred to Tor. "But what makes you think the other guy won't kill him?"

"You don't punch people in a knife fight if you want to kill them.

That's so totally moronic, he has to be the good guy!"

"I guess so. Hmm, I swear I've seen him somewhere before…"

The little faerie peered hard at Groeke, then shook her head, giving up. It was too dark to see clearly, and they had risked enough by staying this long. She stood wary watch on the bedpost, fully expecting one more crazy to burst into the room with a newly sharpened blade and an attitude. Giving the assassin a final pat down, Seline discovered one last item. With a curious hum, she reached into the man's tunic and retrieved an ornate scroll. It was bound in purple ribbon and sealed with black wax. The image of a spider devouring its prey was pressed into the seal.

"Let's go, Seline!" Tor urged nervously.

The nymph tucked the scroll—somehow—into her clothing, gathered Sarah's garments, then mouthed a few incantations. The wind picked up outside, howling fervently. Tor pulled open the shutters and was thrown across the room by the blast of air.

"You overdid it again," she complained, as soon as she was able.

"My bad!"

Then, with a lift of Seline's hand, both she and Sarah were hovering in the rush of air current. Seline gently guided the floating girl out the window.

"How long do you think she'll sleep now?" asked Tor, following close behind.

"Hmm." The nymph looked worried as she multiplied, carried the seven, and promptly forgot what measurement unit she was working in. "Like, either a couple of days, or a couple of thousand years."

"Thousand?"

"Well, give or take!"

The two flew from the confines of the inn room with Sarah in tow, the shutters slamming behind them. In their wake, they left a sword, a dagger, a man knocked violently unconscious, two more slumbering peacefully, and a disheveled sock drawer.

CHAPTER 4

Sarah's brain lurched into consciousness from what felt like the longest sleep in her life. She was dimly aware that her face was clammy, her hair was sopping, and there were bits of leaves and twigs clinging to her skin. In her overpowering daze, she wondered how someone had sneaked a rain forest into her bed without waking her up.

"Hey! Like, she's finally coming around!"

Gentle slaps on her cheek and an overly perky voice annoyed her into opening her eyes. The bright light of the room passed right through her pupils and cut directly into her brain. She grunted in pain and brought her fists to her eyes, rubbing the sleep out of them. When they focused as clear as they could without glasses, she was greeted by two strangers who were not supposed to be in her room, followed by the revelation she was no longer in her room.

"Where am I?" Sarah stumbled to her feet with a small shriek. "Who in the Underpflats are you?"

After returning to Seline's hut with their "guest," the two faeries had tried everything to wake her, from emptying a pitcher of water over her head to rolling her down a small hill. In the end, they decided to wait it out, reasoning the combined powder and charm had to wear off eventually. Thinking a familiar face would calm Sarah, Tor dove a foot in front of her face and tried to explain. The error in judgment was immediately obvious. Sarah took a panicked swing at the sudden intrusion, and Tor barely missing being swatted flat. Seline raised her illuminated index finger with a dark frown.

"No! She's slept enough!" Tor darted between the two—taking care to place herself much closer to her friend. Seline's eyes flashed angrily, but she lowered her hand, the glow subsiding.

"Would you chill out long enough for us to explain what's going on?" The nymph straightened the disheveled grass dress-wrap she was wearing.

"What's going on," Sarah fired back, "is a kidnapping! I demand to know who you people are and where you've taken me!"

Dahn chose that moment to shuffle into the kitchen with a titanic yawn. Seline had been unsuccessful using her charms on him—magical or otherwise—as his typical reaction was to recoil and smile the nervous smile of those cornered by the mentally deranged. Still, he needed to rest before his body deteriorated, which had led to the following conversation that morning, between Tor and Dahn:

"Hey, Dahn?"

"What, Torzzzzzzz."

"That," the sprite had smiled, brushing the remaining sleeping powder from her palms.

Conscious and mobile once more, Dahn had come into kitchen to see what all the ruckus was about (and maybe get a cup of water while he was up). He made eye contact with Sarah. They regarded each other silently.

"Great," she snorted. "I should've known."

Dahn grimaced, clutching the blankets closer. He minced directly back to the bedroom.

Sarah shook her head, checking her surroundings. The hut was simple—not really primitive, but certainly basic. Her clothes were washed and folded in the corner, her glasses on top of them. The occupants didn't appear to be hostile—or at any rate, Sarah didn't feel particularly threatened by them.

While stretching her aching muscles, she noticed the room had fallen silent. The sprite and nymph were giving her looks that would get them arrested for attempted homicide in some cities.

"What?" she asked pointedly.

"What do you mean, what?" Tor scowled. "Are you blind?"

Sarah stared at her.

"What did she just say?"

"She wants to know what your deal is," Seline angrily translated. "If you don't help him, he's going to die! Like, fer sure!"

"Do I look like a healer? What the blazes do you want me to do about it?"

"A lot more than you're doing now!"

"You kidnap me out of my inn room, you drag me halfway across the world to Jar'lin knows where, and then, you want me to patch up an overly flirtatious cat-boy who, in my humble and amateur opinion, looks perfectly fine?" She bundled up her clothes, replaced her glasses, and marched to the front door. "I'm checking out of this hellhole right now. You should consider yourselves lucky I'm not pressing charges."

Tor fluttered in front of Sarah, hands outstretched despite the size difference. Babbling melodiously, she made it clear the ranger wasn't leaving with several shakes of her head.

"Listen, insect." Sarah's patience was finally running out. "You have approximately three seconds to get out of my way before I use you as a stickball."

Tor puffed out her chest, set her chin, and motioned to it.

"Fine. Your funeral!"

Sarah balled her fist and threw a perfect right jab. Her fist smacked into the faerie's open palm, which—despite being a hundred times smaller—absorbed the blow with no apparent damage. With a crackle and pop, the ruby on Sarah's ring dimmed. A cyan aura began to shimmer around the hovering faerie. But the final surprise, the grandest shock of all, came when Tor slapped away Sarah's hand, grabbed a handful of her shirt, and hoisted her into the air!

As the flabbergasted young woman struggled, Tor sung something that sounded a lot less flattering. Seline attended to a pot of tea on the stove with a smile.

"I see you're totally familiar with sprites' mimicry magic." She poured her beverage, then added with a sarcastic flourish, "NOT!"

•

After an abusive monologue and a dozen threatening shakes, Tor hauled Sarah to the bedroom by the back of her collar. She roughly deposited her in the middle of the floor with a mighty two-handed lob.

"And don't come out until you help him!" she added, no longer caring if Sarah could understand her. The cyan aura around her was already fading. She dusted off her hands with a satisfied huff and flew back into the kitchen in search of tea.

Sarah grumbled and stood, rubbing her sore tailbone. She crossed the room hesitantly to confront the figure on the bed. The grey, furred ears poking out of the wrapped blanket made his identity unmistakable.

«Has everyone around here lost their damned minds?» she began.

«I suppose you could say that. There's nothing here but fae and—» He searched for a clumsy translation with a pained expression. «Walkers of the Ground.»

«Argury. Well, at least I know where I am now.»

«I have to apologize for all this,» he sniffled. «I think it might be my fault.»

«What, did you put them up to it?»

«No, but I think Seline heard about you from Tor. Maybe they thought you could help.»

«Didn't they think I'd object to being kidnapped? Or, here's a thought, of just asking me?»

«Between a nymph and a sprite? Not a chance.»

«Great.» After considering her next course of action (and the sprite's threats), she bluntly asked, «What's eating you?»

«Oh, you don't want to hear about my problems.»

The Pflatlands

«If I don't, the Winged Wonder out there is going to break both my kneecaps.» Her tone softened. «Besides, you look awful. It can't be healthy to stay like that.»

Dahn was caught in an internal struggle behind his empty gaze.

«I fell,» he finally admitted, humiliated. «Out of the trees.»

Sarah waited for the rest of the explanation. None came.

«Okay...are you hurt?»

«Oh, no.»

«Eight more lives to go, huh?» Sarah laughed. Dahn gave her a blank stare. She sighed and turned away.

«I wish I could understand your jokes. They seem very amusing.»

«You wouldn't know it. Anyway, you're still breathing, and you've got a couple of cute girls waiting on you hand and foot. Where's the problem?»

Dahn looked at her, then looked away. Sarah noticed how red and bloated his eyes were. He had clearly been crying for days. All the cynicism drained out of her; his mistake obviously meant more than a dangerous plunge. However crackpot their scheme, Seline and Tor had good reason to act quickly. His spirit was broken. It was only a matter of time before his body followed.

«Hey, hey! It's alright! Don't cry!» Taking a seat on the bed, she patted his knee reassuringly. She suddenly found his head on her shoulder as he wept, his fur and hair caressing her arm. She recovered as quickly as she could. «Look, I'm sorry I was angry with you. It's been a rough week.»

«Oh, you had a right to be.» Dahn shook his head with a sniff. «They had no right to bring you here against your will.»

Sarah was relieved. Someone was finally showing signs of common decency.

«Well, I'm here now, might as well take advantage of it. Now, what's this really all about?»

«I told you. I fell.»

«So? You know how many trees I've fallen out of while learning to climb?»

«But you're human!» The look Sarah gave him made Dahn blanch and rephrase. «I mean—it's—well, it's different for you.»

«How so?» she asked sharply.

«For starters, you can still visit your family afterwards. I think. Maybe. Please don't hit me.»

«What, and you can't?»

«No.» He shook his head glumly. «Groundswalkers are forbidden from our society.»

«That's the single stupidest thing I've ever heard! Why would you exile someone for one mistake?»

«It's the earth of this world. It drives a person slowly mad. Even the slightest contact corrupts. For Bejeera's sake, look at what happened when we met! I thought you were the Green Lady of the Forest!»

«Well, that explains the whole tongue thing. Sort of. So you can't go back? Ever?»

«Not unless I join the slave cast in penance. And despite what the elders say, I'd do a lot more honor to my sister as a banished Groundswalker than a tailless vassal.» He spat on the hut's earthen floor in disgust.

«You shouldn't have to put up with that, anyway. If they're going to treat you like that, it's better to leave them behind.»

«But they're all I know! I'm nothing without them!»

«Bullshit! All those so-called friends and family of yours don't make you a person. You do. Besides, you've got two very real friends out there, and they're very worried about you. They don't want to see you waste away in this room!»

«What about family? Don't you have any siblings?» A fresh tear ran down his cheek. «Don't you ever worry about them?»

«I'm an only child—and if my parents were so concerned about me in the first place, they would have treated me better. At any rate, I'm in the same boat as you. The only difference is, I chose to walk away.»

Dahn took a moment to collect his scattered thoughts.

«What do you suggest, then?»

«I suggest you start thinking for yourself. You have to leave your previous life behind and start over. Otherwise, you're going to die with it.»

The Pflatlands

«But how?»

«That's for you to decide.»

Out of the corner of her eye, she noticed his trembling, clenched knuckles turning a pale shade of white. He had been clutching the blanket ever closer during the entire conversation. Afraid he would unintentionally smother himself, she smacked his hands, forcing him to release his grip.

«What? What?» Dahn rubbed his sore knuckles, confused, but quickly scooped the blanket back up.

«You're going to strangle yourself if you keep that up!»

«I'm sorry.» He shook his head. «It's just, I'm not—wearing—anything under it. And you said—well, you know.»

Sarah rubbed her temples. If this guy said one more dramatic thing that meant absolutely nothing to her, she was going to wring his neck.

«So?» she shrugged with a forced chuckle. «If you've seen one, you've seen them all, right?»

«But you said I should get some clothes, and, um…» He lapsed into thoroughly confused silence. «I don't get it.»

«Oh, for the love of—that wasn't an insult, okay? I'm used to people wearing clothing, that's all! I mean, Jar'lin above, you've got looks most human males would kill for!»

«Really?» Dahn cocked his head, smiling for the first time in a long while.

«Really,» Sarah nodded, before realizing what had flown out of her mouth. She hastily added, «But don't get any ideas and try to, uh, thank me. Or something.»

«Oh. Right.» Dahn nodded solemnly, struggling to comprehend their cultural differences—and failing. Still, he was giving it his all.

«Hey.» She changed the subject quickly. «I didn't quite catch your name the first time around.»

«Dahn, of the Kar tribe—» He corrected his introduction with a wince. «Dahn Groundswalker.»

«Dahn will do just fine. My name is Sarah.» She added with great emphasis, «Just—plain—Sarah.»

«I remembered. Pleased to meet you, though.»

He relaxed, letting let the blanket fall to his waist. There was an uncomfortable gap in the conversation. He cleared his throat and took the initiative.

«You know, in my culture, there's an ancient ritual two people perform when meeting.»

Sarah balked inwardly but kept calm. She was ready this time.

«No thanks. I've, er, got a headache.» She patted his ears playfully. «I'll be back in a little bit, okay?»

Sarah stood and hustled into the kitchen. Dahn looked at his open palm, more confused than ever. How did a headache prevent you from shaking someone's hand?

•

Sarah barged into the kitchen, immediately giving Tor the evil eye.

"You and me are going to have a little talk—"

Before she could reply, an explosion rocked the hut.

"Jar'lin!" Sarah cursed, thrown to the ground with ringing ears.

A pack of dryads and gnomes fled outside, screaming in terror. Inside, a small pair of lily-white legs hung out of a broken clay jar, kicking frantically. Tor screamed as she pulled herself out of the broken utensil. Dahn stumbled into the room soon after, hopping on one leg and kicking the blanket off his other. He tripped and fell flat on his face next to Sarah.

"Kunlah ehrohnd," he grinned sheepishly. Sarah shook her head.

Seline calmly slipped to her feet; she had been finishing her tea before, during, and after the explosion. Placing the cup back in the cupboard, she deposited her rear on the counter, smiling triumphantly.

"Get down!" Sarah shouted. "There might be more!"

"Here." Seline ignored her with a giggle, tossing Sarah the one possession that had gone missing—her necklace. "I enchanted it while you were busy with Dahn. Now you'll totally be able to understand Tor when she chews you out!"

"Thanks." She threw it around her neck. "That's great. I'm touched. Now will you please get the scrag down before you end up dead?"

The Pflatlands

"Oh, calm down! This hut's, like, what's the word…Hermanly sealed."

"What does that mean?" Tor asked. (Seeing as Sarah understood her quite clearly, she assumed the necklace was working.)

"I dunno. I think it's, like, named after some Herman guy who invented it. It's a completely enclosed forcefield. Latest Machinist gizmo. S'really something!"

Tor and Dahn stared in confused silence.

"I think you mean hermetically." Sarah rolled her eyes.

"Yeah! That's it! This place is hermetically —" she pronounced the word with extreme care and another giggle "sealed. Like, isn't that the coolest thing you've ever heard?"

Another explosion tested her claim. Several dishes crashed to the floor, including the cup she was previously using. Everyone else pushed flatter to the ground, nearly deafened by the short range audio shockwave. The soft walls of the hut went nowhere. The stampede of fae continued outside.

"What about the dishes?" Sensing everything but his eardrums were safe, Dahn turned his attention to more idle matters.

"Those old things? There's this way cool gnome around here that makes them for free. I'll just get some more."

"Assuming he hasn't been detonated by now," Sarah remarked.

They rose uneasily. Seline scooped up broken dish pieces, tidying up the kitchen before the next blast. Dahn took a few cautious steps forward, expecting the floor to kick itself out from under him in spite. Sarah, unable to stand the silence, crept towards the hut's shutters. After a few tugs yielded no results, her temper flared, and she put both back and ring into it. The shudders finally swung open with a snap. She startled, convinced she had broken something purely ornamental. She looked at the shutters, which were operating normally on their hinges, then over her shoulder at Seline, who hadn't heard. She shrugged.

Sarah saw no one near the house as she glanced out the window. Semicircular scorch marks decorated the earth around the front door. A pair of iron cannonballs, each indented on one side, rested a few feet away.

"I don't see anything." She spoke quietly, in case someone was out there.

"It had to come from somewhere," Tor suggested helpfully.

"You figure out where, then!"

"All right, I will! Nyeh!" The sprite stuck out her tongue and crossed her eyes. She flew to a bag the size of Sarah's fist in a corner of the room. After a bit of rummaging, she returned with a tiny leather tube.

"What in the world is that?"

"Telescope." She peered through the tube with her right eye and closed her left, sticking her tongue out in concentration. "I gave a machinist a hand once. He gave me this for my trouble."

"Awfully small," Sarah noted astutely. "It must've been hard to deal with parts that size. What'd you do to earn a prize like that?"

"Never you mind." The sprite cut her off mysteriously. "There! That's where it's coming from—a couple of guys in black with a cannon. Hey, Seline! Did you know there's a spot about seven thousand eagles from here that's perfect for blowing up your house?"

"That's news to me..."

When the full meaning of Tor's words registered, the earthenware shards slipped from her hands and shattered on the floor. The color drained from her face.

"They're loading up another shot, too! Looks like they have no clue why the first two bounced off."

"Tor?" Seline said weakly.

"It'll be fun to watch them when the third bounces off, too," Sarah grinned.

"Tor?" She repeated, a little more insistently.

"They'll probably end up kicking the cannon!" Tor laughed.

"Tor!"

"What?"

"You guys, like, opened the shutters, right? Somehow." Seline smiled unstably.

"I did, yeah." Sarah nodded. "What about it?"

"I think it'd be best if we got out of here as soon as possible."

The Pflatlands

"Ooh! He's lighting the fuse!" Tor was still looking through her telescope.

"Why?" Dahn felt a twinge of panic.

"Well, when you opened the shutters?" Seline was currently experiencing the lukewarm thrill of her life flashing before her eyes. "It kind of broke the seal."

Their heads snapped fearfully up in unison.

"Now that you mention it," Dahn commented, "I think going outside would be a wonderful idea."

The four practically fell on top of each other scrambling towards the back door.

•

It is a commonly accepted moral device that, for every positive application of someone's Jar'lin-given talents, there's a darker, more destructive side. Not surprisingly, this applies to the High Kingdom as well.

The three most essential guilds in the Kingdom are the Fighters', Mages', and Thieves' Guilds, collectively known as the "Guild Triad." The latter had the most difficulty obtaining a license, but the High Council eventually thought it best to take some sort of action. Anything was better than letting thieves rob them blind, and besides, the last thing the Council wanted was an orchestrated crime spree over a snub to the oldest profession* in the land. In a rather pleasant surprise, larcenous activity dropped to an all-time low after this grey-market regulation. Either the thieves didn't see a challenge anymore in what was, under constraint of government-permitted guild operation, no longer illegal, or the Kingdom's population, possessing better details of what they were up against, were much more careful.

Additionally, guild understudies were encouraged to research the new regulations that made their thefts legal, and the result was some of

---

*The many priestesses of Bejeera, Goddess of Love, tried using the same logic to apply for a guild license. It produced little sympathy.

the finest lawyers in the Kingdom. This proved the Council's wisdom beyond a shadow of a doubt.

If grand larceny is a positive application, you can imagine how bad the negatives must be. First of all, there's the less scrupulous nemesis of the Fighters' Guild, the so-called barbarians. Based in the mountainous northern Peaklands, the barbarians rose to prominence by destroying anything and everything in their path, armed with nothing more than a toothpick and a bad attitude. The Fighters' Guild can't stand barbarians because they teach none of the chivalry their sanctioned cousins employ. In fact, barbarians actually encourage foul play and cheap shots, reasoning that a battlefield is no place for scruples. Not surprisingly, the other reason the Fighters' Guild hates them is they win so damn often.

On the other hand, the Mages' Guild has the Necromancers' Circle to deal with. Unlike the barbarians—who could be considered good or evil, depending on how much grog they've had and what side of the fur pile they got up on—the Necromancer's Circle is rotten to the core, a collection of mages who have either sold their soul to the Dark Lord Goff or are working out a pay-on-credit plan. The Circle is directly responsible for skeletons, zombies, vampires, lycans, most forms of demon worship, and—in a true showing of their mad, sadistic genius—fried okra. Some of their recruits are so devious that Goff himself has banned living Circle members from the Underpflats. Why? You know all those oaths that end with "...when hell freezes over"? It's a surprisingly binding pact. Let's just say it doesn't go nearly as unnoticed as people believe.

But despite the brash brutality of the barbarians and the decadent deviousness of the necromancers, there's an even worse faction out there. This guild can make the proudest barbarian cry like a baby. This guild makes the ruthlessness of the Necromancers' Circle look like a wholesome family picnic. This collection of men and women cause members of the Thieves' Guild to wake up screaming every night, solely from knowing they will never possess, for even the smallest measurable amount of time, their subtlety and stealth.

This group is the Assassins' Guild.

There are two major reasons the Assassins' Guild is so difficult to

The Pflatlands

deal with. First and obviously, they were never granted an official Guild Fellowship License—so not only is their activity untraceable, but by all estimates to date, they owe approximately one million platinum and 43 electrum in copyright infringement fines. Second, by all accounts, the Assassins' Guild doesn't even exist. There are no officially documented sightings of the silent men and women in black silk. Sure, everyone and their pet familiar thinks they're real. Too many deaths have gone unexplained throughout history to chalk it up to coincidence. In spite of this, no one's willing to go public with their theories. There's something about the up close and personal introduction between the bridge of your nose and the inside of your brain that lulls you into silence.

The fact that assassins are experts at covering their tracks doesn't help, either. The Guild's most successful killers have the willpower to commit suicide in all sorts of ways, at any given time, rather than be captured. Those lacking the conviction are usually found dead in their holding cell after taking their own life.* Even the Assassin's Guildhouse both does and doesn't exist, as the powerful magic of Grawkor, Goddess of Treachery, keeps it suspended between dimensions. Those unlucky enough to stumble upon it are perplexed to find the Guildhouse a vaporous illusion. This is followed by the even more shocking illusion of their head popping like a balloon. Unfortunately, this last illusion is proved quite visceral via instantaneous death by exploding blowdart.

Still, even with the support of an ancient goddess, the best are entitled to an occasional mistake. Not by their own standards, mind you; Grawkor has been to known to brutally torture anyone who leaves so much as a smudged partial fingerprint behind. (Of course, Grawkor also rewards those she favors with brutal torture, but that's another story entirely.) But despite their impressive station, the assassins are only human, or elvin, or orc, or even—in extreme cases—troll. It was only a matter of time before someone, somewhere, scragged up. And badly.

•

---

* The difference between the two is much like the difference between suicide and "suicide".

The lightweight cannon jerked backwards a third and final time, belching flame and brimstone into the air. There was a whistle, then a tremendous crash. From his vantage point on the hill, the overseer confirmed that the hut had been smashed into a thousand splinters. His accomplice—17 years of age, with a lanky, scarecrow form—looked to his boss anxiously. The older man turned and nodded.

"Finally!" The boy heaved a sigh of relief.

"Three cannonballs to take out a faerie hut. Three!" The elder shook his head in disbelief. A hulking blond man in his late thirties, he might have been considered dashing—if you could overlook his being a cold-blooded killer. "In the name of Lady Grawkor herself, can you imagine what will happen when the rest of the Guild hears about this? We'll be laughingstocks!"

"But at least the job's done, right?"

"No, you great twit," he shot back. "Just because we destroyed the house doesn't mean it's done. It won't be done until we have that scroll."

"So? We have spies in every major city. They can't run from us. What's the big deal?"

"The 'big deal' is that we're being tailed by Groeke Farkhis! Or has your simple mind forgotten that?"

"I saw him when he came through my village. Everybody knows Quo'Chi-Ka is fake."

The blond man clutched the boy's throat with one crushingly powerful hand, throttling him for his impertinence. His eyes bulged in surprised as he choked.

"That 'fake' fighting style captured one of our best men! If he wouldn't have bitten his tongue off during interrogation, we'd have a major security leak on our hands!" The larger man hissed blackly, shaking his apprentice by the throat. "You dig him up and tell him it's fake! You tell his arrested client it's fake! You tell Yasgof the Viper it's fake!"

The young man's struggles weakened as consciousness slipped away. The overseer finally released his grip, and the boy fell to his knees.

"Get down there and bring me a scroll and three corpses," he concluded, pulling him up by the hair, "or you'll be one* yourself."

"Yes—Supervisor—" The younger gasped, gulping air down his bruised windpipe.

With a satisfied nod, the older man turned and disappeared into the forest. His apprentice rubbed his neck vigorously, his breath slowly returning. He glared furiously into the trees as he disposed of the evidence, but he still did exactly as he was told. The Supervisor of the Assassins' Guild could be anywhere, at any given time. And, as much as the boy wanted to put a knife in his back, the Supervisor would mop the forest floor with him.

•

The final report of the cannon sounded as the four scrambled madly outside. Seline threw herself out the door just as the cannonball smashed into the hut, imploding it into small, shredded pieces of reed. They kept their heads down and covered, making sure the barrage had finally stopped. The long silence convinced them the worst was over.

The nymph was first to rise, aching and bruised but otherwise unharmed. She tugged her wrap back into place, mud now slathered over the entire front. Sarah caught Dahn staring and nudged him in the ribs. The young feline blushed and kept his eyes to himself.

"I'm so sorry about your house," Sarah offered sympathetically, helping Seline clean herself off.

"Oh, no biggie!" she replied, drawing on her seemingly endless supply of perky. "I mean, it's a bummer and all, but I can always build another one."

"What I don't get," said Tor, sitting on a sapling branch and braiding its needles, "is why the seal let us open the shutters in the first place."

"Well, it wasn't, like, totally perfect. I cut some corners."

Sarah and Tor both rolled their eyes.

"It's not like I expected someone with a Ring of Strength to pull on

---

* A corpse. Just so we're clear.

it!" she protested.

"Actually," Dahn interrupted, "I'm more worried about why they blew up your house. Maybe they were after Sarah? They seemed to show up just after she got here."

"You just make friends all over the place, don't you?" Tor teased.

"I liked you better when I couldn't understand you," Sarah replied.

"I'm pretty sure they were after this." The mud-soaked faerie raised her left hand, which was clutched around the sealed scroll. "I grabbed it on my way out. I figured it was, y'know, important."

Sarah snatched the scroll out of Seline's hand, ignoring protests that the parchment was hers. She examined the unbroken seal closely.

"This looks like an official Guild stamp." She whistled in amazement. "It's too detailed for an independent. No royalty I know would be caught dead with a seal like that, either."

"And just how much royalty do you know?" Tor asked curiously.

"Never you mind." Sarah repeated the sprite's earlier words with an equally mysterious air. "It's not the Fighters' or Mages'. Might be Thieves', but I doubt it. It's too imposing. The Needle's usually more subtle than that."

"What's a Guild?" Dahn quietly asked.

"It's like a caste," Seline answered, "only you get to pick which one you want to be in."

He nodded at her explanation, deciding to ask Seline his foreign culture questions from now on. His common sense immediately barged in and demanded to know why he was trusting a nymph to feed him a steady diet of intercultural updates. The rest of him politely explained it wasn't sure Tor knew which culture she was from, let alone about anyone else's, and that Sarah would probably slug him.

"It must belong to one of the uglier factions, then." The ranger scratched her chin in thought. "Let's see. Your average barbarian can't read or write…the Circle wouldn't bother with a cannon…"

They patiently awaited her decision. She finally reached it, dropping the scroll as if it had burned her.

"Do you know what this is?"

Three blank stares answered her question.

The Pflatlands

"This is an assassin's scroll!"

More blank stares. Sarah gritted her teeth. She was getting really sick of explaining things.

"Do you have any clue what this means?" Before Dahn could interject a patently obvious statement, she continued, "We've seen the official seal of the Assassins' Guild!"

"That's bad." Tor frowned. "Right?"

"Yes!" Sarah was frantic. "The Assassins' Guild is real! All the old legends are true! And now that we have proof of their existence, they've marked us all for death!"

She sank onto a patch of grass by a knobeye tree, still in shock. The other three looked around uneasily.

"So, what you're basically saying," Tor gulped, "is that we're frolicked."

A stiletto whistled through the air, screaming past Sarah's cheek and pinning her hair to the tree. Everyone in the clearing held their breath—Sarah most of all.

"Well, well, well." A chilling voice behind a nearby tree preceded its owner's appearance. "It appears you've put two and two together much faster than we thought."

Seline gathered herself and unleashed the most intimidating stare she could muster. Being a nymph, it came out as cutely annoyed. Tor was frozen to her branch in fright. Dahn sat on his heels, curiously eyeing the assassin. Sarah tried to stand, but her hair was held painfully in place. She reached to free herself.

"Ah-ah-ah," the man admonished. With a flick of his hand, he was wielding a fresh throwing dagger. "I wouldn't do that if I were you. The first was a warning. The next one won't be."

"And, like, what makes you think you can kill us before we kill you?"

Without turning to look, the assassin coolly snapped his other hand towards Seline. Four shiny silver blades percussively embedded in the tree next to her head.

"M'kay," she swallowed. "That's as good a reason as any."

"Now, as I was saying…" The assassin stopped in mid-sentence and glared at Dahn, who was still regarding him with intense curiosity. "What are you looking at?"

"Qerih?"

"He wants to know why you're staring at him," Seline said in Kar.

"Oh, Kushkla de'te." He blushed. "It's just that I've never actually seen an—assassin—before."

Seline screwed up her courage and translated his reply. The assassin did a double take. He could usually bully anyone into submission using a few fancy tricks with throwing knives. Whatever this thing with the cat ears was, it was not only unafraid, but infuriatingly polite.

"Tell him he'll never see one again if he doesn't stop—or anything else, for that matter. In fact, since he's apparently ignorant to our esteemed past, tell him this: You're currently facing one of the most lethal killers in both Kingdoms, and one that's in a very bad mood. I suggest you show me proper respect, or both you and the girl will have several new and painful body openings."

Dahn's eyes widened as Seline relayed the threat. He shrunk back and cast his eyes downwards.

"Wise decision." He laughed sinisterly, then added as an afterthought, "And for Grawkor's sake, get some clothes."

"Qerih?"

"He says you need some clothes," Seline sighed, knowing how he would take it.

"Qerih?" Dahn's eyes narrowed. He looked at the assassin again. This time, the expression wasn't curiosity.

"You heard me," the man cruelly smirked. "No one wants to see you naked, least of all me."

Illumination fell upon Seline. She translated slowly and carefully. Dahn's frown deepened into an angry grimace. He rose to his full height.

"Dahn..." Sarah began, as if he were blindly stepping in front of a hopper stampede. "I don't think you should—"

"Qerih teh pahpahr a'te?" Dahn demanded irately, his tail puffed to twice its size. Inch-long claws extended from under his fingernails. Even with the language barrier, the assassin knew his barb was successful.

The Pflatlands

The strategy was as old as the Guild itself. Watching one of their companions die for insolence would give him an excellent psychological advantage.

"Dahn!"

Another dagger cut Sarah off, the point landing millimeters from her leg. She bit her lip and prayed to Jar'lin Dahn wasn't about to do something as stupid as she thought. Her hopes were not at all bolstered by the inhuman growl rising from his throat.

"I'm going to ask you once—politely and civilly—to take that back," Dahn said. "And then, I'm going to sink my claws into your face.

"You know, I don't take well to being threatened." The assassin hadn't understood the words, but the Kar's aggressive stance spoke for itself. "Say goodbye to your friends." He waved mockingly and, in the middle of the motion, snapped his arm forward. A knife shot towards Dahn's head at lethal speeds.

Dahn calmly plucked it out of the air an arm's length from its destination. Giving it a look of critical disgust, he tossed it over his shoulder and into the forest.

The assassin went slack-jawed, all traces of sneering superiority lost.

Dahn crouched on his haunches with an angry hiss. *Honestly, he thought, it wasn't even magical. He really doesn't think much of me.* With a powerful flex of his legs, he pounced, a picture of breathtaking grace for the full second that he was airborne. He then promptly crashed straight down and skidded to a face-first stop in front of his target.

The man in black silk continued to gape, not believing Dahn's sudden metamorphoses from polite simpleton to frighteningly dexterous monster to hapless fool.

Having freed herself in the distraction, Sarah whirled the assassin around by his shoulder and hit him square in the jaw with her fist. His head spun, his body followed, his eyes rolled back into his head, and he slumped limply to the ground.

"Are you okay?" Seline helped the brave—if unskilled—Kar to his feet.

"I'm fine." He sighed and retracted his claws. "Tremelor above, I'm so embarrassed."

"Why?" she scoffed. "You saved all our butts just now!"

"I shouldn't have lost my temper. Besides, I slipped. Sarah was the one that saved us."

"Yeah. I was." Sarah was still swinging her throbbing knuckles back and forth to soothe them. "You want to explain to me how you missed?"

"It's not my fault!" he protested. "It's the ground! It doesn't even stay firm under your feet!"

"Oh, come on. You're telling me you can catch a throwing dagger without blinking, but you have no idea how to operate your legs in mud?"

"What's mud?" the Kar blinked. "It is anything like a tree branch?"

Sarah shook her head in response and began searching the unconscious assassin. Seline gently swayed Tor's perch to get her attention.

"Tor, like, it's over. Dahn and Sarah totally saved us."

"Really?" The sprite had cupped her hands over her eyes when the knife flew Dahn's way. She peeped through a crack in her fingers in a manner far too cute to be legal. "I was worried there for a—"

"He's not carrying anything except a bunch of throwing knives and some silver pieces." Sarah announced her conclusion the instant she reached it, regardless of who else was talking. "We need to get moving. If he's got friends, they'll be here any minute. And they'll want this scroll."

"What about my village?" Tor protested. "What about all the people? What if they burn it down?"

"Sarah's right." Dahn shook his head. "If we stay here, they'll do something horrible for sure. If we go, there's a chance they'll leave everyone alone."

"But where are we going to go?" Seline lamented. "The entire kingdom'll be crawling with assassins, and they'll be majorly stoked to snuff us out!"

"I don't know," Sarah admitted, "but I do know we're wasting precious time. Our best bet is to head as deep into the forest as we can. If they want to follow us, they can go ahead and try. They may be the most lethal force in the Pflats, but Goff damn them, I'm a ranger. This is my turf."

The Pflatlands

"You go, girl!" Seline cheered.

Sarah stared inquisitively at the applauding nymph. She stopped in mid-clap, then finally dropped the whole thing altogether.

"All right, it's settled! Let's go!" Dahn's grey tail twitched excitedly, his face glowing at the prospect of adventure. He took two or three random steps before slowing to a halt. He hesitantly glanced back at Sarah.

"Wait. Where were we going again?"

Sarah immediately realized how much she liked working alone.

•

An hour or two passed before the assassin regained consciousness, a dull, throbbing pain stuck firmly in his head. A polite cough sent him to his feet in an angry stumble, ready to impale whoever had the gall to sneak up on him.

He turned a sickly shade of green when he recognized the Supervisor. The larger assassin was standing over the unfortunate young man, arms crossed, a darkly amused smirk on his face. His body was sheathed in the standard black silk tunic and pants of his profession. The sleeves of his tunic were cut off past the shoulders, revealing his sizable biceps.

"S-supervisor! I can explain!" He raised his hands defensively as his jaw throbbed painfully.

"Then I suggest you start," the Supervisor replied evenly.

"You see—I'm—playing to their egos!" His clouded brain struggled for a palpable excuse. "I lured them into a false sense of security to get information!"

"And?"

"And it looks like there's a fourth ally they've kept hidden until now. I've never seen anything like him! He was half cat and half human being! He had superhuman reflexes! I'm no slouch with my daggers, you know that—and he caught one of my knives in midair!"

"But you let your mark get away," the Supervisor pointed out.

"I—I admit, I did. But I believed that, if I sacrificed myself, you could follow them without arousing suspicion!"

The young man hastily bobbed his head, seeing light at the end of the tunnel. His superior finally nodded in satisfaction, his dark blond hair waving behind him.

"Karl, you've done the Assassins' Guild proud." He broke into a smile and warmly wrapped one arm around his charge. "You've taken a serious disaster and turned it into something amazingly positive!"

"Well, th-that's what my parents always told me—make the best of a bad situation. Uh, sir."

"Of course they did. And so you have."

Karl sighed in relief. The more experienced assassin brought his other hand from behind his back, burying a jagged knife between the young man's ribs with a quick thrust. He inhaled sharply at the explosion of pain and looked into the Supervisor's face, astonished. The larger man was still smiling warmly.

"And so have I."

He shoved Karl away, who sunk to the ground as his strength dissipated. He flopped backwards with one last gasp, his muscles went limp, and his spirit vacated his flesh. Satisfied with the results, the Supervisor removed the dagger from the dead boy's chest, and it made a sickening squelch. He plucked a nearby leaf and cleaned his knife on it, then returned the weapon to a sheath under his tunic. He looked over the body while he donned a pair of black silk gloves. The knife wound would be the hardest part to cover. Still, with a minimum of work and a quick change of clothes, it would look like a garuda snake ambushed the "lost" man. The fact that he died with a look of surprise on his face would make it even more convincing.

"I wonder which was worse, Karl?" the Supervisor asked the corpse. "Letting them live, or lying like a blubbering idiot?"

He'd have to move fast. The neighbors would shake off their panic and start investigating soon, and he wasn't quite so confident in his abilities to face a horde of angry fae alone. Nevertheless, he couldn't resist turning an eye towards the future. There was still the matter of the group fleeing him. He wasn't really worried about capturing them. Sooner or later, they'd have to emerge from the forest. The real problem was what to do with them. They would have to die in a manner most foul, of course, but business before pleasure. He had to find out how much they knew and who, if anyone, they had told it to. This was already a disaster of monumental proportions. If Yasgof found out before he could apply damage control...the Supervisor shuddered at the thought.

The only exception was the feline. No, he thought with an evil smile, this fantastic creature would have to stay alive. The Supervisor had much bigger plans for him.

R. D. Hammond

CHAPTER 5

Night crept over Argury, spreading blackness, despair, and mild discomfort. True to her word, Sarah had led the group straight into the deep grass and never looked back. The ranger was clearly in the best shape; everyone else struggled to match her pace through the steadily stranger vegetation. She had good reason for the grueling tempo. The deep Argury was every bit as dangerous as the villains tailing them. Besides, the faster she got them to safety, the faster they would stop their incessant whining.

The breakneck pace also meant there was no time to clean up, which Dahn complained about increasingly often until Sarah threatened to hang him by his tail from the nearest tree. She didn't know what he was so upset about, anyway. Sarah herself was parading through the deep forest at night in nothing but a nightshirt and glasses. This was how pulp-grade horror novels got started.

"Look—would it be possible—to stop—for just a second?" Tor panted. "My wings are killing me!"

The Pflatlands

"No time." The answer was the same as the previous six. "It's best to assume they're breathing right down our necks."

Or if they're not, she added silently, then something is.

As risky as it was, she had opted to cut through the tallest grass to obscure their tracks. She was managing an impressive, weaving gait which picked a drunken path right through the undisturbed underbrush. It was amazing to watch, as well as impossible to replicate. While the occasional brush against Seline's leg or menacing growls from the darkness spurred them into proactivity, Sarah spent most of her time waiting for her companions. Constantly having to collect the others was an unbelievable irritant, but it beat leaving one of them behind, no matter what she told herself to the contrary.

With a sudden thump, there was one less person walking than before.

"Hey! Like, are you okay?" Seline looked down with concern. Dahn had fallen to his knees with a sour frown. Tor landed near him, thankful for the rest, and hugged his ankle sympathetically.

"We need to keep going." Sarah waded back through the greenery with a mix of disgust and impatience. "We're never going to make it if you stop to catch your breath every five seconds."

"Oh, go chase your tail. My ankles are ready to burst right now."

"Keep thinking that when they put a dagger in your throat."

"I'm not taking another step. If they want me, they can come get me."

There was an ominous pause. Everyone held their breath, expecting an unseen force to take him up on it.

"Fine," Sarah continued icily, after none appeared. "We'll set up camp for the night. But we'll have to make one last push towards a decent spot—if you don't mind, that is."

"Oh, this'll do perfectly!" Dahn replied after a glance around.

"What?" She looked around, confused. There were dim lights dancing just beyond her field of vision, lights that were unquestionably less cheerful than Tor's faint glow. She shuddered. "Dahn, it'd be suicide to—"

He wordlessly lifted a finger. Sarah turned her head and followed it.

Behind her was a forking net of branches, winding between three trees like a wooden spider's web.

"Of course. How silly of me," she muttered. Dahn beamed in triumph.

She sighed and approached the nearest trunk, cracking her knuckles. With a strained effort, she hoisted one foot onto a large knot, then pulled herself to a low branch, looking for another foothold. She had no clue how she was going to navigate to the center of this tangle, let alone sleep.

"You're going to help with the hammocks?" Dahn called up from below.

"Hammocks?" Sarah echoed back.

"Well, yes! We can't just sleep on the branches. That'd be downright uncomfortable."

He extended his claws, hooking into the side of the tree and bounding straight up. He hoisted himself onto a high branch with all four limbs and walked as if it were a mile wide. Sarah stared.

"Coming?" he inquired curiously.

"No," she said glumly, slipping to a hanging position, then dropping. She winced as her ankle twisted slightly. "No, I don't think I am."

She put some distance between herself and the others, then tugged herself into the shrouded, leathery branches of another tree. She turned her back to them, resting her head in her hands.

"What's up with her?" Tor asked.

"Beats me." Dahn pulled a few select vines down. "Hammocks'll be ready in a little bit."

"I'll go find food!" Seline volunteered.

"I'll see how far we are from—from—" Tor frowned. "From wherever it is we're going!"

"Yes," Dahn agreed, equally concerned. "It'll be good to know where Sarah's taking us."

Seline concentrated briefly, then wandered off in a carefully chosen direction.

Bounding from branch to branch, Dahn situated himself in the high treetops. He dutifully peered into the distance as he worked, occasion-

The Pflatlands

ally switching branches with a soft rustle of leaves.

Tor was ultimately left alone with Sarah. She fluttered to the vexed girl.

"What's wrong?"

"What do you mean, 'What's wrong?'" Sarah snapped back. "Are you trying to rub it in?"

"Now why in Mab's green forest would I do a thing like that?"

"I scragged up this whole thing up! All our lives are in danger, and I can't even get out of this stupid forest!"

"Actually." Tor folded her hands cutely behind her back. "That's the reason I'm here…"

"So, you're the ambassador now?"

Ambassador, martyr, same difference, Tor thought.

"We just want to know where we're headed." The faerie made it sound as polite as possible, the notes of her voice sliding up an octave and trilling. "That's all. Honest! Cross-my-heart-and-hope-to-die."

Sarah looked away and said something in a low tone.

"…I'm sorry?" Tor was sure she misheard her.

"I said, I don't know where we're going!"

"But—" Tor faltered, her ruby eyes unfocused. "But you said—"

"Take a look." Sarah stabbed a finger straight up. "See anything?"

Tor glanced up. A gorgeous, leafy canopy stretched as far as the eye could see, luminous and luxurious.

"Trees," she noted blandly.

"See anything missing?"

A pause. The information began to sink in.

"Not trees?"

Though not deep enough.

"I can't see the sky."

"Oh. Oh no!" Tor gasped. "That's awful. Right? It's awful."

Sarah raised a hand in a tight claw. For the briefest of moments, she looked like she was going to do something desperate. She managed to force it back down.

"We don't have a compass. If I can't see any heavenly bodies, I don't know what direction we're going in. If I don't know what direction we're going in, we're lost."

"Oh." Tor swallowed. "Yes. That's awful."

"Okay!" Dahn called down from the treetops. "I think I've just about got the—oh sweet Tremelor this isn't a vine!"

A loud din of hissing and growling erupted above, as well as several harsh, dull thumps.

"What in the Sulphur Pits did I do to deserve this?" Sarah wondered out loud.

"Well, everybody has a bad day now and then…"

"Bad day? Today has been the worst experience of my entire life!"

Something twisting and coiled fell into the grass from the trees, where it emitted a ghostly cry of displeasure.

"I'm fine!" Dahn called back down. "Just a howler snake! Nothing to worry about!"

"I go peacefully to bed one night, my only worry what I would do when my next paycheck ran out…"

"Might want to stay out of the grass for a while, though," he concluded. "They use paralyzing venom when they're angry. And I think I made it angry."

"…And the next thing I know, I'm running from assassins with some over-dexterous sex fiend and two bimbos who couldn't fill a thimble with their collective brainpower!"

"Hey!" Tor objected. "I'll have you know that Dahn and Seline are actually smarter than they—"

"Oh, stuff it," Sarah snorted. "First you kidnap me. Then you knock me around for no good reason. Then you nearly get me blown up. And now, your oversights have forced me to take drastic measures to avoid a knife in my back! Could you just leave me alone right now? Is that so much to ask?"

Dahn gathered the last of the vines he needed and turned his attention away from the forest floor. A jagged, seven feet tall shadow of fur and glistening tusks emerged from the grass, rising on its hind legs behind Sarah and Tor. The hulking figure grinned demonically at such easy prey. In its arrogance, its foot fell carelessly on something twisting and coiled. It looked briefly shocked before it fell rigidly back into the grass. The eerie, shrill cry echoed again, followed by soft squishes. No one noticed it over the growing racket of the Argury nightlife.

"Sorry." Sarah sniffed a halfhearted apology.

"It's okay. You're right." Tor looked at the ground in shame, focusing on a bit of red grass that, unknown to her, was previously blue. "It's just—"

"Just what?"

"We should've known better, but when those two guys were trying to kill you, we just wanted to get you out of there. I guess we didn't have time to think."

Sarah shook her head in surprise.

"Pardon?"

"Oh? Oh! That's right! In all the rush, we didn't have time to tell you! When Seline and I were in your room, we had to hide from a couple of humans. One of them was an older man with a limp, and the other was—well, I guess he was one of those assassins. He was dressed in that shiny black stuff."

"Wait a minute. The old man—was he about six feet tall, white hair, bloated face?"

"Yeah! Do you know him?"

"You're damn right I do," she spat. "He came after me with a few of his friends a little while back. What else happened?"

"The assassin blew some powder in your face to keep you from waking up, then the older guy told him to kill you."

"What?"

"We were getting ready to do something when another guy burst in, and he started beating up the other two..."

"Another one?" Sarah grew more astounded with every new detail. "So, you're telling me there were five other people in my inn room, all at the same time, and I didn't even wake up once?"

Tor nodded.

"Huh. That must have been some strong sleeping powder."

"Sure was." The sprite hummed innocently.

•

Seline whistled a little tune, kneeling to work at a root. Wiping off as much dirt as she could, she placed the tuber in her makeshift basket made from waxy hillocks leaves. She looked proudly at the results. Already, she had amassed an assortment of fruits and vegetables that would last them another two days—and even better, they were nutritionally balanced and low in fat.

"Like, sometimes I even amaze myself," she chuckled.

Her amazement was greater at the hand which clamped over her mouth, dragging her into the bushes from behind.

•

"And so," Tor concluded, "we decided not to risk anything. Seline knocked both of them out, and we got you out of there as soon as possible."

"I—wow." All of a sudden, Sarah felt like an enormous heel. "I'm really sorry, Tor. I had no idea."

"Oh, no, it's okay! We should have planned it out better. Or asked your permission to kidnap you, at least!"

"Well, the important thing now is how we get out of this mess." Sarah pat her fist determinedly into her open hand. "We can hash out the rest later."

"Mm hmm," Tor agreed. "But you still haven't answered my question. What's wrong?"

"Huh? With what?"

"With you, silly. I mean, so you're lost! Big deal! Between the four of us, we can find some way out of here. It's not like we'll be wandering forever!"

"You shouldn't have to help me, Tor."

"Why not? We're in this too, aren't we?"

"I can't depend on other people all my life. I should be able to do this by myself."

"Oh, please. If you ever lean on anyone that much, I'll cut my own wings off. Honestly, letting someone help you now and then would do you a world of good."

The Pflatlands

"Why?" Sarah laughed bitterly. "I'd be all weak and helpless then."

"Nonsense! Besides, it's better than facing it alone!" Tor took to the air and tugged on Sarah's hair, gently urging her up. "C'mon! Everybody's out getting our camp ready."

"Okay," she relented, swinging one leg over the branch and dropping down. It was a lower, softer fall, and one which barely missed the surrounding piles of furry parts hidden in the grass. "Hey, can I ask you a question?"

"Sure!"

"Why are you so concerned about me? I mean, we didn't exactly start off under the best conditions." Sarah briefly recalled the faerie's near-annihilation during their first meeting.

So did Tor.

"Well, " the sprite said, weighing her words carefully, "it simply wouldn't do to leave you on your own. Besides, you know more about the assassins than we do."

"I wouldn't go that far. The only information I have are the old legends. Any part of those stories may or may not be true."

"That's more than we've got, though. All I know is that they've got very good aim and very bad manners."

Sarah laughed a little, which made her feel much better.

"Yeah, I guess we should go get everyone. We ought to post a watch, too. Even assassins have to sleep, but it never hurts to be sure. And Tor?"

"Hmm?"

"Thanks."

"Not a problem." She smiled.

The lack of falling leaves and rustling drew Sarah's attention. She looked into the treetops. Dahn's lithe form and grey-furred tail were noticeably absent.

"Hey, where's the fuzzball?"

"You know, that's a good question." Tor scanned the surrounding treetops in concern. "Where did he get off to?"

•

A word should be said at this juncture about Quo'Chi-Ka.

A long time ago, the Lower Kingdom began training their citizens in hand-to-hand combat. Necessity alone facilitated this. Swords and their ilk were generally frowned upon in the hands of plebeians, and besides, it was less of a hassle to use your own fists and feet than to blow all your gold pieces on a new katana. (Far more conducive to your health, too, since the Emperor had first dibs on your gold.) So precious was the advantage of martial arts that, after the formation of the High Kingdom, their eastern neighbors jealously hid their fighting styles from outsiders. In the opinions of the great and past Emperors, unarmed monks killing fully armored knights would give the Lower Kingdom a significant psychological edge. The observation was predictably astute.

Despite the national effort at secrecy, a few forms managed to leak their way through Argury's dense shield. Most were simple styles that visitors could pick up by watching; while flashy, they were mostly worthless. All this changed drastically about a century and a half ago, when the Emperor declared Chi-Ka, the ancient "Way of the Grappling Fist," to be a "great joke" and "unworthy of national support" (sic). With the technology of warfare advancing and the stakes of each skirmish piling higher, a "slow and ungraceful form" like Chi-Ka was, in the Emperor's opinion, now utterly useless. The actual reason was that His Omnipotence and Ruler of All Surveyed had just failed a Chi-Ka test. We don't mean run-of-the-mill failure, either; we're talking "get laughed out of the dojo by white belts" failure. With his proclamation, the Emperor thumbed his nose at an entire culture which had humiliated him. Unfortunately for him, the result was thousands of displaced and disgruntled Chi-Ka monks defecting quietly to the High Kingdom…bringing their fighting style along with them.

The bulk of Chi-Ka is nerve holds and joint locks. Practitioners are taught to home in on a single body part and bend it all sorts of ways Jar'lin didn't intend it to go. Additionally, they are trained to rob opponents of their balance and force them to the ground, where a submission of one's choosing can be applied more easily. A well-trained Chi-Ka practitioner could do all this with rapid and precise movement, to the point where you would be down and screaming before getting

The Pflatlands

your head up from the first bow. A person not well trained? They usually end up falling down a lot and looking silly, which is how our poor Emperor spent most of his time. Unlike him, however, the High Kingdom went absolutely crazy over Chi-Ka. Maybe it was the physical domination, or maybe it was the attraction of proving who the better fighter was without risk of being rendered somewhat dead. Whatever the reason, though, Chi-Ka was in—and it was in big. It soon became a major staple of the Fighters' Guild, and just like that, the High Kingdom wasn't helpless at fisticuffs anymore. The Emperor realized his blunder as a new wave of settlers pushed into his marshlands, compacting the Lower Kingdom's borders tighter than ever. In an effort to correct the oversight, His Omniscience and the Light in the World's Darkness re-legalized Chi-Ka. Unfortunately, before he could fully repair relations, he met his untimely demise by a nasty case of food poisoning.* The next Emperor picked right up where he left off, taking great and immediate strides to reconcile the throne with the remaining Chi-Ka monks, as well as great and immediate strides to hire a food taster. The damage was already done, however. Chi-Ka was the national fighting style of the High Kingdom.

But what does this have to do with Quo'Chi-Ka?

About fifty years ago, Chi-Ka enthusiasts were demanding more action and less of the strategic give-and-take that began matches. Of course, the enthusiasts themselves didn't want to suffer the more extreme style. No, they wanted to watch other people go at it, fighting to the last in a no-holds-barred Chi-Ka slugfest. The idea caught on and grew like peat moss on an ironwood log. A new variation of Chi-Ka was developed, one which added full body takedowns and manhandling slams to the usual joint locks and submissions. It was most certainly not in the original spirit of Chi-Ka, and yet, the High Kingdom stubbornly continued to love it. Naturally, the more extreme things got, the worse health the fighters found themselves in. Duelists began pulling blows to preserve the careers of their respected opponents. Eventually, the moves became so unbelievably dangerous that the grapplers stopped doing

---

*Or poison food. You decide.

them altogether. They put on very convincing acts instead, making it seem like they really and truly did just drive their opponent headfirst into the stone ground. The fans never caught on—or if they did, they didn't say anything. For whatever reason, they ate up the new "fighting" style without a second thought. As an afterthought, the word "Quo" was affixed to the new style, meaning "higher" or "more complex"—or, perhaps more accurately translated, "professional."

Believe it or not, this ties in to the talented monk from the Rangers' Guild. As a baby, Groeke Farkhis was orphaned in the Lower Kingdom during an era of stormy relations. In response to an invasion of a major border city, His Magnificence and the Source of All Knowledge ordered the execution of several legitimate tourists—including Groeke's parents—to send a statement to those darn High Kingdom crusaders[*]. Just to show he wasn't all bad, he decreed that baby Groeke would be given to foster parents and raised as a Lower Kingdomer. The ruling Emperor was nothing if not all heart. This was probably why his killer had such an easy time stabbing him to death.

As he grew, young Groeke gravitated to Chi-Ka on a seemingly natural impulse. By 17, the adopted foreigner had won several local tournaments and a major district title. At 19, he won the highest honor a Chi-Ka grappler can receive, the prestigious Trophy of the Emperor's Favor. At 21, with his fame was running wild throughout the Lower Kingdom, his foster parents decided it was time to tell Groeke the truth. Shocked, the young monk swore a passionate vow to find out who his real family was. Bidding his adopted parents goodbye, he packed his things and left on the long trek through Argury. It was an emotional moment for the entire Lower Kingdom, and they gathered at the marshlands for a send-off of national proportions, watching Groeke bow to them one last time before disappearing into the forest. True to his reputation, he survived the perilous journey, arriving in East Dunsbar without a silver to his name. Realizing he wasn't going much of anywhere without money, he sought employment as a prize fighter. Needless to say, he rarely worried where his next meal was coming from.

---

[*] And that statement was, "Scrag you."

The Pflatlands

He went undefeated in two hundred competitions before his first loss, a fluke occurrence in the last round of the national finals. Nobody's perfect, but Groeke was as close as it got.

One fateful day, a Quo'Chi-Ka scout caught one of his fights. He was blown out of the water by Groeke's depth of talent and, more importantly, the way he commanded the crowd. Groeke could enthrall anyone, simply by dominating so completely that you couldn't help but cheer. The scout approached Groeke after his match, offering a tryout. The pay was good, and the travel would help him scour the country for his lost past, so the monk accepted. His fluid movements and stone-faced nature were an instant hit with the fans. He adapted to the new "style" as quickly as the old one, combining Quo'Chi-Ka slams with Chi-Ka fundamentals to become something truly special. The booking committee—responsible for match-up arrangement, in-ring choreography, and wet towels to soothe the chairman's forehead after the latest profit reports—scripted win after win for him. Fans throughout the High Kingdom dished out huge amounts of silver to watch his limb-twisting submissions. And before long, he was known by one famous, fearsome epithet:

"The World's Most Dangerous Monk."

•

Seeing the stirrings of trouble from his lofty perch, Dahn bounded to the tree above Seline to warn her. Unfortunately, he was too late. Fortunately, she didn't seem to need it. The man who had tried to ambush her was already rolling around in pain. With the threat gone, Dahn was content to watch. Seline seemed to know him, and she genuinely regretted her vicious back kick between the legs.

"Mr. Farkhis," she gasped. "I am so, so sorry for that."

"Quite—all right—" Groeke was finally on his feet, but still doubled over. "Should have—given you—advance warning—"

"That, like, might of helped some." Noticing his dark brown skin was turning a pale tan, she helped him stand as upright as possible. "You shouldn't grab innocent girls from behind! It's, y'know, not right."

Groeke was just thankful his breath was coming back. He indicated, through various grunts and hand gestures, that he would remember her advice.

"What are you doing in Argury, anyway? Didn't you, like, have a championship match this week?"

"Something came up at the last minute." Groeke sighed, the pain finally subsiding. It was so hard to keep the circus of Quo'Chi-Ka out of his personal life. "I was offered a very lucrative contract. It was in my best interests to fulfill it."

"Bummer. I had season tickets to the East Dunsbar arena."

"Yes, yes," Groeke said briskly. Honestly, these fans sometimes. "I am pleased to hear that."

"No problem!" Seline bit her lip in excitement. "Like, wow! This is so cool! Groeke Farkhis, right here in front of me!"

Groeke shook his head. If she asked for his autograph after kicking him in the groin, he was turning around, right on the spot, and forgetting his assignment altogether. He tried to change the subject. "I do not believe I caught your name, madam."

"Uh huh." Seline was still gazing admiringly.

"And your name would be?" he prompted helpfully.

"It isn't." She shook her head.

"Excuse me?"

"I don't have a true name. Isn't that rad? I'm, like, totally immune to magic and junk."

Groeke's head throbbed. He wasn't sure if it was the nymph's bubbly voice—and logic—or the aftershocks of her attack.

"Do you have some sort of title your friends call you by?"

"Oh, yeah! Like, Tor—she's my best friend and all that—she calls me Seline, and I guess everybody else does, too, and it's better than just saying 'Hey you!' all the time, because, y'know, this way I know which 'you' they're talking—"

"Indeed." Groeke cut her off, searching desperately for an escape route. "Well, as I was saying, I am on assignment. I really should be moving along…"

"Really?" Seline pouted. "Wait. If you're in such a big hurry, why did you, like, pull me into the bushes?"

"It is funny you should ask that." Groeke's mind raced for excuses. "You see—"

"Waaaaiiit a minute." Seline's lips curved into a mischievous smile. "I think I know why."

The monk silently panicked. If the jig was up, it was only a matter of time before they warned Sarah.

"You wanted to do more than talk, didn't you?" Seline circled Groeke, running one hand lightly around his shoulder.

Relief that his mission was still secret turned back into to panic, as he realized she had misunderstood him entirely.

"Ah. I am sorry to disappoint you, madam—"

"Oh, trust me," Seline purred. "You're, like, totally not disappointing."

"Thank you. I think. But I believe we have a case of mistaken identity on our hands." It was a lame excuse, but it was all he could think of. It was in the general neighborhood of the truth, anyway. Maybe not on the same street, but definitely in the same suburb.

"Oh?"

"Yes. I am currently searching for a certain young lady on behalf of her concerned parents. I mistook you for her."

"Oh," Seline repeated, a little less energetically.

"At any rate, my sincerest apologies. I assume there are no ill feelings?"

"Yeah, no ill feelings," she mumbled.

"In that case, I bid you good day, Miss Seline. Thank you for supporting Quo'Chi-Ka, and I hope to see you again."

"Yeah," she sourly agreed. "Oh, wait a sec! I've got a couple of friends that might know the way back to—"

She stopped, realizing there was no one left to talk to. Groeke had melted back into the forest at first opportunity. With an exasperated huff, she secured her food basket on the crook of her arm. Twice this week, she had met a nice sample of what the male gender had to offer. Both times, she couldn't even get them to flirt back. She was beginning to think she was losing her touch.

Wrapped up in her thoughts, she was completely oblivious to the creature lowering itself behind her, dangling upside down from a low tree branch.

"Boo," a whisper hissed in her ear.

Seline shrieked and clobbered the creature with her food basket.

•

After a few minutes, Tor and Sarah noticed Seline storming out of the bushes in a huff, a basket hanging from her arm. Dahn followed, rubbing his head.

"You could have checked who it was first!"

"And just how long were you up there?"

"Long enough to make sure you were all right," Dahn replied, with the noblest intentions in the world.

"Then you should've known not to sneak up on me! Didn't you see what happened to Groeke?"

"Groeke?" At the mention of his name, Tor darted excitedly around Seline's head. "Groeke Farkhis? As in, 'The World's Most Dangerous Monk' Groeke Farkhis?"

"Oh, yeah. He was here on this totally dangerous rescue assignment." She played it cool to impress her friend. "He mistook me for someone else and grabbed me from behind, and I had to fight my way out of his grasp! And, like, he ended up on top of me…lots of struggling and rolling around…"

"That's funny." Dahn cleared his throat. "I remember it happening differently."

"Wow! He's such a hunk." The sprite's eyes took on a dreamy expression.

"Who's Groeke Farkhis?" Sarah asked, feeling entirely left out.

"When he found out who I really was, he, like, tried to get me away from everyone else." Seline continued her fantasy. Tor eagerly bobbed her head at the details. "But I tried to be coy…"

"I said," Sarah repeated, "who is Groeke Farkhis?"

The Pflatlands

"I didn't want to leave you guys alone and all. But when I turned around next, he was totally gone! He just vanished into thin air!"

"You should have gone with him!"

"I know, I know. It was a once in a lifetime chance—"

"Hey!" Sarah shouted. "I really hate to interrupt this nice little scene you've built for yourself, but who in the Nine Rings of the Underpflats is Groeke Farkhis!"

Tor and Seline exchanged pitying looks. Dahn smoothed the tangled fur of his tail back into place, not really understanding any of this.

"You really don't know who Groeke Farkhis is, do you?" Seline was in disbelief.

"No. And it's fast getting to the point where I no longer care."

"Groeke Farkhis is the best Quo'Chi-Ka monk in the Pflats!" Tor explained. "He's 'The World's Most Dangerous Monk'!"

"And the world's sexiest." Seline shivered. She and Tor looked at each other, then giggled again.

"Quo'Chi-Ka?" Sarah looked vaguely pained. "That stuff is so unbelievably fake that it's not funny. Look, while you two live out your fantasies with burly, untalented actors, I'm going to find something flammable. I'd rather not spend the rest of the night tripping over things."

She jostled past them roughly and, illustrating her point nicely, almost tumbled over Dahn. He was crouched in the grass, still ensuring his fur was free of mud.

"You know," he murmured as she regained her footing, "she actually kicked him in the groin and scared him off."

"Somehow, I'm not surprised." Sarah smirked. "Hey, show me how to get into these fancy hammocks of yours."

She carefully made her way towards the web of branches, which now had three pods of tangled vines swaying in its clutches. Dahn shrugged and bounced up after her.

The two faeries exchanged confused looks.

"Do you think she actually likes guys?" Tor asked.

•

After finishing their meal and extinguishing their firepit, the four tucked themselves into their hammocks for the night. Being the most culturally diverse, Seline had few problems squirming into hers, with the aid of the gentlemanly Kar. Dahn tried providing the same service for Sarah, but received nothing but a swat and a shoo. He was kind enough to hang her hammock lower than the rest, but it still required a five minute athletics course to struggle into. In spite of Dahn's reassurances, Sarah was extremely wary of the rickety fabrication of vines.

"It's really safe once you're inside," Dahn had insisted. "See, you climb this vine here, then pull yourself up with these supports."

"These?" She pointed at a pair of extrusions in the weave.

"No, that's the emergency release."

Sarah hadn't asked for further elaboration and still didn't want to know. She eyed the "emergency release" like it was going to pull itself, then leaned her head over her interlaced hands with a sigh. They had put out all the lights after eating, reasoning it would make them less of a target. Still, Argury was neither dark nor silent. Life teamed in every nook and cranny, strange, beautiful, dangerous, and all points in between. The distant glow and giggle of sprites could be seen and heard in the horizon. Blue flames exploded noiselessly above certain trees, dancing mischievously before dissipating back into their hosts. Sarah was familiar with will-o-wisps, but seeing them ten feet away was very different than reading a textbook. Their appearance violently startled her the first time, and she wasn't really getting any more comfortable with them. Looking into the canopy, she saw dancing pinpoints of light—some of it faint starlight peeking through the leaves, some of it internal to Argury in one weird form or another. The glows made Tor's telltale luminescence indistinguishable. For this, Sarah felt very glad.

Sarah also felt, looking into the expansive and tree-filled sky, that she was on a completely different planet.

"Ow! Hey, quit hogging all the room!"

Laughter and rustling above confirmed that Tor and Seline were still awake. They were happy and carefree, as if it were a giant slumber party. Sarah couldn't help but envy them. They had no apparent fear of death.

"Well, excuse me!" Tor responded. "I guess I'll have to scoot over!"

The Pflatlands

Sarah inhaled deeply, then exhaled, rolling her eyes.

"You guys are still up?"

"Yup!" Tor replied. "You?"

"Obviously," she muttered under her breath.

"Sarah?"

"Yeah, Seline?"

"Like, I know we're going into the forest and all that junk, but where are we going after that? We need to go somewhere. I mean, we could wander around endlessly and all that, but some parts of this forest, like, totally gag me out. Y'know?"

Sarah stared vaguely in the direction of her voice. Despite her necklace, she still wasn't entirely sure what had been said.

"Yeah," Tor chimed in, trying to help out. "When are we leaving the forest?"

"I haven't gotten that far yet, honestly." Sarah thought for a few moments. The idea popped out before she realized its conception. "Lower Kingdom. It's our best chance. They're probably waiting for us back in the High Kingdom."

"Sounds great! I know you like to do things yourself and everything, but, like, I have this idea…"

"Oh?"

"Yeah! There's this one type of leaf that's totally easy to find here, and then we can use some gahngis fruit for ink, and—"

"Seline?" Sarah realized what she was getting at. "Are you saying you can make a map?"

"Oh, yeah! It's a piece of cake for me! I so totally have this affinity for spatial perception."

Since Seline had just said "affinity" and "spatial perception," Sarah decided she was either partially asleep or already dreaming.

"We'll worry about it tomorrow. Get some sleep for now. You have the watch next."

"Actually, you have the watch now."

Dahn's voice floated from the trees, lazy and soft. Seline gave a little shriek of surprise, followed by a shriek from Tor, followed again by Seline for good measure. Sarah slid her glasses from her face and shook her head.

"Oh. It's just you!"

"So it is. Your turn."

"Bummer," she pouted. "I haven't slept at all."

"I know," he chuckled. "That's why I'm taking it for you."

"Aw! You're such a sweetie!"

"Yeah, why don't you hold on to my glasses while you're at it?" Sarah grumbled.

•

It was well past midnight now. The rest of the party slumbered peacefully in their hammocks, rocked to sleep by the gentle sway of their beds. The two glowing lenses of Dahn's eyes were barely visible in the treetops, reflecting back what little light there was. Cradling Sarah's glasses in his palm, he alertly scanned the area for the thousandth time, watching for approaching assassins.

He felt nothing but the forest's gentle, still warmth.

He heard nothing but the usual night sounds, a cacophony of cries and caws and hisses from unseen figures—along with Sarah's soft and pained moans.

And he saw nothing in his field of vision but his sister Shoh's face.

Without knowing why, he balled his fist and slammed it into the tree trunk, hard. It wasn't the tree's fault, of course. It was his. But it was easier to punch the tree.

"Dahn?" Seline's sleepy voice wafted up from below, concerned. "Like, are you okay?"

"I'm fine," he replied in an even tone. "Nothing to worry about. Sorry to wake you up."

He waited until the nymph was breathing evenly again, then wiped his brimming tears with the back of his hand. He was alone now in the trees, with nothing but the night surrounding him.

CHAPTER 6

High atop the Assassins' Guildhouse, the Supervisor looked out into the murk between dimensions. His blond hair flapped gently in the wind between worlds.

"They have emerged." A hissed whisper, like metal grinding painfully against metal, came from behind him.

Even an experienced killer like him couldn't have been prepared for it. Still, he had trained himself not to be startled. To be startled was to be surprised. To be surprised was to be dead. To be surprised by her, however, was to be punished—which was far, far worse. He turned as calmly as he could, glancing at a familiar figure in a black silk robe. Only a smooth chin and bloodless female lips were visible inside the raised hood. Knowing Yasgof as he did, he was glad he couldn't see more.

"They have? Why haven't my men informed me?" he asked.

"Because your men are incompetent."

He forgot himself for a moment and lashed back angrily. "I'll have you know my men are the best in—"

Yasgof raised a hand, and his voice cut off, as if his throat was being crushed in a vice. He struggled for breath, just like his underling a day before.

"Your men are fools—just like you." She spoke plainly and without emotion. "You are indeed fortunate that Lady Grawkor allows all of you to live."

He clutched at his throat, trying to get the precious air he needed. Yasgof finally dropped her hand, and his neck was released from the unyielding supernatural force. He choked down gasp after gasp of air, desperately resisting the urge to surrender consciousness. He had a vivid mental image of what would happen, and it involved being splattered on the ground a dizzying height below.

"For such proud followers of the Lady of Treachery, you are all simpletons. They have found the one deceit your precious forces did not plan for."

"Deceit?" The Supervisor croaked the words, rubbing his neck. "We have assassins posted at every viewpoint along the Lower Kingdom's border. If they leave the forest, we'll know instantly."

Her hand rose once more. Fortunately for him, she only extended a finger—long, bony, and covered in greenish-brown scales. The nail was a razor-sharp talon.

"There is one place you do not have guards posted, and they have escaped there." Yasgof shambled off, her robe dragging on the ground. "We do not have to warn you about further failures. Bring us the scroll."

"As you wish," he murmured.

His mind raced as she disappeared into the Guildhouse's inky darkness. The one place he didn't have guards posted? He had arranged one of the largest dragnets in the guild's history! If they so much as set one foot out of the forest, he would know by now! Surely Yasgof was mistaken...

He shook his head, turning back to the displaced surroundings. No, Yasgof's words came from Grawkor herself—and he would not question the goddess' commands under any circumstance. He leaned his elbows on the railing and pondered the remaining question—if not the Lower

Kingdom, then where? Where could they have possibly gone to avoid his gaze?

He thought. A slow, evil smile spread across his face. Of course. How stupid of him not to realize it. How brilliant of them to think of it. He was amazed at the brazen nature of his marks, but their plan had worked with perfect efficiency. They had the headstart they needed.

He spun and followed the path Yasgof had treaded, avoiding the trail of glowing slime left behind. Despite their bumbling facade, these were no amateurs. These were savvy, battle-hardened masters of the unorthodox. He should have realized that the moment they captured the scroll.

•

The travelers finally emerged from the trees, squinting as the light of the newly risen sun burned into their eyes. It had been a hard journey with scant meals, little rest, and lots of frantic fleeing, but they had done it. They had traversed the Faerie Forest and lived.

Seline threw herself onto the grass field with a sleepy smile, savoring the prickling of the blades. Sarah sat on a log to check their makeshift map. Tor rested on the ranger's head, a habit which Sarah was far too tired to be annoyed with.

"Um, okay. This? This is new." Dahn nervously played with his tail, glancing dubiously at the wide open space.

"Don't worry about it." Tor fluttered to the ground beside him, no longer possessing the energy to hover. "Once we get into town, it'll be just like the forest! Except there'll be really tall buildings instead of trees. And lots of humans. And they'll probably all point and gasp at your ears."

"Oh, that's—comforting? No, that's not the word I'm looking for…"

"Wait a minute." Sarah frowned at the surroundings, then the map. "Wait just a Goff-damned minute. This doesn't look like the Lower Kingdom at all."

"Like, what do you mean, doesn't look like the Lower Kingdom?"

With her pathway to a peaceful nap barred, Seline scowled and pulled herself to her feet. "According to that map, we should be in the land of Emperors and gold pieces and all that junk!"

"This should be a marsh, not a plain! We're nowhere near the Lower Kingdom!"

"Oh, sure. Like, since I'm a nymph, I'm such an airhead that I can't make a good map. Is that it? What, are you going to make blond jokes next?"

"Don't tempt me."

Dahn padded over and peered at the map.

"Oh, that's just great!" Seline shouted. "Never mind that I calculated the scale totally perfect! Forget the fact that I spent, like, an hour looking for the right type of berries for ink! Seline must be a total idiot, we can't rely on her! That's just scragging fine!"

"Good thing, then. I was about to say a lot worse."

"Gag me. You just did not say that."

"Wish I could. The silence would be nice."

Dahn cleared his throat politely.

"What?" they both shouted.

"I'm sorry for interrupting, but I think I can help. Seline, would you take another look at the map?"

"Sure. I bet you think I can't read a map now."

"Just do it. Please."

Seline snatched the map from Sarah and held it up to the sun, peering at the faint lines.

"See, look. Here we are." Seline stabbed a long fingernail at a specific point. "Or, like, do you have a problem with that?"

Before Sarah could unleash whatever nasty thought she was devising, the Kar took the map out of Seline's hands, flipped it widthwise, and handed it back. She looked once more at the curled leaf.

"Oh—my—Gods. I feel so, so stupid right now."

"You had the map backwards?"

"Well," she shrugged meekly, "like, you didn't know what direction we were going in, so I couldn't tell…"

"You couldn't tell? We're being chased by a whole horde of assas-

The Pflatlands

sins, and you couldn't tell the map was backwards?!"

"I did wonder why the lines were so faint!"

Sarah tried to sputter a response through her rage but couldn't manage it. Fearing she might tackle Seline to the ground, Dahn put himself between them.

"Come on, Sarah." He led her gently away by one arm, ready to duck if the other swung his way. "What's done is done. Let's take a few steps back and calm down."

"She—had—the map—the wrong—backwards—aaarrrgggh!" Sarah spit out random sounds in anger. Nevertheless, she allowed herself to be led away. "I'm going to scragging kill that airhead if I have to spend one more minute with her!"

"Just calm down," Dahn repeated. "We're hot, we're tired, and we're starting to get cranky. Believe me, nobody wants to be in this situation—least of all me."

"Is there a point to all this?" she asked testily.

"The point," he replied, rather testy himself, "is that I would still be wasting away in a hut—or worse, blown to bits—if you hadn't convinced me to make the best of things. I know Seline's scatterbrained sometimes, but she's our friend. We need all of those we can get. You said so yourself."

Sarah fumed quietly.

"I wouldn't have done anything to her," she finally admitted, defensively.

"Glad to hear it. But seeing as you've been cantankerous since the day I met you, I'm not taking any chances."

"Of course, I've been cantankerous! Thanks to you three, my whole life's been derailed!"

"Yes, and thanks to you and your Goff-damned unannounced appearances, my little sister is an orphan again! So kindly shut the Infernus up!"

Dahn's shout echoed off the trees. He clutched at his mouth as soon it left his lips. He began to apologize, then shook his head sadly. Sarah watched him slink away, her jaw left hanging. The force behind his words was uncharacteristic. The hurt in his eyes was painfully obvious.

R. D. Hammond

•

There's a lot to be said about predictability and adventuring.

They'd never admit it, they may not even know it, but the average adventurer lives by a set of unspoken laws. It may seem preposterous at first, but it makes sense if you think about it. You don't see people running around in chain mail and looking for dragons with reckless abandon, do you? No, of course not—assuming your part of the country doesn't suffer from widespread brain damage. And do you know why? Because there's rules against that sort of thing. See, it all makes sense.*

An example: A hero or heroine fresh off the proverbial starting blocks tends to fight goblins and run from...oh, let's say a lich. That's just common sense. The squat green thing is less likely to end your fledgling career than an omnipotent, undead wizard. You just don't fight things straight out of training that could use you for an iron-enforced after-dinner mint. It's unsanitary, not to mention suicidal. But the reason it's common sense? The reason every adventurer knows it a priori? It's in The Rules.

Another example: Adventurers can and should accept female virgins as payment for services rendered. In this day and age, many are campaigning against this exploitative practice. The sensitive modern adventurer sees it for the cheap and degrading ploy it is, while the older, jaded adventurers have learned non-virgins are more fun, as far as things you expect from virgin payments go. Nevertheless, it's still a Rule, and it must be followed. Yes, even by female adventurers. (And no, there's no rule that says what you have to do with them.)

Problems always arise with amateurs, however. Having never received formal Guild training, they don't know the rule set long standardized by the Universal Guild Union (or UGU, if you prefer). Don't get the wrong idea here. UGU's stripped down re-interpretation of The Rules has generally been a good thing. For instance, their hard work has brought to light the previously overlooked "Competence Appeal" [Section III, Paragraph 4, Sentences 2-3], which states:

---

* And if you don't agree, you haven't had enough beer.

The Pflatlands

> "[A]ny contractee (also ref. as 'adventurer', 'hero(ine)', et al.) may thusly be granted the right to refuse a job for which he or she is not fully qualified (e.g. is not of the proper experience 'level'). Furthermore, this right shall be granted without reprieve or prejudice should the proper conditions as stated above be met."

In a nutshell, any adventurer can turn down a job he or she is unsuited for without a black mark on their record for abandoning people in distress. This is but one of the many good things to come out of UGU. (Where are The Records? The same place as The Rules. It's best not to ask any further.)

Still, while amateur adventurers don't know all their rights, they also don't know their limitations. There is a large difference between the unionized Rules (the result of numerous translations over thousands of years) and the actual Rules (which came straight from Lumina's trembling, aching hand). In the case of our disgruntled adventurers, the unionized Rules suggest hiding in some third world city-state, where "They"—being the deadly, organized group pursuing you—won't be able to find you. This buys you time to prepare an amazingly clever counterstrike against Them, which, by standard measurements, takes anywhere from three weeks to twelve years. Normally, this isn't a problem. You can say what you want about the skullduggery of evil, but they live by The Rules, too. Even the vilest necromancer in the Circle would rather hold important prisoners hostage than kill them. Do you honestly think Goff wants to deal with the cosmic legal overhead of a Rules violation?

The Assassins' Guild, however, doesn't care two pieces of dung for all this. With a history dating back to the original version of The Rules (which Grawkor memorized very, very carefully), the assassins have all sorts of back-doors and loopholes to justify doing whatever they please. Sure, it's dirty pool—but not only do they not care, they'll use it as an excuse to knife you in the ribs. This is the single greatest handicap in the centuries of cold war against them.* The professional heroes' hands are bound by the (unionized) Rules. The amateur, unsanctioned heroes can't muster the resources they need to fight. And meanwhile, the Assassins' Guild continues to do whatever in the bowels of Infernus they want, delighting in their opposition's misery as if they were flies with their wings pulled off. It's all one big, vicious cycle, really.

This answers a question you might have been asking for some time now: If the Assassins' Guild is everywhere, and even neonates are highly efficient killing machines, how has a bickering and patchwork party of amateurs lasted this long? Simple. Tor, Dahn, Seline, and even Sarah have a sum UGU Rules knowledge of exactly squat. Had they followed their original plan and emerged from the eastern end of the forest, they would have been slaughtered by assassins in waiting, and the author could've packed it up early and went home. But, whether from serendipity or sheer dumb luck, they're still alive...and all because they're as willing to bend The Rules, however unintentionally, as the assassins.

•

The ragtag heroes trudged onwards for what seemed like eons. The last voice heard was Dahn's, who tersely suggested they get off the plains and into the nearest town. He still wasn't entirely sure what a town was, but it had to be better than waiting around for their executioners in an open field. Besides, after all the grass he'd slogged through, he imagined it would be heaven by comparison.

As they plodded along, Sarah slowed to walk with Seline. The nymph gave her a critical look. Sarah searched for the right words, then shrugged and spoke gruffly.

"Sorry about earlier."

Seline considered, then shrugged as well.

"Ah, it's all good. Don't, like, have a cow or anything."

"No. You made a simple mistake, and I was being a bitch."

"Don't sweat it. I was, like, all defensive and crabby, too. We'll both

---

*The loopholes. Just so we're clear. (Although the knifing doesn't help.)

feel better after some rest."

Sarah nodded, increasing her strides to retake the lead. She sneaked a glance at Dahn as she passed and caught him smiling in approval. She shot him a scowl, and he quickly focused his gaze forward.

They continued across the fields. The silence was much less tense now, the result of exhaustion rather than dissension. The distant brown line they were waiting for finally appeared on the horizon, growing larger with every step.

"Thank Jar'lin," Tor mumbled. She was riding on Seline's shoulder, her wings too stiff to beat anymore. "We made it."

Only Dahn had the strength to quicken his pace. When they finally caught up with him, he was standing in front of the wide dirt path and gazing at a nearby sign, his tail swishing back and forth excitedly.

"Look!" He pointed. "A sign!"

"You really don't get out of the woods much, do you?" Sarah asked.

"Hey! I know what a sign is—"

"But you've never seen this particular sign, right?"

Tor made a choked sound, which was obviously an unsuccessfully stifled laugh.

"Now, wait just a minute—"

"Like, don't worry about it." Seline rolled her eyes. "They're just pulling your tail. What about the sign?"

"Oh. Well, if this sign's here, that means there's people nearby!"

"You have an amazing grasp of the obvious, you know that?" Sarah forced a few more steps towards the object of Dahn's exuberance. She adjusted her glasses, reading the words in the mid-morning sun.

EAST DUNSBAR (3½ k. North)
HOUSE OF YOSEPH'S TAVERN AND INN (1 k. South)

She thrust her back against the signpost to keep from falling down and sobbing.

"Well? What does it say?" Tor asked expectantly.

"I've got good news and bad news."

"Like, give us the bad news first," Seline said.

"We are currently three kilolengths south of where this entire mess started."

Three hands slapped three foreheads in a perfectly coordinated display of disbelief.

"Well, at least there's good news," Tor sighed.

"Actually, I just remembered—Yoseph's is closed for repairs. We've got three more kilolengths of walking ahead of us."

"But at least we found a town, right?"

Like any good Kar, Dahn easily ducked the rock Seline winged at him.

Two hours later, they finally reached the outskirts of East Dunsbar, hungry and exhausted. Dahn couldn't even muster constant excitement at every new discovery anymore. In fact, he was a bit cross that the hot sun was burning his skin in very painful places.

"That's it," Seline declared with firm conviction. She flopped down on the hill overlooking the town. "My cute little butt isn't going a step farther."

Sarah silently agreed. Her legs were screaming to her brain that they weren't meant to perform at this level of stress, and that if she took one more step, they would leave her lower torso in protest. She tried to shut out the aching. Her job wasn't done.

"You should all stay here, anyway. Faeries pass through East Dunsbar every now and then, but they're still rare. Seline would be okay, but they'd raise eyebrows at Tor —and they'd really freak over Dahn."

"What? Why?" Dahn, lying on his back and staring dreamily into the sky, glanced up at his name. "I mean, I know I haven't bathed in a while, but—"

"Don't worry about it!" Tor said. "We'll wash you up, get you some clothes, and you'll fit right in. Isn't that right, Seline?"

"Huh?" Seline, watching Dahn sun himself on the grass, glanced up at her name. "Oh, yeah. Sure."

"Oh, good." Dahn sighed in relief, his eyes closing sleepily.

"Uh. I think there may be a little more than—"

"Of course, silly!" Tor tossed her hand nonchalantly at Sarah. "We'll need a place to live, too. And we'll have to hide from the assassins!"

The Pflatlands

"No, really," Sarah urged. "I think there may be something else you're overlooking—"

"Like, let's just get a room somewhere and crash." Seline yawned. "We can work out the rest later."

Sarah looked at Dahn's furry tail and ears one more time, still worried.

"Just promise me you'll stay out of sight, alright? There's an outside chance the Assassins' Guild doesn't know where we are. If they don't, we should try to keep it that way."

"Don't worry," Tor assured her. "We'll be careful."

"Good." She summoned what little energy she had left. "I'll send someone trustworthy after I reserve some rooms. I'll probably be asleep when you get there."

"It's okay," Dahn murmured. "We probably will be, too."

Sarah shuffled off towards town, reassuring herself that they'd be fine on their own. After all, they may be an odd bunch, but they had made it this far.

•

Tor watched Sarah descend the hill towards East Dunsbar, torn and sullied nightshirt flapping in the breeze. She turned to Seline and found her eyeing the napping Kar again. She prodded the nymph gently in the neck with her elbow.

"Now what?"

"Hmm. Like, she said to lay low, so—hey, I've got a great idea! Let's go into town and get some clothes!"

"I don't know," Tor said distrustfully. "Sarah said to stay here."

"Oh, c'mon. She'll, like, be a lot happier if we take care of things ourselves while she's gone. Besides, we'll blend in a lot better once we have them!"

"Oh, okay! We'll have to be careful, though. Remember what Sarah said!"

"No prob!" Seline smiled cheerfully. "I've dealt with shop owners before. If you're really polite, and you buy enough stuff, they don't care how you look!"

"Then it's settled! We'll have to move fast, though. We need to be back before the messenger."

" 'Kay!" Seline eyed Dahn one last time—this time, in consideration. "Should we wake him?"

"He'll be okay by himself. It's open terrain, so no one can sneak up on him. Besides, you know how fast Kar wake up when they're in danger!"

He snored loudly in response.

CHAPTER 7

Rudrick Romanoff sat at the same counter he sat at every day of the year, answering the exact same questions—all of which should have been obvious to anyone with three or more brain cells. ("Do these green tights go with my orange tunic?") He had originally opened Romanoff's Wardrobe in the hope of obtaining a coveted Merchants' Guild license. After three years of consistently mediocre income, he had fallen on less lofty desires, like wishing a flaming meteor would strike him full on the temple.

Rudrick was explaining to an elderly, three-fourths deaf woman that the fashion style of floral pastel had long since passed on when he noticed a commotion around the store's entrance. He sighed. More than likely, someone had knocked over a row of cloth rolls (again). When he saw the awestruck patrons at the door, he realized the disturbance was larger in scope. He craned his neck forward with mixed emotions. True, someone might be scaring his business off…but it was a rare opportunity to break the monotony of his day.

It didn't take long to discover what all the gaping was about. A long-legged, well tanned, blue-eyed blonde strolled casually into the shop, wearing only a dirt-covered grass wrap that ended at mid-thigh. The sea of (mostly male) onlookers parted like she was royalty. Stunned by her appearance, Rudrick silently thanked Bejeera for the magnificent lady approaching his desk. She spread her pouty red lips into a dazzlingly white smile and spoke.

"Like, hi!" She tossed the wavy locks of her blonde hair. "I'm here for some clothes."

"Are you sure?" Rudrick stammered reflexively.

"Huh?"

"I mean, of course, miss!" He hurried from the counter to her side, almost tripping over his own feet. "What would you be interested in today?"

"Hmm." She eyed the racks with obvious experience. "I'll need a good dress or two..."

"For you?" he asked hopefully.

"Yeah. Like, I would get one for my friend, but she would be so mad at me! She loathes clothing. Totally gags her rotten."

"Really! Is this friend of yours around?"

"Tor? She's waiting outside. I also have to get some clothes for this guy—"

"Ah," Rudrick said, disappointed. "How long have you two been seeing each other?"

"Oh, it's totally not like that! I mean, he's a hottie and everything, but he's got too many things on his mind right now."

"Of course! My apologies." He sounded much less disappointed. "We should fit you for something to wear, then!"

"Sure thing!" she nodded cheerfully. She remembered her manners and extended her hand. "By the way, you can call me Seline. Everybody else does."

"And you can call me lucky," he murmured suavely, kissing the back of her hand.

"Charmed!" She giggled at the extravagant show. "So, Lucky, do you work for Mr. Romanoff, or are you his business partner, or...?"

The Pflatlands

•

Sarah minced down East Dunsbar's cobbled main street, the rocks cutting into her bare feet. She had been spoiled by grass. The pavement, in stark contrast, hurt. A lot.

"Hee-eey! Get a load of that!"

But not quite so much as that.

She was already tired of the wolf whistles following her down the street. Could these people not see she was in obvious distress? Why was the standard male reaction, when confronted by a female in a torn nightshirt and a scowl, to check what they could see through the holes? She shook her head as the stables went by, the general store went by, both boxy, wooden buildings with large billboards on top. With a block left to go, she gritted her teeth for the absolute joy and pleasure that walking past the Beer-O-Rama would be. Predictably, it was as if someone had revealed the Holy Grail to a room full of downbeat Paladins.

"Woah-ho-HO! Check that out!"

"I'd like a piece'a that! If you know what I'm sayin'!"

"Oh, I think I do!"

"Oh, no, no, no! I don't think you do know!"

"Oh, I do! Y'see, it's one of them there innuendos."

"What?"

Sarah darted into the Happy Boar, enduring one last round of gawks. She marched directly to the counter, recognizing the same clerk from before.

"Hello!" he began, turning from the pigeonhole mailboxes. "Can I help—"

He froze, face to face with the familiar ranger. She was half naked and looked like she had gone through the Mountain Wars twice over. She looked at him. He looked at her.

Your move, Sarah thought, staring him down.

"Good Gods!" He ripped off his long red cloak and furled it around her shoulders. "What happened to you?"

Good call.

"It's a long story." Sarah clutched the cloak to her. "Is my room still here? And all my things?"

"Of course! I've been taking your rent out of the money you had delivered. Here's the remainder. And here, here's a spare key." He came around the rough counter, a key dangling from a metal loop in his fist. "I'll walk you to your room."

"Really, that's not necessary."

"I insist," he cooed, offering his arm.

Too tired to fight, Sarah humored him with a roll of her eyes. Besides, Tor was right. She could stand to let people help her every now and then. She leaned her weight against him, giving in to exhaustion.

"Much better." The bellhop grinned brightly as her body pressed against his.

Sarah realized his hand was on her ass. She suddenly saw everything in shades of crimson.

•

Tor perched on the wooden sign above Rudrick's Wardrobe, enjoying its gentle swing in the light breeze. She had been surprised to find the average city dweller didn't look so much as an eagle* above the door they're entering, let alone at signs hanging from the roof. She was initially delighted she could wait for Seline without arousing suspicion. When it became apparent the nymph was taking her sweet time, delight turned to sheer boredom. She was weighing the risks and rewards of dropping something spherical and filled with water on a passerby's head when Seline finally emerged. She was wearing a black strapless dress—which didn't cover much more than the grass wrap—and a matching pair of high heels. Draped over one arm was a single piece of grey clothing. Tagging along behind was a pudgy and middle-aged man.

"Really, Mr. Lucky, you are such a sweetie for letting me try on all those dresses! I feel so bad that I only bought two things!"

---

*The diminutive sprite measurement for distance. Named after the bird and not the golf score.

The Pflatlands

"No, no, no," Rudrick rattled off without a second thought. "Don't think a thing about it. It's perfectly okay."

"And you let me have the clothes on credit! I swear I'll pay you back when I have the money! Honest. Fer sure."

The tailor nodded dumbly, his gaze on the nymph's legs. He remembered something.

"You said you had a friend out here?"

"Yeah!" Seline frowned. "Where is Tor, anyway?"

The little sprite perked at the sound of her name and hovered silently down behind them. Seline (looking in the completely opposite direction) and Rudrick (gaping at Seline) didn't notice a thing. Tor had been mulling over what Seline said concerning shopkeepers and politeness. She also remembered Sarah's insistence on blending in. With these two things in mind, she decided to try out the first word of High Common she had ever learned. From watching the people milling around the store, she deduced it was a greeting. With men Rudrick's age, it seemed the louder and more jovial it was said, the better the response—especially when accompanied by increasingly violent hits on the back. She cleared her throat and put on her happiest tone. Syllables were much more problematic than notes. She wanted to get this right.

"Hi!" she shouted as loud as she could in Rudrick's ear, whacking him across the back of his head.

Rudrick screamed in surprise. All at once, the noise cut off in his throat. His eyes widened, his hand went directly to his chest, and he fell to the ground with a thud. People on the street stared in surprise, alerted by Tor's emphatic greeting. There was definitely something wrong with the man on the ground, as well as the two women beside him.

"Maybe we should, y'know, make ourselves scarce." Seline edged away.

"Yes." Tor looked at the poor, unconscious man, who was still clutching his chest. "That would be a very good thing to do."

•

For the first time in days, Sarah was in good spirits. For one thing, she was wearing pants again, which was a delight in and of itself. For another, her belt pouch was noticeably heavier than before. The sight of all that silver did more to energize her than any amount of rest. Invigorated, she decided to fetch the rest of the party herself.

While passing the brass gates of the market district, she noticed a throng of people clustered around a certain shop. She slowed to a halt, bewildered. When she caught sight of the white and red healer wagon, it immediately felt like something ugly and slimy was clutching at her stomach. She shoved her way through the crowd without a second thought. The store's sign identified it as "Romanoff's Wardrobe," a crappy little tailor shop she had passed countless times on the way to Walter's. With silver holy symbols dangling from long chains around their necks, the healers were applying medicines and magic to a middle-aged man. His face was slowly fading from an unnatural pasty white to its normal pasty white. The crowd murmured and applauded.

"What the Infernus happened to him?" Sarah asked.

"Heart attack," a young man in a yellow tunic and feathered hat replied. "Rudrick's been getting along in years. His doctor said this would happen if he didn't take care of himself. The healers got here fast enough, thank gods and goddesses, but he might not be so lucky next time."

If this was supposed to have reassured Sarah, it didn't.

"So, what, he just went on the spot?"

"Not really. A couple of real oddballs were here earlier—probably faeries from Argury or something. The two of them must've pushed Rudrick over the edge."

Sarah's only acknowledgment of the explanation was a slight twitch of her left eyebrow.

"Let me guess. One was about six-feet tall, blonde, really long legs?"

"That's right!" The young man blushed with a big grin. "Hard to forget her. The funny thing was, the other was a little thing with wings and—hey! Where are you going?"

Sarah didn't hear a word after the initial confirmation. She was already storming out of town at twice normal speed.

The Pflatlands

•

Back at the grassy mesa, Seline presented Dahn with his new garment. The grey satin robe was fairly high quality, the type that master wizards decorated with arcane symbols to impress—even though the symbols often held as much relevance to magic as chocolate cake recipes.* The robe fit him well. For the first time in his life, the Kar was wearing human clothes.

"I feel so incredibly ridiculous." Dahn looked himself over one final time.

"Like, don't worry about," Seline reassured him. "Humans really go for this kind of thing."

"Why? I can't even move my tail more than half a length! It's annoying!"

"Hey, I got the loosest thing I could find. You're lucky I didn't, like, pick you up a pair of jeans!"

"Really? Well, thank you," Dahn relented. "What are jeans?"

"Actually..." Tor buzzed around him appraisingly. "I like it!"

"I appreciate it, Tor, but stop trying to make me feel better. We both know this is completely unnecessary!"

"Well, humans are silly about things like this. Besides, when Sarah comes back, we can cut a hole for your tail with her knife. It'll be so comfortable, you won't even know you're wearing it!"

"Speaking of which..."

Seline noticed the ranger coming towards them with a noticeable head of steam. All three faced her expectantly. She stomped to a halt and lifted a single finger, pointing lethally and accusingly at Seline. She opened her mouth to speak, but nothing came out. The rest of the party looked on in concern.

"Sarah?" asked Dahn, concerned. "Are you okay?"

The well-meaning question only made her turn an even more vivid shade of red. She finally found her tongue.

---

*Very often, they *are* chocolate cake recipes. This is exactly the sort of thing master wizards laugh themselves silly over.

"The next time—you go—into a tailor's shop." The words were choked, but audible. "Don't—give the owner—a heart attack."

"Heart attack?" Seline repeated feebly. She and Tor winced.

"Yes, you simpering git! A heart attack! You were supposed to keep a low profile, and you nearly killed off some poor scrag in one of the city's busiest areas! Goddesses above, I can't leave any of you alone for five minutes without someone getting kidnapped, blown up, or killed!"

"Oops?" Tor offered simply.

"Oops," Sarah echoed hollowly, with a laugh that was not altogether stable. "Just oops. Well then, that's all well and good. All's forgiven! Let's go back to the inn, Little Miss Oops."

Tor rested one of her tiny hands on the ranger's shoulder.

"Sarah, we're really—"

"Do not touch me right now." Sarah whirled to face her, not looking completely sane.

"Er, right. Sorry." She backed away quickly.

•

Stan Chryzdolf sat in the dungeon of Walter's Guildhouse and bleakly stared into his nearly empty mug. He wondered if Walter had served him a tankard of cleaning fluid by accident. He eventually decided against it. The quality would have been noticeably better.

He sighed through his depressed and thoroughly drunken stupor. His career was in shambles. His friends were shunning him for getting the living hell beat out of him—first by a woman, then by a Quo'Chi-Ka exhibitionist. And to top it all off, his leg now ached acutely when it rained. He would still be in the town barracks if someone hadn't sprung for his bail. He still didn't know who anted-up the money. Bail for attempted homicide was steep. He figured he owed the guy a beer, at the very least. (Or whatever it was they served here.)

He raised his eyes to Walter for a refill. That's when he noticed his view was blocked by something resembling a tanned stone wall with muscles. Stan nearly fell out of his chair. Either the man's approach had been completely silent, or he was more drunk than he thought. He ruled out the latter, having long since realized his goal of drinking as much as he could without vomiting.

"Mr. Chryzdolf." With a warm smile and a smooth voice, he extended his hand. Stan figured him to be a diplomat of some sort. "I've been looking for you for a while now."

"You're not gonna beat me up, too, are ya'?" Stan took the hand and shook it.

"Of course not." The man's grip was firm and powerful. He laughed brightly, taking a seat nearby. Stan tried to focus on him and failed miserably. He managed to make out a long, blond ponytail and a black silk cape. "In fact, I'm rather distressed about your new female nemesis. She's quite the little hellcat, isn't she? Pity you were caught, it would've made both our lives easier."

"How did you know about that?"

The blond man looked over his shoulder. Walter caught the look in the his eyes, stopped cleaning his tankards, and left for his workshop. The iron door was quickly closed and barred, leaving the two alone. Turning back with the same glossy smile, he continued in a lowered voice.

"I represent a group of friends that you called upon mere days ago—friends meant to aid you in services you couldn't perform on your own."

"If you're from that one Temple of Bejeera, I already told you a thousand times. I paid in full."

"Come now, Stan. Surely you're not that drunk."

Stan had an obscenity-filled response primed, but in a modern miracle of biology, his memory of recent events collided in his inebriated brain with the man's black silk cape. His mouth snapped shut immediately.

"Ah. I see we're on the same page, then." The man's demeanor seemed smoother than ever now that Stan was fearing for his life. "No need to worry, Mr. Chryzdolf. I'm just here for a friendly chat."

Stan shifted on his seat uncomfortably. He lowered his voice to a whisper, despite no one else being in the room.

"No offense, mister, but my pal from Harkshire, he sent me to someone who was s'pose to be one of your best guys. We could've beaten the monk to the punch if he wouldn't have gotten greedy. And what in the name of Goff was Farkhis doing there, anyway?"

"Please, please! One thing at a time! It's a shame we had to lose one of our most talented employees, but he paid for his greed in full. As for Groeke Farkhis, that was a complication no one could foresee." He leaned his massive elbows on the table and placed his fingertips together. "But enough pleasantries. You owe us a favor. After all, that's what friends are for, isn't it? You scratch our backs, we'll scratch yours."

"A favor?" Stan scoffed. "Your guy landed me in jail. You botched your job. I don't owe you squat."

"I'm afraid it wasn't a question, Mr. Chryzdolf." The man seemed neither afraid nor particularly sympathetic. "You see, the Guild paid for your bail."

Stan noticeably shifted in his seat again.

"Obviously, we're willing to right our error and clean up the charges against you. But our time and money is very valuable, and we would appreciate repayment for services rendered. After all, as a gentleman, you'd want to repay your debts. Wouldn't you?"

"And if I refuse?"

"Honestly, Stan. I would think you'd have learned not to ask us that by now. If you refuse, you go back to jail, you're convicted, you're put in solitary confinement, and you die in the worst possible way we can imagine. And believe me—we can imagine far worse deaths than the state can."

The charming smile on his face contrasted sickeningly with the death threat. Stan had no problems believing him.

"I guess I don't have much of a choice, do I?"

"No." The Supervisor stood. "I guess you don't."

Stan looked into his tankard despondently.

"But how'm I—"

He looked up, but the blond man was gone. Lying on the table was a rolled-up piece of parchment. With trembling fingers, Stan unfurled it and read. His lips drew thin. His favor was simple, but there was no margin for error. The stranger had made that point abundantly clear. As per the instructions, he lit the parchment's corner when he finished, then deposited the flaming scroll into an ashtray. He knocked back the last suds of his drink to bolster his courage.

•

The two healers finished strapping their medicine into their wagon, checking off the tailor shop on their list of chores.

"That's all for today, brother," the taller said.

"Praise to Exultus and Jar'lin," the shorter nodded. "It has truly been a long day."

A cry in the distance caught their attention. Following it back to its source, they found a young man in a bellhop's uniform running down the street. He was waving frantically for their attention, in clear need of their services. His cheeks were bruised and puffy, one eye was swollen shut, and blood was trickling from both nostrils.

"I'll get the potions," the taller sighed.

"A shame the church does not pay overtime," the shorter remarked, retrieving his tools.

His companion gawped at the unexpected display of avarice.

"Well, it is," he repeated meekly.

R. D. Hammond

CHAPTER 8

"Ohm nah mahn tih kah qeh rah."

Every race in the Pflatlands has a trait they're known for. Sprites giggle, elves lord and rule, humans blow things up, nymphs do things we can't discuss in this account, and Kars meditate. (They also do things we can't discuss in this account, but that's beside the point.)

The Kar aren't attractive just by means of fur, pretty eyes, and cute derrières. Their philosophy holds that life is beauty, and all beauty emanates from three places: betih, me, and ahlnima (roughly, the body, mind, and soul). Without a sharp mind and loving soul, a good set of curves is all but pointless to the Kar. Besides, among an attractive and polygamous race, experience dictates that solely physical relationships last anywhere between 30 minutes to six hours—depending on combined stamina—and are pretty much over before they begin. This isn't to say they're perfect by their own standards. Even in Kar society, you have the occasional lavender-haired, gorgeous femme whose IQ points couldn't fill a teacup. But if said airhead is trying her hardest to better herself, then by golly, it's the thought that counts. Even if she doesn't have many of them.

"Ohm nah mahn tih kah qeh rah."

This is why Dahn has crossed one leg on top of the other and begun chanting, if you were wondering what that noise was. Self-improvement permeates every aspect of a Kar's being, and in this quest for personal beauty, the ideal starting point is to know thyself—inside and out. Once one's limitations have been uncovered, they may be pushed gently past. Like everything else in Kar philosophy, the idea is better on paper than in practice. Still, it does have inherent advantages, one of which is developing a calm center within a Kar's mind. This grants him or her the ability to make quick, logical decisions uninhibited by stress or irrational desires—a trait every good Kar unarguably possesses.

"Ohm nah mahn tih kah qeh rah."

And if you believe that, we've got a goose for sale that lays eggs you won't believe.

•

Dahn was roused from meditation by a gentle tapping at his door.

"Cheh'kulu!" he said cheerfully.

The door was nudged open, and Tor's glowing form slipped into Dahn's room. The inn room was a standard paint-by-number deal, available throughout the Happy Boar. A single oil lamp provided light, a worn feather mattress provided rest, a cheap oak dresser provided storage, and the unvarnished floor provided splinters. Tor glanced at Dahn's robe—on the opposite side of the room—and sighed.

"You really should keep that on. These people are too uncivilized to go without clothing!"

"I know, I know." He swatted his tail out of the way. "But it's so unbelievably baggy! And it itches!"

"You'll just have to make do."

"What about you? You're not exactly overdressed."

"That's because I'm a sprite, silly." She shook her undersized body at him flirtatiously. "Humans don't expect me to wear clothing!"

"Lucky you. Don't you have somewhere else to be? I have to finish meditating."

"No can do. Sarah kicked me out of her room."

"Whatever for?"

"I got bored and started poking around in her stuff." With an impish grin, she added, "Want to know what she's got in her underwear drawer?"

Dahn considered. Sprites were innately curious creatures. Perhaps he could take advantage of...

"No, no, no." He felt the need to say it several times. "I've more manners than that."

"Whatever lights your torch. Hey, after all we've been through, I could really use a bath. Think you can help out?"

"Hmm. Maybe." Dahn scratched between his ears in thought. "I'll see if those nice people in red suits will help. Sarah said they're supposed to."

He rose from the bed, bounded gracefully to the other side of the room, and struggled into his robe.

"Thanks," Tor smiled.

"You're welcome," he smiled back. He flipped up his hood and walked out into the hallway.

The second floor of the inn was dimly lit by half-melted candles. The walls were dotted with small porthole windows, and the red carpeting was more than a little trampled. As Dahn passed the neighboring room housing Sarah and Seline, a brief flash of lightning illuminated the hallway, followed by a thunderclap. He could clearly hear both of them over it.

"The Infernus you are!"

"Oh, yeah? If you're so great, how come men don't, like, flock to you?"

"Because I'm not an airheaded floozy like some people!"

He continued down the rickety stairs to the lobby. Like most inns, the lobby of the Happy Boar also served as bar and diner. Several patrons were already taking dinner and drinks for the night, in groups or in quiet solitude. Not much conversation was heard over the rattle of silverware and clinking of tankards. Dahn felt several pairs of eyes on him as soon as his foot touched the floor. He shrugged it off without looking. Of course he was being stared at. He was new. Besides, the irritating hood mashing his ears flat to his head made him look like everybody else.

He approached the counter, waiting politely for the clerk. Several minutes passed. Dahn coughed. Several more minutes passed. While drumming his claws on the counter, he noticed a device on the corner and remembered what Sarah had done to get service. Since he wasn't good at threat of bodily harm, he tried the device instead, pushing the little button on top. A sharp chime made him leap back in fright. He looked behind him guiltily. None of the patrons seemed to notice, but the ominous feeling of being watched persisted.

In response to the bell, the clerk glanced up from his paper, and Dahn saw he had two black eyes.

The paper's headlines blared:

DETAILS OF SCANDAL STILL A MYSTERY
High King Unhelpful, Downright Surly

"Good day," Dahn said. "I'd like some water, a thimble, and a cup."

The clerk glared at him. Dahn smiled back, unfazed, and rocked on his heels. The man behind the counter didn't budge.

"Oh! Please," he added, remembering his manners.

The young boy still refused to move.

"Kushkla de'te," Dahn continued. "Tihj beh nohn bihnu…?"

"Look, buddy," the bellhop snarled, "I don't have time for this. Either speak High Common or go back to your room until you can."

Dahn was startled by the stream of angry gibberish. Too late, he realized this particular human didn't have a translation necklace. He tried his sentence in Elvish, but the clerk's expression didn't change. Finally, he made a last-ditch effort to point at what he wanted. The bellhop turned back to his broadsheet, ignoring him completely. Dahn fidgeted, then hung his head in defeat. He dejectedly padded back up the stairs and to Sarah's door.

"Did not!"

"Did too!"

"Did not, did not, did not!"

He knocked softly. The door flew open a fourth of the way, Sarah's flustered face behind it.

"What?" she shouted, then noticed Dahn cringing on the other side. She calmed and spoke again. "Dahn, what do you want?"

"I'm sorry to bother you," he said, nervously smoothing his ears under his hood, "but the people downstairs are being very mean."

"So? Welcome to life in the city."

"But I'm trying to get some stuff so Tor can take a bath, and they won't give it to me, and the guy downstairs with the red robe and weird eyes says things I don't understand at all, and they sound pretty mean, and—"

"Okay, that's different."

She lulled him into silence with a surprisingly gentle hand on his shoulder. She slipped through the door and strode determinedly to the front counter, leading him reluctantly by the arm. Upon seeing Dahn's return, the bellhop rolled his bruised eyes.

"Look, pal. If you came down with your lady friend to complain, she better speak our language. I'm getting real sick of—"

He suddenly realized who Dahn's "lady friend" was. His eyes widened in sheer, unadulterated fear, and he turned to bolt from the room. Sarah calmly relocated his large wooden desk with one hand and lifted him by the back of his shirt.

"Dahn," she said quietly. The lobby fell silent as the bellhop kicked. "What was it you wanted?"

"Reh ahkwa, reh cutoh, nahr reh thihm."

"Right. Water. One goblet. One thimble. And make it snappy, pinhead."

She released his shirt without warning. The bellhop dropped to the ground, stumbled forward, and slammed into a wood wall with a grunt. Dahn felt eyes on him again, but this time, he knew where it was coming from. Everyone in the lobby was openly staring. Sarah whirled with one of her patented glowers, and they went back to dining, avoiding eye contact. Satisfied, she dropped the desk inches from the clerk's toes and led Dahn off.

" I don't get it," he said, as they walked up the stairs together. "I thought you didn't want to make a scene."

"It's a little late for that," she replied tersely, all but proclaiming the conversation over.

He followed her the rest of the way in silence. Sarah stopped at her door.

"Besides, they shouldn't have treated you like that. You don't deserve it."

"Really?"

But Sarah was gone by then, shutting the door gently behind her. Dahn walked back to his room with a huge smile on his face.

Inside hers, Sarah leaned on the door, shaking her head in disbelief.

"Like, what are you so contemplative about?" Seline asked.

"None of your business," Sarah snapped back.

•

The lobby of the Happy Boar was well within regulations for a B-Permit inn house: shoddy boar-shag carpets, warped floors and walls, and just enough candlelight to annoy people trying to read. The bellhop muttered, stuffing the night's mail into the proper boxes. While normally cordial, his morale (1) ebbed after suffering a broken nose (for something which was, quite frankly, worth the pain), (2) had declined after his father's near-lethal heart attack, (3) worsened considerably when a member of some unknown nation made him feel like an idiot with his incomprehensible babble, and (4) bottomed out when his new nemesis completely manhandled him, in spite of his having six inches, 40 pounds, and a Y-chromosome on her.

He was so wrapped up in his thoughts, he didn't notice the bellhop he was thrusting a tray at wasn't a current employee. He also didn't notice the bellhop's uniform wasn't his. And furthermore, in the foul mood he was in, he completely missed the ugly red stains around the uniform's wrists."Here," he grumbled. "Some babbling freak in room

207 wanted this. Watch out for the girl next door, she's as vicious as a cacodemon."

A smirk crossed Stan's face as he silently accepted the tray. This was going to be much easier than he thought.

•

Tor continued her pacing on Dahn's nightstand. A knock at the door roused the Kar once again. He yawned and groused. If this is what it was like trying to meditate, sleeping was going to be an unmitigated disaster.

"One moment!" he called sweetly, no longer caring if anyone could understand him. He picked up his robe and commenced with the usual amount of fumbling. The knock sounded again, more impatient. Emitting a nasty string of syllables, he pulled the garment on and stumbled for the door. Tor flitted behind him as he reached the doorknob, flipping the hood over his ears. He bowed in silent thanks. She smiled and returned to her pacing.

Finally and properly cloaked, he opened the door as far as the chain latch would allow. He peered out into the hallway, his eyes shining reflectively in the candlelight.

"Room service!" the old man on the other side smiled, leaning on a cane for support. Dahn furrowed his brows in confusion, not understanding a word. He lowered his tray and pointed helpfully. Realizing these were the items he was waiting for, Dahn bowed politely, then closed the door to remove the chain.

As luck would have it, Sarah had woken minutes earlier with a full bladder and a pressing need to do something about it. Emerging from the restroom in a fire-red nightshirt, she took one look at Stan Chryzdolf's crippled figure and instantly sobered, no matter how much ale she drank to survive rooming with Seline. A scream of alarm rose to her lips, and Stan turned just in time to catch four knuckles and a magic ruby right between the eyes.

Unfortunately, Stan didn't come alone. The innocent guests at the pub downstairs suddenly weren't so innocent anymore, unsheathing weapons and surging towards the staircase.

"Sarah?" Seline stuck her groggy head out the door. "What in Queen Mab's name is all the noise—"

"Move!"

Sarah pounced at the door and careened through it, sending the nymph reeling with a shriek. Dahn's door was already tightly shut and locked. Sarah followed his example, and just to be sure, shoved the ponderous weight of the oak dresser in front.

"They're here!" she exclaimed in panic.

Seline mutely nodded, grabbing the scroll from the dresser. Sarah snatched up her shortbow, ducked her head and shoulder through it, then flung open the shutters.

"But we're leaving behind all those great clothes!" Seline bit her lip and gave one last look at Sarah's wardrobe.

The ranger heard swords and axes hacking away at the door. She shoved Seline through the window, nearly sending her off the outside ledge.

•

Dahn walked calmly to the bed after shutting and locking his door. Tor was sitting in the goblet and dumping a thimbleful of water over her head. She looked up inquisitively.

"I'm afraid you'll have to skip your bath. Those people in black are back again."

"What?" She gave a terrified squeak.

"I know. Just hop in." He patted the chest pocket of his robe. "We can get away over the rooftops."

"Won't they follow us?"

"Oh, we've got nothing to worry about." Dahn ignored the strange noises outside, stepping to the window confidently. "Most of them appeared to be human."

•

Sarah scrambled onto the narrow outcropping after Seline. They pressed themselves against the wall and shivered in the pouring rain. Despite the pressure from their pursuers, Sarah moved very carefully on the slick ledge. It was a good thing she had put her glasses on, or she might have ended up in a dumpster, below, instead of the ledge outside.

"Like, should we hide or run?" Seline whispered.

A graceful blur cut through the night air from a neighboring window, landing on the roof across the street. An explosion rocked the inn afterwards, flames blasting out the windows. A strong rush of stormy wind pinned them to the wall, keeping Seline and Sarah from plunging off. The wall they were pressed against held. The roof above was not so lucky. Rain poured into the blackened and smoldering remains of what used to be their inn room.

"Run," they nodded in agreement.

The figure on the roof turned and looked back. In the pale moonlight, Sarah could make out a pair of glowing yellow eyes.

"Sarah!" Dahn cried.

"Go!" She waved at him blindly. "Get out of here! I'll meet you on the outskirts of town!"

"But—"

"Go!!" she screamed, hearing the assassins hacking their way through the collapsed roof. With only a split-second of that worried look, the one which Sarah refused to let melt her heart, Dahn took off like a black, liquid arrow.

Suddenly, her ears caught the blood-freezing sound of bowstrings being drawn taut. The assassins were threatening from below, as well. They were caught in a vice, and there was only one option.

"We're going to have to jump!" Sarah shouted to Seline.

No response came.

"Seline! We have to jump, or we're dead!"

Still no response. Hoping she would follow, Sarah pushed hard against the wall with her heels and hands, rising up into the air—and up, and up some more! To her shock, Sarah found herself flying over the rooftops. Seline's hand was wrapped tightly around her arm.

"Sorry I didn't answer earlier," Seline yelled over the howling gusts.

The Pflatlands

"I was concentrating on getting the wind currents just right, and—"

Sarah winced as black-shafted arrows zipped past her ears, barely driven off their mark by the wind blowing around them. She tried hard to ignore them—much like the cold air blowing up her nightshirt, exposing her undergarments to anyone who happened to look up and squint.

"I thought you were a water nymph!" Sarah shouted back.

"Sorry! I totally can't hear a word you're saying!"

The roar around them increased as the two rose higher, leaving the assassins' hit squad behind.

•

As Dahn leapt from roof to slippery roof, he extended his claws through his toenails in a desperate attempt to hang on. Every now and then, a slight slip caused Tor to emit a muffled shriek. The scream was always worse than the actual loss of balance. By the fifth or sixth shriek, he decided it wasn't worth the risk. He had already fallen from a dry tree under mildly distracting circumstances, and this was worse than any situation he ever thought he'd be in. At first opportunity, he bounded off the edge of a building into the night sky. Tor felt like the bottom had dropped out of her world. The sensation ended jarringly, as Dahn hooked onto an outstretched rail and swung onto the cast-iron fire escape of—

Iron. Dahn realized what he had done a moment too late. A piercing scream, followed by much thrashing in his front pocket, reminded him that faeries and iron didn't mix. He reflexively placed one hand on the railing and vaulted over the side. As he sped towards the ground, he realized he technically should have looked before he leapt. He barely had enough time to reason breaking a leg was better than killing Tor before he crashed on top of someone. A large knife—which might have qualified as a shortsword in some circles—slid from the figure's hands. Dahn looked under his feet at the unconscious man and scrambled off. Concern turned to disgust when he noticed the black silk robe. He gave the assassin a swift kick in the ribs for good measure and turned to leave the alleyway, shivering in the rain.

Three figures, wrapped entirely in black except for their eyes, melted out of the darkness to block his escape. Turning the other way, Dahn was met with a brick wall. He was completely trapped. His only escape route would kill his friend, and Tor wouldn't make it very far on her own with wet wings. He grimly extended his claws and crouched, ready to meet his fate.

Several moments passed before Dahn realized they weren't attacking. In fact, they were hanging back in confusion, as if they had a general lack of—leadership? The man he landed on must have been the squad leader, waiting in ambush. Apparently, the assassins didn't know enough about Kars to watch above instead of around.

Serves him right, thought Dahn.

The middle assassin took a few hesitant steps and assumed control.

Tor peeped out of Dahn's pocket, wondering why they had stopped. Seeing the situation, she dove back in and trembled.

"Give us the scroll!" The assassin's voice was clear and haughty, carrying easily across the alleyway.

"Qerih?"

The assassins stared. Dahn stared. He resolved then and there that, if he ever got out of this mess, he was going to learn High Common. He conveyed his feelings in a more universal fashion with an obscene gesture. A pair of throwing knives hurtled towards him. The Kar simply ducked, too cold and tired to do anything fancy.

«Spider-Legged Grawkor!» the female assassin swore in Elvish. "It's true! He can't be killed by ordinary weapons!"

"I've got something that'll do the trick, then," the assassin on her left sneered.

Dahn caught a glimpse of something shiny on the man's left hand before a massive ball of flame rocketed down the alley. He clenched his hands over his head and flattened his ears in comically inutile defense. Surprisingly, no flaming magma smashed into his body. The roar dissipated into a hiss, and all he felt was a warm breeze. Opening his eyes, he saw the three assassins staring at him, shocked. He looked down in disbelief, patting himself to make sure he was alright. A cyan glow was

The Pflatlands

radiating from his body—specifically, his chest pocket. The glow intensified into white-hot light and, with a deafening crash, another fireball exploded into the original caster. The man screamed as he burst into flames, ran blindly through the rain-soaked street, and leapt headfirst into a horse trough. Steam rose into the night air.

"The cat-man is immune to magic! Retreat! Report to the Supervisor—"

That was as far as the woman got, before catching a muscled arm in the throat, delivered by a figure in a brown sackcloth cape. The rain shimmered from his ponytail as he spun and impacted his wooden sandal square on the forehead of the remaining assassin. Satisfied both were incapacitated, he vaulted over them and landed by Dahn with a splash. The young Kar backed away, hissing. The man raised his hand...then extended it, palm up. Dahn warily sheathed his claws and took it. The stranger shook it vigorously.

"Come," he said simply, squeezing the water from his goatee.

Dahn dumbly followed him to a cart outside.

"How in the world...?" He scrambled into the back of the getaway vehicle.

"Wise man once say," the stranger replied in broken Kar, "well-formed plan is grease that slicks fate-wheels."

He snapped the reins. The cart took off into the dark, rainy night, thundering down a twisting series of back roads and alleyways. Eventually, the cramped scenery of the city's underbelly fell away, and Dahn found himself on a familiar dirt road. He exhaled. He was finally safe.

His respite was over as suddenly as it came.

"Stop!" he shouted. "We forgot Sarah and Seline!"

"Can't stop!" the driver shouted back. "We will die!"

"If we don't stop, they'll be killed!"

"They survive! Know Sara wants you live, not dead!"

Dahn sunk back into the cart. The wind howled, billowing his clothes around him. The chill in his body matched the emptiness in his heart. Sarah had saved his life, and when the time came to repay her, he had failed. First Shoh, now Sarah and Seline...the elders were right about the Groundswalkers. He felt like a miserable excuse for a Kar.

Moments before the tears started to fall, there was a small tug on the collar of his robe.

"It's pretty windy for such a small storm, don't you think?" Tor had pulled her upper torso out of his pocket, looking up with a mischievous smile. Dahn stared down at her, confused. In response to his unspoken question, she pointed straight up into the air. The Kar followed her tiny finger and squinted, seeing an inky void, twinkling stars, a billowing red nightshirt, and a pair of black, lacy underpants.

"Sarah!" he screamed, leaping to his feet.

Seline was knifing gracefully through the night sky, holding onto the scroll with one hand and Sarah's wrist with the other. Her black dress clung aerodynamically to her ample figure as she guided the two through the heavens. Sarah was alternating between holding her nightshirt down and violently kicking to stay horizontal, both of which were obviously futile.

Dahn hopped up and down in the rickety wagon, his superhuman balance the only thing keeping him from hurtling out onto the road. The gesture was unnecessary. Seline and Sarah were already descending, growing larger and larger until Seline landed softly inside the cart…and Sarah lurched ungracefully forward, knocking Dahn into the soft hay.

"Nice landing." He blushed, pinned under the huntress' weight.

"Shut up," she grimaced, glaring down at him.

A small moan of pain caught both their attentions.

"Tor!" Dahn shoved Sarah off, who fell to the side with a grunt. He held his pocket open and peered in hopefully. The sprite pulled herself out, gasping for air.

"Are you okay?" he asked, concerned.

"Try—laying—sandwiched between two ogres," she panted as soon as she was able, "and see if you're okay!"

"Looks like we all made it!" Seline exclaimed in relief. "Who do we have to thank for this totally bodacious rescue?"

"Hello, Miss Seline." Recognizing the voice, Groeke turned his attention from the road and flashed a charming smile. "We meet again."

"Bitchin'," murmured the suddenly starry-eyed nymph.

CHAPTER 9

After exchanging escape stories, the adventurers gave in to exhaustion, one at a time, until Seline and Groeke were the only two awake. After giving him some directions, Seline drew up the cloth tarp to shut out the dying rain and conceal the cart's cargo. She soon joined her teammates in slumber.

The last to fall asleep, Seline was also the first awake. She stuck her head outside; the sun was shining cheerfully, and Groeke was nowhere to be found. It was as good of an excuse as any to wake everyone. She clambered out and rolled back the tarp, revealing Dahn settled against a bale of hay, Sarah snuggled into his side, and Tor wrapped cozily in Sarah's hair.

"Aww!" Seline grinned as they stirred in the chilly breeze. "You guys look totally adorable!"

Sarah blinked groggily. When she realized where she was, she bolted upright. Tor yelped and tumbled on the cart floor, her unprotected flesh savagely exposed to the cold air.

"Huh," Sarah mumbled, rubbing her eyes. "Must've gotten cold during the night or something."

"Fer sure," Seline nodded, straight-faced.

"Although that still doesn't explain how his arms got around me." Sarah glared accusingly at Dahn.

"I was just trying to keep you warm!" he weakly protested.

"Where are we, anyway?" Tor took to the air, shivering.

The cart had been parked in a deep and rounded valley—rounded being the operative word. The entire countryside was perfectly bowl shaped, with wildflowers of lavender and orange dotting the scenery. Despite the bright sun, cold wind constantly poured through the valley. The only creatures present that didn't seem to mind were the cart's horses, which were happily chomping away at the vegetation. Something about their languid and unimpressed manner struck Sarah as familiar. She glanced at the side of the cart.

HAY IS FOR HORSES™
A Division of Sweenie and Sons
"Our Hay is as Insane as Our Owners"

"I had Mr. Farkhis take us to a couple of old friends," Seline explained. "If they can't help us, we're totally screwed."

A reply sprang immediately to Sarah's mind, but she held her tongue.

"They live here?" Dahn asked. "But it's so cold!"

"Well, like, not in the valley itself."

"Where, then?"

"Right over there!"

They turned and looked. A tower rose high into the sky, dead center in the grassy vale. It was a smooth and windowless piece of marble, perfectly cylindrical save for the jagged and twisted crown. Giant gold runes lined the sides, and the surrounding air crackled with magenta energy. Drafts of cold air whistled from its surface. Every so often, a silent bolt of electricity fired out the broken top into the sky above.

"A Tower of High Sorcery?" Sarah gasped.

The Pflatlands

"Well, not really high sorcery," Seline elaborated with an odd expression. "I guess you could say it's, like, moderately lofty..."

"Oh, wow!" said Tor, delighted. "You mean an archmage lives in there?"

"Two, actually..."

"Two?" Sarah was flabbergasted. "What are two archmages doing in the same tower? What's their guild numbers?"

"And what's an archmage?" added Dahn.

"Well." Seline still looked as if there was something she didn't want to admit. "Zero and 23."

"Zero and—wait, that sounds way too low. Even the conjurers only go down to 150."

"Let's get inside, 'kay?" Seline waved off the entire conversation. "Trust me, it's not going to get any warmer out here. The wind's, like, a side effect of their generators cooling off."

"You mean we're going inside that thing?" Dahn gave the pulsating piece of marble a dubious glance.

"Don't worry about it!" Tor reassured him. "We'll be fine!"

"Unless they forget to turn the force field off," Sarah pointed out, "in which case, we'll fry like bugs."

"That's never happened before, has it?" Dahn gasped.

"Of course not!" Seline lied, leading the way.

The others fell warily in line, filing towards the tower in impressed silence. Luckily, the magenta haze faded as they approached. Now that they were closer, they could see runic patterns carved into the smooth surface, starting from the base and twisting upwards in a spiral. The effect was magnificent. Dahn would have slid his fingers across them in awe if he wasn't so afraid he'd lose one. Instead, he peered at the dizzying heights and nervously chewed his fingernails.

"Where's the door?" Seline wondered out loud, stopping a foot from the wall.

"You don't know where the entrance is?" Sarah exclaimed. "I thought you'd been here before!"

"It's not my fault! They, like, move the stupid thing almost every time I come here."

"Maybe they're trying to tell you something."

"The best path inward is often the least obvious."

Groeke's deep voice startled everyone, and they spun towards the source. The monk was leaning out of a rounded hole in the grass, which was definitely not there before. Dahn looked more confused than ever, his head tilting back and forth in a fruitless attempt to understand.

"Omigod! They moved it off the tower completely?" Seline cackled. A pair of bickering voices rose from deeper inside.

"It was Zero's idea!" one said.

"You went along with it!" a second, more polished voice shot back.

"Way rad! Move it, Groeke!"

The monk shifted slightly to accommodate her. Seline peered down the hole for a moment, then swung over the lip and disappeared from sight.

"You will find a ladder inside." Groeke followed her down. "Use caution. It is much deeper than it appears."

Pausing only to shrug at Dahn, Sarah descended as well, Tor flying down after her. Dahn sniffed around the entrance in distrust, then knelt to look inside. It appeared to be a metal chute with thick, rectangular rungs jutting out. He shifted his weight distrustfully onto them and, finding them suitably sturdy, began his cautious climb down. The chute was actually a small tube attached to a larger wall. When he reached the ground, a metal iris closed around the top. He hopped back, startled by the sudden motion.

"Jumpy as a cat, eh wot?" came the polished voice behind him.

He proved it right by nearly leaping out of his skin.

Dahn had apparently descended into a spacious den. A square, fuzzy rug with black and white stripes covered the floor. Surrounding it were couches and chairs made of black leather. An intriguingly twisted and semi-clear shape sat in the middle of the carpet, a glass disk on top. On it was a double-sized mug of steaming liquid. Multiple doors lined each wall in mathematically precise divisions, with paintings of gnolls playing cards between them. A crackling fire—burning cheerfully despite a complete lack of fuel—was located in an alcove in the rear. The brick fireplace surrounding it was obviously for decoration, since the fire also

The Pflatlands

lacked smoke. Finally, hanging over the mantle was a portrait of a blonde woman. She was clad in a white dress and smiling, her hair tied back with a red ribbon.

It was a picture perfect vision of Seline.

As he gazed around in wonder, Dahn slowly became aware of other presences. Seline and Sarah stood next to two unfamiliar men. Groeke hovered silently in the background, Tor seated on his head with a mischievous grin. Seline embraced one of the two strangers, laughing. He was at least as tall as the nymph, if not taller, but incredibly thin. He had angular features, grey eyes, and a shock of bowl-cut, carrot-orange hair. He was also dressed in a bright red robe and fez, complete with a bright yellow tassel. His partner was dressed in a similar robe, but he was far more robust in girth. He had brown hair, hazel eyes, a thick goatee covering his chin, and a constant smirk covering his mouth.

"Like, how are you guys?" Seline said warmly. "It's been ages since I've seen you!"

"One year, four months, three weeks, and two days," the thin man stated.

"Not that you've kept track or anything, right?" his partner deadpanned.

"I have no idea what you're insinuating!"

"C'mere, you!" Seline laughed, giving the thin one a bone-crushing hug. He panted for breath afterwards, straightening his fez and smoothing his robe.

"How many times have I told you not to do that?"

"Like you care!" the larger smirked.

"Oh, I didn't forget about you, Geoffrey!" She stood on her toes and gave him a kiss on his cheek. His expression remained steadfastly cynical, but he flushed noticeably.

Seline turned to address everyone else. "Guys, may I present two of the most totally awesome archmages I know: Dougglas Arthur of Machinists' Guild Zero and Geoffrey Chauntecler of Machinists' Guild 23."

"Charmed!" Dougglas replied, tipping his fez with a bow. Geoffrey made an abstract hand motion which could have been interpreted as a wave.

R. D. Hammond

•

Perhaps a brief explanation of magic in the Pflatlands is in order.

Magic, as both an art and science, has come a long way since the days of old. For one thing, it's no longer necessary to dance around a cauldron/crystal ball/fire/coffee table for hours. This isn't to say some people aren't into that sort of thing. Perhaps it's become religious, or maybe a superstitious custom, or perhaps some magicians are stark raving loonies. This is all beside the point; whether the preliminaries last five seconds or three days, the actual channeling of magic is a simple five step process. First and foremost, the magician evokes a power source. This varies widely from order to order: Clergy call upon their god or goddess, druids invoke the power of nature, mages channel mana from a ley line, etc. Next, having tapped this mystical energy, the magician crafts his or her spell. Third, the caster selects a target. (Sight works just fine, though methods for longer distances do exist.) Fourth, the magician channels power through the spell to the target, bringing the entire ordeal to fruition. Finally, having successfully done his or her job, the magician wanders off to have a beer. It's a very easy process to follow, but it can take years upon years* to learn, let alone master.

All of this assumes you're not a machinist; if you are, the whole five-step process goes right out the window and lands in the hedges below. People usually take one of three stances on machinists: You're a big fan; you hate them and stay the Infernus away from their insanely dangerous inventions; or, being a big fan, you know to stay the Infernus away from their insanely dangerous inventions. Most shy away from the first option, due to sanity being more common than its alternative (by however slim a margin). As an unfortunate result, machinists garner little respect.

But this simplified history is both unfair to machinists and insensitive to the issues at hand. For the benefit of the reader, we will now explain in full.

Technomancy, the machinists' line of mystical study, is a brand new

---

* And beer upon beer.

The Pflatlands

form of magic which is already threatening to overtake older arts. This is both its greatest boon and detriment. In order to learn traditional magic, one must normally possess what is called "The Gift"—the inherent ability to channel forces greater than yourself through your body. Whether this Gift is the result of genetics or psychological factors remains to be discovered, but ultimately, you either got it or you don't. Those who have it are often downright snotty about it, feeling themselves to be genetically superior to the Giftless. To these snobby elitists, the worst thing about technomancy is that anyone can do it. It's the casting of mystic pearls before swine.

So, how do machinists work magic without The Gift? Technomancy is really just a conglomeration of science and enchantments—and anyone, regardless of Gift possession, can work an enchantment. Although this magical jury-rigging is by no means easy, it doesn't involve the Infinite Powers of the Cosmos crashing through your veins. Thus, the field is open to all. However, it does involve the Infinite Powers of the Cosmos crashing through your machines, which sometimes leads to smoking, bulging, and in extreme cases, detonation. Fortunately, this only happens if the device wasn't correctly built. Unfortunately, machinists have a long way to go before they can consistently get it right on the first (or second, or even last) try. In spite of this, machinists are an undaunted bunch. They merrily putter along without a hint of daunt, pausing their studies only long enough to shriek and dive behind protective barriers. They are getting better at it, though—however slowly. And occasionally, all that diving and shrieking leads to wondrous things.

•

The rest of the day was spent on a whirlwind tour of the tower. Douglas (or "Zero," as Geoffrey and Seline called him) felt obligated to explain the odd choice of entrance. In the past, he would alter the tower's door from time to time—partially for technomantic practice, but also from want of change. Over time, he became disillusioned by traditional entryways. Drawbridges had lost their appeal, iris portals snagged and ripped robes, and automatic doors had a distinct history of falling on people. The archmage sat down with a cup of coffee to think, and after the fifth refill, he stumbled upon a brilliant solution: He would move the entrance off the tower altogether. Geoffrey was quick to point out it happened while he was buying supplies, and that he was barred from his own tower for two full hours before his absent-minded partner finally noticed.

Zero was quick to ignore him.

Sarah, Dahn, Groeke, and Tor were led through a dizzying array of portals, doors, ladders, and staircases, each leading to an entirely new room, each room decorated with the same odd fashion sense as the den. It was soon evident the inside of the tower was somehow larger than the outside. Zero, whose profession afforded him fluency in Elvish, offered a reasonable explanation to the inquisitive Dahn.

«We've actually done very little dimensional distortion, since that type of enchantment makes power spikes rather dangerous. What you're seeing is separate levels of the tower spliced together; almost all the doors are teleporters to new levels and locations. The process is seamless enough that the illusion of giant floors is created.»

«Oh,» Dahn replied, most of the explanation sailing right over his head. «What's a power spike?»

«A common occurrence, sadly. We occasionally see an unexplainable interruption in the mystic force powering a machine, then a noticeable surge thereafter. Most of the time, it causes harmless abnormalities, but it has been known to have…dramatic results.»

"How dramatic?" asked Sarah, who had been eavesdropping.

Zero exchanged glances with Geoffrey, who distracted her with a story about the giant white teddy bear tucked in the corner of the room.

The tour concluded well after sunset, and the party was shown to their individual rooms. Each chamber was decorated to order by odd metal spheres with telescopic arms and seemingly limitless supplies.

Groeke was content to leave his room the way he found it, requesting only some weights, padded mats, and a few sand-filled bags.

When Seline was finished with hers, it looked much like the bedroom of her old hut.

The Pflatlands

Tor's room, while too small to enter, was apparently to satisfaction. Squeals of joy came from inside as extra-tiny spheres zipped in and out at maddening speeds.

Dahn had requested an extra large living space, tediously filled with a jungle of trees and a free-swinging hammock—none of which he actually expected to receive.

And Sarah's was the most complex of all, with stone walls, fine tapestries, torchlight, a feather bed, a wardrobe full of fashionable clothing, a bookcase full of famous works, and a small window to view the valley. She recognized she had been given full run of the facilities, and she was going to milk it for all it was worth.

After settling in, bathing, and changing clothes, they were all invited back to the den. Geoffrey and Seline were first to arrive, Groeke in tow. Zero showed up with Tor and Sarah next, then excused himself to fetch Dahn, afraid he would get lost in the complex maze of teleporters. The rest were making idle chitchat when the two finally descended a twisting staircase in the corner, which didn't exist as early as five minutes ago and retracted into the floor as soon as they stepped off. Unsurprisingly, Zero was explaining something.

«So, what we're trying to do is optimize space,» he concluded. «We create rooms and entrances only when needed and delete them when we're done. It's all very economical—conservation of resources and all that rot.»

«But what happens if a bunch of—what did you call them?—power spikes happen, and you can't get out of the room?»

The machinist thought about it.

«Well, you would have to lean out a window and scream for help.»

«But what if there's no windows?»

"Sit down, will you?" Sarah ordered playfully, tugging on Dahn's tail. He peeped in surprise, taking his place next to her on one of the leather couches. Seline sat on the floor with her legs crossed underneath, clad in one of her completely immodest grass wraps and sipping a cup of tea. Tor sat beside her in the exact same position with the exact same mug, only a tenth of the size. Sarah was now dressed in a long red kimono, her glasses, and her necklace. Geoffrey sprawled on one of the leather armchairs, turning sideways to prop his legs on the arm. Groeke chose to remain standing, leaning against a wall with arms crossed over his chest.

"Now that everybody's here—" Geoffrey began.

"One moment," the other mage grumbled. A black metal sphere floated near him, emitting dripping noises at constant intervals. He tapped his foot impatiently.

"Zero, your coffee can wait."

"We've been over this a million times. My coffee waits for no one."

Hissing steam ejected from the back of the sphere. Gleefully, Zero raised his oversized mug. Steaming black liquid poured through a small tube extended from the bottom of the machine. Finally satisfied, he flopped into a chair opposite Geoffrey. The black sphere floated away.

"Now." Geoffrey sat upright and folded his hands. "With everyone here, I'd like to—"

"Wait, wait!" Zero cried again. Geoffrey rolled his eyes, but let him continue. «Some of our guests don't speak Common! Madam, could I borrow your necklace?»

«She's not a 'madam,'» Dahn reflexively offered.

«And yes you can,» Sarah finished, removing her necklace and handing it over.

She smiled at Dahn with something he swore was pride. Zero hurried to the fireplace and pulled a series of cleverly camouflaged connectors out of the wall. He fooled with the tangle of colorful wires.

"Not so bright, Hans," he frowned at the fire while he worked. The reprimanded flame whimpered and shrank noticeably. Finally satisfied, he rested Sarah's necklace on the mantle, now fully ensnared in colored cables. He retook his seat and cup.

"Fire elementals," he sighed. "Helpful, but overzealous."

"Hey!" Tor exclaimed. "I didn't know you spoke Sprite!"

"And last time I checked," Sarah said, "you didn't speak Common. What's going on?"

"My doing, I'm afraid." Zero chuckled. "I've wired your necklace's enchantment into the room's audio. As long as we stay in the confines of the den, you'll find we all speak the same language."

The Pflatlands

"Convenient."

"Assuming the necklace doesn't overload," warned Geoffrey, "in which case, you'll need a pair of tweezers to get it all back. Now, can we please get started?"

"Of course. Seline has already told me the abbreviated version of your last few days. It sounds like quite the adventure."

"More like a nightmare," Sarah sighed. Dahn bobbed his head in agreement.

"Nevertheless, you're safe from the big, bad Assassins' Guild inside this tower. No matter how well versed in the arts of deception they may be, no one goes in or out without our express permission."

"Don't get me wrong." Tor shook her head. "You guys have a really nice place, but we can't stay inside it forever!"

"Why not?" Geoffrey asked. "Zero does."

"Scrag you," the thin mage replied brightly. "I'm afraid that may be unavoidable at this point*. Until we can find out what this scroll of yours is and why the assassins are so intent on getting it back, you'll have to stay here."

"How long will it take to translate it?" Sarah asked.

"I doubt the assassins would leave sensitive material lying around in the open, so it's probably encrypted," Geoffrey conjectured. "We might be able to break the code, but it'll be a difficult crack. It could take months. Maybe longer."

"Terrific. Not like I had anything planned for the next three years."

"Really?" Dahn said. "You must lead a very boring life."

"I was being sarcastic, hairball."

"Oh."

"I suggest you not worry about it for now," Zero reassured them. "You've had a long, hard road to this point. Get some rest. In the morning, we'll haggle over the finer details."

"Very well," Groeke replied, the first words he had said since arriving. Just like that, he turned and left through one of the many doors.

"I think I'll call it a night as well," Tor yawned. She hovered by

---

*Staying in the tower. Just so we're clear.

Zero, returning the tiny cup and patting his cheek affectionately. "G'night, everybody."

"So, Seline." Sarah changed topics as Tor disappeared through a chute in the ceiling. "How did you, Zero, and Geoffrey first meet?"

"It's a rather personal relationship, my dear." Zero cut in hastily.

"I'm not your 'dear,' either," she scoffed back. "And that was way more information than I needed to know."

"Hey!" Geoffrey exclaimed. "Give us some credit, will you?"

"Like, what's that supposed to mean?" Seline scowled.

"You see—" Zero continued hesitantly. "We—ah—that is—"

"Come off it, guys! They're cool! You won't tell anybody, right?"

"I—guess not." Sarah shrugged.

"Well." Zero hummed. "We created her."

Dahn and Sarah's mouths fell open at the exact same moment.

"I could turn you two in for inhumane experiments," Sarah said sternly. Both archmages looked extremely uncomfortable until she deadpanned, "What with you being responsible for her and all."

"She's got us there," Geoffrey noted. Seline shot him a dirty look.

"You created a living being? By yourselves?" Dahn was astonished. "That's amazing! That's incredible! That's—"

"Something machinists had the technology to do five years ago." Geoffrey rolled his eyes. "Where did you get this guy, blondie?"

"The deep Argury Woods. He, like, doesn't know much about magic except for druidism."

"That explains it."

"Explains what?" Dahn asked, somewhat offended.

"Seline was our first project after we got our Archmage Licenses," Geoffrey elaborated. "We had to prove we were the real deal, so we decided to piece together our own cloning tank."

"Besides," added Zero, "there was a dreadful lack of interns in our line of work. Someone has to fetch the coffee, you know."

"But the use of cloning tanks was banned by the High Council," Sarah pointed out.

"Quite," Zero nodded. "They have a nasty tendency to explode or give you something completely unexpected. Or both."

The Pflatlands

"And you did it anyway?"

"We were desperate for recognition," he guiltily replied. "So much so that desire for fame eclipsed common sense. And naturally, we were forced to use homemade parts to complete the tank...with the addition of such unpredictable elements, we were lucky to get anything near what we wanted, flaws or not."

"Flaws?" Dahn blinked. "But Seline's perfect!"

The nymph smiled sexily at him. Sarah whacked him on the shoulder. He rubbed it through his cloak with a frown.

"Maybe by popular standards," Zero readily agreed, "but there were many inconsistencies with the original design."

"For starters," Geoffrey said, "there's her intelligence level."

"Yeah, I noticed that," Sarah grimaced.

"Right. It's too high for a nymph—abnormally so. We wanted it up from the average, but we seriously overdid it."

Sarah gawked at him, then Seline, expecting her to break the punchline to this absurd joke. In response, she handed Sarah a napkin she had been doodling on. She glanced at it and realized the doodles were, in fact, mathematical equations.

"New calibrations for the force field. Hand that to Geoffrey for me." Seline winked. "I told you I wasn't stupid."

"But—" Sarah passed the napkin along. "You—the map—the wrong way—"

"So I'm absent-minded. Like, sue me!"

Sarah decided not to think about it—for the sake of her own sanity, if nothing else.

"You mentioned there were more flaws?" Dahn was curious.

"Quite," Zero continued. "There were also problems with her elemental alignment."

"I wondered why a water nymph could control air currents," Sarah said. Seline shrugged at her with a cheesy grin.

"But that's just the symptoms, really," said Geoffrey. "The cause is her True Name. You guys know what that is, right?"

"Right," Sarah replied. "Formulaic representation of someone's essence gives you complete magical access to them, yadda yadda yadda."

"Yeah! Simple!" Dahn added, clueless.

"Hey, good for you. You get a cookie. Anyway, Seline's True Name was marred midway through the cloning process, which is why we ended up with something a little more random. Bottom line is, no one knows her True Name. Not her, not any mages, and certainly not us."

"So, she's immune to magic?"

"Like, to a point," she elaborated. "People can still fling spells at me if they can see me, but I'm immune to really nasty stuff, like curses. It's sooo rad! I could have someone directing voodoo at me all day, and I'd never feel a thing!"

Sarah shuddered at the thought of invincible perky.

"And, so," concluded Zero, "after cloning our little nymph—the act of which sent tank and top floor sky-high, might I add—we sensibly decided to follow the High Council's suggestions from now on. We gave her the option of picking her own name, as a sort of consolation..."

"Which was totally unnecessary!" Seline insisted. "I don't really need a name. I didn't even bother with them until I met Tor. You have to understand, I totally knew from the start that they didn't create me because of, like, a God complex or anything. These two are the absolute sweetest guys you'll ever meet, hands down!"

"I wouldn't go that far," Sarah smiled mysteriously.

"Sarah," Dahn interjected, "that wasn't very nice."

"Quite all right!" Zero replied cheerfully. Unlike the unobservant Kar, he saw where the smile was aimed.

"But there's still one thing I don't get," Sarah admitted. "Why in the world would two archmages risk their licenses and lives to create a fully grown, smarter than average, blond-haired, blue-eyed, curvaceous...water...nymph."

She trailed off with a look of disgust, answering her own question. Seline giggled. Both mages looked extremely guilty.

"I'm going to get some more coffee," Zero announced, leaving his partner to explain. Geoffrey fidgeted uncomfortably, drumming his fingers on the armrest.

"It was a phase," he said simply.

"Riiiiight." Sarah still looked disgusted.

The Pflatlands

"She's got a point, though. Why did you feel a need to prove yourselves?" asked Dahn. "I mean, you two are already important, right? That's what being an 'archmage' means?"

"There were certain...circumstances...involved with our licensing."

"Like what?" Sarah wasn't letting up with her narrow-eyed look of disapproval. Having practiced it so often over the past few days, she was starting to get really good at it.

"Well, the Mages' Guild office was really busy when Zero applied, so they told him to just pick a guild number. They meant from the standardized machinist range, but they didn't bother to put that on the form, and Zero's always been unique in everything he does..."

"He picked zero, didn't he?" Sarah could see where this was going.

Geoffrey nodded.

"And he was the only person in Mages' Guild Zero, wasn't he?"

Geoffrey nodded again.

"And that's why he's the archmage, isn't it?"

Geoffrey nodded one final time.

"And what about you?" Sarah leaned back on the couch, her hand on her forehead. "I guess you didn't come by your title honestly, either?"

"Actually, I did. I've been at this for a couple of years. I was lucky enough to land in Guild 23—nothing but machinists, one of the first of its kind. You learn your craft really quickly in an environment like that, or you end up a blackened, charred lump on the ground."

"That's good!" Dahn replied.

"Not really. Out of all the original members, I'm the only one who's not a blackened, charred lump on the ground."

"Oh. That's bad."

"Yep." Noticing Sarah didn't look entirely well, he added, "Don't worry too much about it. I know it's an unusual set of circumstances, but me and Zero know what we're doing. Trust me. We run this place like a well-oiled machine."

One of the silent, floating spheres rammed solidly into the marble wall in the background. It recoiled slightly, realigned itself, and continued along a different path. Geoffrey winced.

CHAPTER 10

After saying goodnight to the others, Dahn and Sarah ambled down a torch-lit stone corridor together. Sarah was once again wearing her necklace, relieved its disconnection hadn't blown it to bits.

Dahn limped along uncomfortably on the unforgiving stone floor.

"Do I have some sort of hex on me?" Sarah sighed as they walked.

"I don't believe so. Why?"

"It's just this entire situation. First you, then Groeke, then Tor and Seline, now Zero and Geoffrey. I haven't met one marginally normal person since this started!"

"If it makes you feel any better, neither have I."

"It's different for you."

"How so?" he asked, with a surprisingly dangerous edge. The question seemed vaguely familiar.

"You're out of your element. I could understand feeling uncomfortable around foreigners, but I should fit in with other humans."

"I don't know about that." Dahn leaned against the wall to rub his

The Pflatlands

aching feet. "Just because you have the same appendages and physical form and some of the same internal organs doesn't mean you have the same type of soul."

Sarah tapped her necklace to make sure it was working. However kindhearted he may be, she had estimated Dahn's intelligence somewhere between a rock's and a sprite's. That last thought was a little too deep.

"I guess you're right. I'm just sick of surprises and…weirdness." She waited until he was done, then continued down the hall.

"Life would be really boring without weirdness."

"I'd be perfectly happy to lead a boring life right about now."

"Maybe for a week or two. But then it would get old, and you'd want something new and exciting again."

In the back of his mind, Dahn wondered where these words were coming from. It certainly couldn't be him.

"So, I'm scragged either way?" Sarah laughed.

"Not really. You just have to concentrate on the positive—you know, get something constructive out of your situation. The elders say everything has a lesson to teach you."

"These same elders want you to spend the rest of your life of serving wine, right?"

"Well, yes. But it proves my point, if you think about it."

"I'd rather not. It's been a long couple of days." They finally reached the elaborate wooden doors of the ranger's room. Sarah rested her back against them, facing Dahn. "Want to come in and take a load off? I mean, if you're even half as tired as I am…"

"Sure," Dahn shrugged. "I probably won't sleep for a while, anyway. This place gives me the creeps."

"Yeah, I know what you mean. Too artificial."

"Yes! I mean, Zero and Geoffrey are great hosts, but—I don't know, all of this is so weird and scary."

"I'm sorry you were dragged into this mess, Dahn. I know you'd rather be back home."

"You know, if it wasn't for my sister, I…wouldn't." He looked away, uncomfortable. "I guess that's what scares me. There's never a dull moment down here, is there?"

"This whole thing is pretty unusual. Still, I guess we have some interesting things. What's wrong with liking it? You always said being a Groundswalker was bad, but you never told me why."

"Well." He chewed his bottom lip. "It goes back to the history of Jahk the Lifter and Narr Groundswalker..."The Kar turned to spit, then stopped himself. He glumly remembered there wasn't a point anymore.

"This could take a while." Sarah shook her head. "You should probably come in and sit down."

"Oh. Okay."

•

Zero sat on the bench in his workroom. Sparks flew as he welded his latest gadget together. On the other side of the room, Geoffrey peered at a flat, floating piece of glass. Dark green numbers flashed under his diligent perusal. He paused only long enough to offer useful input (and snide remarks) to his compatriot.

Adding Zero to her long list of heads sat upon, Tor was holding a tiny leather tube in her hands and cleaning its lenses with his hair. She had left her bedroom an hour after retiring, too tired to do anything but too bored to sleep. In her restless wanderings, she had stumbled across Zero and Geoffrey working hard in their lab. The faerie was delighted to find an enchantment similar to Sarah's necklace's in the laboratory—an absolute necessity, due to the diversity of races who sought their skills. Conversely, it was rarely needed in the den, since most people were not comfortable socializing with machinists. You never knew when something was going to break down and explode.[*]

"It was nice of you to make me a new telescope!" Tor said politely. "I lost the last one when we ran from the assassins."

"Think nothing of it!"

"Mainly because I had to deal with the micro-technomancy."

"Nobody forced you to make the device, Geoffrey."

---

[*] Including the machinist.

The Pflatlands

"Details, details."

"Admit it! You like to help people!"

"No! And you can't make me!"

"What are you two working on?" Tor asked, breaking up the argument.

"Well, right now, I'm refining one of Zero's inventions." Geoffrey motioned to the screen he was so carefully studying. "I've got my own project to work on after this."

"Oh?" Tor left Zero's head and bobbed in front of the glass, watching numbers fly by at dizzying speeds. "What's this thingy do?"

"It operates on the same principal as a crystal ball," Zero expounded, "plus a few improvements of my own. I found that flattening the crystal makes it easier to read images."

"Kind of like wide-screen palm reading!"

"Kind of," Geoffrey agreed. "But you can do a lot more than just predict the future."

"Quite, which ties into the true nature of my project. My goal is to relay images and sounds happening many kilolengths in the distance."

"Can't people already do that with magic?"

"Yes, but like all magic, the results aren't consistent. And you can't follow, just fixate. With spells like that, you might as well use a pair of binoculars. My device will absolutely revolutionize long-distance communications!"

"Hmm, interesting!" Not a single word failed to go in one of Tor's pointed ears and out the other. "You said you were working on something too, Mr. Geoffrey?"

"Yeah. I got an idea a few months back for a gizmo that'll really set the world on its ear."

"What does it do?"

"That's the ingenious part. Nothing."

"....huh?"

"Geoffrey's working on an advanced espionage device," Zero clarified. "On the surface, it performs mathematical computations at a rate heretowit unheard of in the entire Pflats."

"Oh. Neato!"

154

"Which is exactly what you want your enemies to think," Geoffrey grinned. "You wait for them to raid or pillage you or whatever, you leave it where they can find it, then you get the Infernus out of there. They take it home, hook it into a ley line, and react the same way you did. Especially if they're a magician."

"You wouldn't believe the amount of machinists who fell for it during field tests," Zero interrupted.

"Once they figure out its potential, they start using it to do their most difficult work. They store their best spells and information in its pocket dimension. They have a huge swell in productivity. Pretty soon, they're completely dependent on the Goff-damned thing to do their work for them, just because it's faster and more accurate than they could ever be."

"That doesn't sound bad at all!" Tor frowned.

"But that's the great part! It's not—until just the right moment. It's preprogrammed to completely scrag them over when they need it the most. And not just a little failure, either! It completely obliterates the pocket dimension and self-destructs!"

"Wow!" Tor exclaimed, impressed.

"Every single subject we've tried it on has fallen hook, line, and sinker. The only people who showed any long term benefit were those of the clerical inclination—which is to be expected, what with divine intervention and all."

"But discounting those extreme cases," Zero boasted, "all tests have been successful except for one—which wasn't really our fault, per se. We sent a prototype to an interested party and never heard of it or them again. We're assuming it was lost in transit, since they have yet to storm our front door and scream for a refund."

"I'll have you know the first model left nothing but a greasy smudge on the wall," Geoffrey proudly proclaimed.

"So, what are you going to call it? The Smoking Black Harbinger of Death?"

"I like it, but it doesn't have the subtlety I want. No, we need a user-friendly name. Something completely trustworthy. Something that makes you want to use it for all your computations."

They brainstormed in silence.

"How about 'computer'?" Tor proposed.

"I like it," Zero nodded sagely.

"Me too," Geoffrey agreed.

•

"Wow! This is amazing!" Dahn's gaze flickered like a nervous butterfly inside Sarah's room. What little of his tail that was visible twitched back and forth.

"Well, I'm glad you think so." Sarah sprawled on the bed in relief. "It's a pretty accurate copy of where I used to live."

"Where did you live? A cave?"

"No, I didn't live in a—" She caught herself and began again, softer. "Sorry. I forgot, you've never seen the inside of a castle. But no, I didn't live in a cave."

He scampered to a tapestry and stroked the brilliant purple and blue cloth. A weave of thorns and leaves was stitched around the border. Notes, arrows, daggers, quills, and countless other items formed a giant, inverted pyramid, all resting precariously on a silver tiara.

"What's this made out of?"

"That? Wool."

"What's wool?"

"Oh, for crying out loud! I know you haven't been in the real world for long, Dahn, but I can't stop every two minutes to explain things!"

"Just because it's your world doesn't make it real! Besides, you asked me for a history lesson. It's only fair."

"Alright, alright. It's like fur, except you don't kill the animals to get it. You kind of, uh, give them a haircut. And then…you make stuff out of it."

Never in her life had Sarah felt so silly explaining a concept so simple.

"You make blankets out of hair? Why?"

"That's not a blanket, it's a tapestry. It's for decoration. And what do the Kar use?"

"Fur. I guess there's not that much of a difference, especially if the animal gets to live. It's very pretty. Being made out of hair makes it even more impressive."

"You're not supposed to focus on what it's made out of, you're—"

"Who made it?"

The question took Sarah by surprise.

"Well...I did. The original version, anyway. This is just a replica."

"You? You're kidding."

"What's that supposed to mean?"

"You don't seem like the domestic type." He padded around the room, poking his nose into anything that didn't have a lock on it: cabinets, other tapestries, musical instruments, and a giant wooden trunk in the corner of the room.

"You don't seem like the type to philosophize at the drop of a hat, but you don't see me making jackassed comments about it. Besides, there's nothing domestic about weaving. It's as much an art form as anything else."

"Hey, what's this?" Dahn pulled something very skimpy out of the trunk.

"Get out of my clothes!" Sarah screamed.

He threw it back in and slammed the trunk shut, sitting on top of it and his hands.

"Sorry! I didn't think it was clothing! There wasn't enough there!"

"Just stay out of my stuff altogether, okay?"

"Sorry," he repeated. After she calmed, he added, "You wanted me to tell you about Jahk and Narr?"

"Sure."

"Mind if I sit down? My feet are killing me."

"Make yourself at home."

She moved over on the bed to make room. Dahn flopped onto it, ran his fingers through his hair, and began.

•

The Pflatlands

Many centuries ago, the Kar were still relatively few. We lived in the Argury, worshiped Lady Green, and kept to ourselves—much like today. What little interaction we had with the outside world was through the fae, who brought us terrible tales of brutal violence and madness. To keep our people safe, the decision was made to retreat deeper into Argury...but not all agreed.

("Makes sense," Sarah guiltily interjected. "That was right around the Second Dark Age. It wasn't a real high point in our history.")

At this time, there were two brothers, Jahk and Narreh. Sons of the great protector and warrior, Numah'hih the Striped, they were respected for their wisdom and leadership by Kar and fae alike. But, they disagreed on the matter of the Kar homelands. Jahk wanted to relinquish the old lands to the fleeing fae, believing Lady Green would reward the act of kindness with a new home. Narreh disagreed. He was proud of his heritage, and he wished to remain in the land of his father and his father's father. Jahk would win the debate in the eyes of the people. Narreh took his supporters and respectfully withdrew into the woods, contemplating what the decision meant.

He would come back changed.

The first sign of Narreh and his followers was the slaughter of his fellow Kar. The raids were fast, efficient, and bloody. They struck hard and melted into the forest before anyone could raise an alarm. Jahk was horrified; his only consolation was that Numah'hih was no longer alive to see this. Now calling himself Narr Casīdērā, "The Crusader," Narreh's goal was the elimination of the fae and any of their sympathizers. There was no beauty in Narr now, only bitterness and hatred. This was not the Narreh that had left us.

Jahk felt somehow responsible. He left to ask Lady Green for her aid, bringing nothing but a blanket to sleep under. He searched for twenty days and twenty nights while the deaths of his friends mounted. Fearing the same fate that befell Narr, he finally returned—starving, empty-handed, and defeated.

Fortunately, she found him.

Lady Green came at last in his fevered dreams of exhaustion. If his opponents were masters of the ground, she said, why fight on the ground? When he awoke, Jahk knew what had to be done. It took months of clumsy, slow work—but Lady Green had given us the trees, and the Kar had accepted. Narr's single-minded ferocity never prepared him for an attack from above. Day after day, Jahk's troops grimly purged the forest of the murderers. Ultimately, the Groundswalkers were erased from Kar society. The threat was over. Jahk had become Jahk Nahngteh, the Lifter and First Chieftain. And, in his selfless act, the Lifter had also found the Kar's new homelands: the treetops. Peace reigned in Argury once again. The Kar were finally home.

•

"Uh huh." Sarah gave him a highly skeptical look.

"That's why the ground is so dangerous. It took one of our greatest and turned him into a violent madman—just like your people during this 'Dark Age' of yours."

"And I suppose you buy into this?"

"I used to..."

"What happened?"

"My fall." Dahn grimaced. "The branch felt completely safe, right up to the very last moment. I just don't understand. There was no temptation or fanfare. I even wanted to stay in the trees! I don't understand why an accident makes me evil, but—"

"Maybe you were destined to fall," she replied sardonically.

"Maybe..."

She rolled her eyes.

"Look, you shouldn't use the concept of fate as a crutch. You can't go spouting mysticism out the ass and expect it to solve all your problems!"

"But it's real!"

"Real? You can't even see past your own story!"

"What?"

"This Narr wasn't an honorable guy, Dahn. He was rotten from the start. He took off as soon as he wasn't going to get his way, and as soon as everyone let their guard down, he started killing anyone he could get

The Pflatlands

his hands on. It was a tēcha cūtē* from start to finish. Where he was standing when it started didn't matter."

"I didn't think you'd understand," Dahn sighed. "But it's alright. I wouldn't except a race born on the ground to see the difference."

"What the scrag does that mean? What makes you an expert on right and wrong all of a sudden?"

"I'm not an expert," he peeped with a hurt look. "It's just a very simple process to understand. The stories say this, therefore, you do it."

"Oh, go stuff your tail in your mouth. I really don't want to listen to your useless drivel, especially if you're going to judge my entire race on some half-assed guesses."

"To Infernus with you! They're not guesses, they're fact! Just look at this place! You're all insane!"

"Whatever." She dismissed the entire conversation with a wave. "Get out of my room."

"Godless cynic!" Dahn scowled, his patience finally at an end.

"Naïve airhead!" Sarah shot back.

"Stubborn tomboy!"

"Idiotic hornball!"

Dahn remembered what Groeke called her the night before. He was unfamiliar with the word, but given the way Sarah behaved, he assumed it was derogatory. It was worth a shot.

"Cold-hearted Sara!"

Sarah's eyes went wide as ten-silver pieces.

"What did you just say?"

"Ha!" He laughed triumphantly. "I win."

She grabbed the scruff of his neck and ran to the door, then threw him out so harshly that he smacked into the opposite wall. The wooden doors were quickly slammed and locked.

"Ow." He righted himself and limped down the hallway, rubbing his bruised back and neck. "At least, I think I won."

Meanwhile, Sarah jammed her back against the door and struggled to get her breath under control. She threw herself onto the bed and

---

*Elvish for "broken house"—or, less literally translated, a coup d'état.

stuffed her face into a pillow, alternately swearing in Common and Elvish. Three even, heavy knocks rattled her door. Sarah blindly charged the wooden portal and yanked it open.

"Dahn, leave me alo—"

The muscular torso that filled her vision definitely didn't belong to Dahn. Her eyes traveled upwards to meet the unchangingly aloof expression of the World's Most Dangerous Monk.

"We need to talk, Sara Danoor."

She simultaneously cringed, paled, and wished for the monk's death.

"Have a seat." She gave a suitably biting reply as soon as she was able. "You've obviously come a long way to make my life miserable. The least I can do is offer you a chair."

"Sara?"

"Sarah!" she interjected forcefully. She stomped her feet in punctuation, her anger degenerating into a tantrum. "Sarah, Sarah, Sarah!"

"Sara Danoor, we both know that is not your name."

"It is now! And I order you to address me by it!"

"Perhaps we can reach a compromise, your majesty," Groeke sighed. "Elizabeth?"

"Whatever. And for Jar'lin's sake, will you get in here and close the scragging door? It's bad enough you and the fleabag know about this…"

Groeke maneuvered his massive frame through and shut the door softly.

"Sara Elizabeth—"

"Don't call me Sara!"

"Elizabeth," the monk repeated through clenched teeth, "I will be frank with you. Your father has hired me to bring you home."

"Keep dreaming." She jerked her thumb towards the window. "I'll leap out that first."

"May I remind you, Elizabeth, that you are the High Sara, the first daughter of High King Richard Danoor and his bride. You are the future High Queen! You cannot run from that!"

"I've been doing a damn good job so far," Sarah/Elizabeth grumbled, collapsing into a mound of pillows on the bed.

"Your parents want you home," he appealed.

The Pflatlands

"So they can use me as a pawn again? Scrag that. I'm not their nationalistic poster girl. Goddesses above, they don't even let people take my picture! I'm a person, not a concept!"

"Think of your people, then. Do you want your father in sole control of the High Kingdom?"

"Hmm" Sarah stopped to consider. "You have a point. The entire High Council's in his back pocket, and mom's useless outside of...well, come to think of it, she's pretty useless in general."

He nodded, relieved to find something they agreed on.

"But I can't go back, Groeke. Mom won't let me hunt because it's not proper for a Sara. Dad won't let me compose or paint because he thinks it's a waste of time. The only marginally enjoyable activity they don't give me Infernus over is weaving, and that only goes so far. I can't be an ethereal figurehead all day! I'll go absolutely insane!"

"I am sorry to hear that. But you should know I was instructed to bring you back at any cost, Sara."

"Don't call me that!"

Groeke swore mightily for the first time in years, diving away from a crystal vase given flight by Sarah's temper. It disintegrated into dust as it hit the door, the full power of her magical strength behind it.

•

Dahn perched on the highest branch of a faux ironwood and sighed. No matter how much she berated him, no matter how much time they spent at each other's throats, he still couldn't get his mind off Sarah. Every time he tried to meditate, his mind's eye would fill with visions of her: the way her glasses caught the light like a shining silver mirror; the way her fits of rage exposed her raw passion; the way her petite, pear-shaped body would look in the tiny outfit he discovered earlier...

«Visitors!» a voice called out, interrupting his thoughts.

He shook it off, tree-hopped to his hammock, and struggled into his robe as fast as he could. Fed up with the discomfort, he had finally ripped a small hole in the back with his claws. Threading his tail through was yet another awkward step to deal with.

«Hello?» the voice called again. «Anyone here?»

«Just a minute!»

Dahn finally adjusted robe and tail to satisfactory levels, then began his journey downwards, leaping from branch to branch until he landed noiselessly at the entrance. Standing just inside the archway of twisting branches was Zero, who had witnessed the entire trip.

«Bravo! You impress me more with every meeting!» Zero clapped enthusiastically.

«Are you making fun of me?» Dahn sniffed.

The mage stopped applauding, bewildered. «I—don't believe so, no.»

«That was terrible! I had to use my claws the entire way, I missed one branch completely, and I took forever to get here!»

«Really? It looked perfectly fine from where I was standing!»

«I suppose it's the robe throwing things off, although the trees aren't helping, either...»

«Oh? Is there something wrong with them, then?»

«There certainly is! There's nothing wrong with them!»

Zero did a double take.

«Pardon?»

«There's nothing wrong with them! That's the problem!»

«Could you elaborate?»

«No matter where I want to go, there's always a clear-cut path there. The trees are all set up so there's a branch every twenty lengths up, right on the dot. And the surfaces are smooth—no bumps or knots. Every last one of them is a perfect launching pad!»

«And...this is bad?»

«Yes! These trees all have the exact same pattern. It's like they're completely soulless!»

«Now I see!» Zero chuckled. «Our attempts to simplify your primary means of travel make you feel as if you're in an unnatural environment, yes?»

«Exactly!» Dahn was relieved someone finally understood.

«Well, you must realize that the feeling of unnaturalness can't be fully avoided. Even if we could get the simulation perfect, it would be

The Pflatlands

just that—a simulation. Nevertheless, there are steps we can take to alleviate your discomfort—adding a few more elements to the forest generation fractals and whatnot.»

Dahn nodded merrily along, assuming this was beneficial.

«We'll handle that tomorrow. I do apologize for the inconvenience, but we'll work on it at first opportunity. Will you be needing anything else, then?»

«No, thank you.»

«Very well! In that case, I wish you a good night's sleep.»

The archmage turned to leave. Dahn stayed where he was.

«Zero?»

«Yes?» The wiry machinist turned back.

«Nothing.» Dahn looked to be debating something, but shook his head. «You've been a tremendous host so far. I don't want to burden you with my silly problems.»

«Nonsense! The entire purpose of my visit was to ensure you were all right. If you have any concerns, personal or otherwise, please don't hesitate to share them.»

«Well. Let's say there's this girl, right? And she's completely uninterested in me. But I've really fallen—» He winced. «Really fallen for this girl, but she wants nothing to do with me, and we don't seem to get along at all, and—»

«Dahn!» Zero held up one hand to stop his jabbering. «Listen to yourself! If it's a hopeless situation, just forget about it.»

«I can't.» Dahn rubbed his eyes. «She's so beautiful. And smart. And strong!»

«I think you need something to take your mind off her, then, until you can handle the situation more rationally.»

«What do you suggest?»

«Well, whenever I'm lost in a problem, I find it best to curl up with a good book.»

«Book?» Dahn echoed.

«Your culture has literature, don't they?»

«Oh! Of course. I used to love reading the stones at our chieftain's hut! In fact, I've read 'Kuntar the Longtailed' seven times. It's the greatest epic in Kar history!»

«Really?» Zero jumped at the chance to gain insight into a new culture. «What's it about?»

«Okay, there's this Kar named Kuntar. He's a really strong warrior—right? And he fights this big, mean monster.»

«Yes, yes!» Zero nodded. «Do go on!»

«The battle rages all over the land, and it looks like he's going to lose the fight badly. But, right at the height of the battle, at the most climactic moment—»

Zero eagerly awaited the ending, enthralled by Dahn's exciting recount.

«He wins!»

Zero waited for the rest. He eventually realized there wasn't any more.

«And that's your culture's greatest epic?»

«Of course! Isn't it beautiful?»

«Dahn? You can read Elvish, yes?»

«Of course!» Dahn scoffed. «What do you take me for? A barbarian?»

«I'm sorry, I didn't mean to offend. I'd like you to accompany me to the library. If you don't mind, of course.»

«Sure!» he shrugged. «What's a library?»

•

Groeke sighed, holding the First Daughter of the High Kingdom to her bed in a complex hammerlock.

"How the hell are you doing that?" she shrieked. Even with her Ring of Strength, she couldn't break free.

"It is called the suo-on-kata—the Self-Binding Arm. It uses one's own strength against them. Will you please stop attacking me, Sara Danoor? This is the third time I have had to do this."

"Best of seven!" the huntress challenged, voice muffled by the bed. "I can take you with one arm tied behind my back!"

"You already are—and failing." After a bruising tirade about his

The Pflatlands

profession during the second suo-on-kata, she was beginning to sound like his last opponent. He was struck by the irony of it all. "Your highness, while it is not in my nature to do so, there are much worse things to be done to your arm. Please cease."

Sarah stopped struggling. Satisfied she was properly sedated, Groeke released her. She sat up and rubbed feeling into her numbed elbow, her gaze knifing into him. "Okay, Groeke. You've hunted me, you're caught me, you've humiliated me. You've won. Slap on the cuffs and put me back into royal slavery." She held up both wrists. "Let's get this over with."

"I admire your admission of defeat, however grudgingly it came. But that is not the course of action I have decided on."

"And just what did you have in mind?"

"Firstly, I want an apology for the shameful disrespect you have shown my fighting style."

She scoffed.

"I can put you back in the suo-on-kata, if you wish."

"All right!" Elizabeth grumbled, still rubbing her elbow. "Quo'chika is not fake—just scripted. There, I said it. Are you happy?"

"Quite. Secondly, I will not return you to your father."

"You won't?" She blinked in genuine surprise. "Wait. You're serious, aren't you?"

"Yes. I quite agree with your previous statements. From what I have witnessed, the High King is a boorish, obnoxious, conceited old man."

"Don't forget balding. And manipulative."

"So, if you do not wish to return, I respect your decision. As a truly wise man once said—"

"Yeah, that's great." She cut him off quickly. "So you're violating a direct decree from the High King? I'm touched, but that's not too bright. I mean, I should know."

"My dear Sara," Groeke replied in his best shocked tone, "I am doing no such thing. I shall return you to the throne. Eventually."

"Oh, of course. But this is still a little too good to be true. What's the catch?"

"My only stipulation is that I be allowed to protect you, until such time when you no longer require it. As long as you are safe, I am safe. And, more importantly, the future of the High Kingdom is safe."

"Have you follow me around all day? No way. Dahn's bad enough."

"It is what I have done thus far, with or without your approval. Those are my terms. I will not negotiate."

"On second thought," the princess speculated after a long staredown, "it's better than being in the su-kata-arm-hold-thing. You got a deal."

"It is done." The monk shook her hand.

"But here's my terms, Groeke. Outside this room, Sara Elizabeth Danoor doesn't exist. You call me Sarah, or you don't address me at all."

"Understood." He stifled a yawn. "And now, having concluded my business, I bid you farewell. It is late, and we both require sleep. Goodnight...Sarah."

"Night to you, too," she replied. As he left, she added under her breath, "And don't let the door hit you in the ass on the way out."

•

Dahn gaped heavenwards at the single bookcase of Zero's library, built into the silver-white walls of the small room and towering stories into the air. Row after row of thick books, old books, red books, small books, books in Elvish, books in Orcish—books of every size, shape, age, and language imaginable—were separated only by thin metal shelves.

"It's totally cool, isn't it?" A familiarly bubbly voice broke Dahn's trance. He looked to the left of the bookshelf, where Seline was leaning.

"It's certainly awe-inspiring." He stared back at the dizzying heights, squinting in a futile attempt to see all the way up. "How far does it go?"

"Gag me if I know."

"And how do they get all the books up there?"

His question was answered by a large silver sphere descending from above. Clamped between two metal fingers was a large book bound in blood-red leather. The orb presented it to Seline.

The Pflatlands

"Thanks," she said with a smile.

Having done its job, the sphere retracted its arm back into its body, becoming perfectly round once again. It bobbed silently out the exit and towards Zero, who was moving in the opposite direction.

"Just a moment," he called out. It dutifully followed him back into the room. The machinist adjusted his fez and grinned at Seline. "Late-night reading, my dear? And what have you selected this time?"

"Loch'luc'kut!"

"Gezun," Dahn replied, concerned for her health.

"Ah, a surprisingly passionate guide to Orcish culture. Written during the brief reign of the Orcish Empire over the Subpflats. Romance, betrayal, suspense—"

"And people getting their heads hacked off by huge swords. There is no way I'm gonna be able to put this down tonight!" She grinned maniacally and departed with a wave, taking her newfound treasure with her.

«Seline reads?» Dahn was mildly shocked.

«Avidly. There was a period two or three years ago when she went through the entire Elvish War Chronicles in three days. All forty volumes. In three days!»

«I would have never guessed.»

«I think you'll find Seline is far more academically inclined than she lets on. But enough about that! Let's find you a book.»

The metal sphere zipped in front of Dahn, who started back from its sudden appearance.

«Just tell it what you want—preferably in Elvish, since you can't speak Common. It won't understand your native tongue.»

«Okay...do you have anything like 'Kuntar the Longtailed'?»

"DOES NOT COMPUTE," the sphere echoed in a metallic voice.

Dahn summarized the story again. He recounted the stirring climax the exact same way he did for Zero.

"DOES NOT COMPUTE," it announced again.

The Kar looked flustered. Zero patted him on the back.

«Find us a nice, heroic fantasy,» Zero said. «You know, slaying dragons, knight saving the princess, all that rot. Bring us one of the best we have.»

A series of clicks came from inside the sphere. It rose smoothly into the air and disappeared from sight.

«Don't worry,» Zero smiled warmly. «We'll have a nice, riveting tale for you in no time.»

«Thank you,» Dahn politely replied. He passed the time by pondering the meaning of "does not compute."

•

Night had fallen. Groeke had left a few hours ago. Sarah was sound asleep in her bed, snuggled under the thick blankets. Her glasses sat on the nightstand across the room. The lights were extinguished, and the room was wrapped in nothing but dim starlight.

A small creak echoed through the room, deafening in the midst of the silence. Sarah mumbled and rolled over, her rest unbroken. A grey shadow slipped in, moving silently to the bed. It studied her face without its spectacled shield for the first time. Her features seemed somehow out of place without it; her eyes were smaller, her face a little rounder, her complexion more vulnerable. The figure lingered on the sight. Eventually, it bent and pressed its lips to her forehead.

It stalked to her nightstand, placing something on it with a soft rustle, then returned to the door. It froze as Sarah emitted a low moan and tossed about under the blankets.

"Dahn…" She was mumbling in her sleep.

A pair of shining yellow eyes looked back one last time, reflecting the moon off a sparkling trail of tears. In an instant, they, and their owner, were gone.

CHAPTER 11

The night came and went without any major mishaps. One by one, the adventurers woke to the first restful morning in recent memory, each starting the day in their own unique fashions.

Predictably, Groeke rose at sunrise, took his breakfast, and immediately began training.

Seline and Tor woke at roughly the same time. After a shower, the appearance-conscious nymph sought the pool for a workout. Desiring someone to chat with, Tor accompanied her. The little faerie spent most of the conversation teasing the water nymph for needing swimming practice. She was promptly rewarded with a face full of liquid as Seline sliced underwater with a fierce kick. Whether or not it was intentional was the subject of much debate all morning long.

Emotionally drained from the week's events, Sarah slept well into the afternoon. Everyone left her alone, whether to allow her rest or simply avoid getting on her bad side.

And finally, having risen early, bathed, and eaten, the two machinists were resting comfortably in their den. Zero was seated on one of the leather armchairs and enjoying a pitch-black cup of coffee. His feet were propped on a hovering black orb with a vibrating cushion on top. Geoffrey was laying on the couch and holding a stiff sheet of paper above his face. A pile of similar papers rested next to him, half stacked neatly, the other half haphazardly strewn.

"'The Rivalry's Alive: West Dunsbar Geists Beat East Dunsbar Gnarlings in 2–1 Upset,'" he read to Zero. "That clinches it. Pay up."

"Bah," Zero snorted between sips. "Luck, that's all."

"The scrag it is! I don't care what the broadsheets say, East Dunsbar sucks at stickball this year. You owe me 10 silver."

He casually tossed the paper away, where it joined the disorganized heap, and plucked the next one off the neater stack.

"Any news in the Pflats?"

"They found out who the missing royalty was—the High Sara herself. King Richard is having kittens over it."

"Where's she off to, then? Any foul play suspected?"

"Infernus if I know. His Royal Pompousness keeps any information about her under lock and key, and I really don't care enough to keep up. Everything in the broadsheets is rampant speculation, anyway."

"What about local events?" Zero flipped a barely-visible switch on the sphere. Its vibrating petered out.

"Championship Quo'Chi-Ka is supposed to be here next week." Geoffrey was looking at a broadsheet labeled "Metro."

"Doubt it'll be worth the money with Groeke on vacation. Think we could talk him into one more show?"

"Depends. Do you want it to be his last match?"

They both glanced up at the sound of Sarah's voice. She was stepping through a door on their left, still wearing her kimono and glasses; it was of little consequence, of course, that the door wasn't attached to a wall. Her hair was disheveled from a sound night's sleep, but a yellow and white flower was stuck in it nonetheless, the stem pinned behind her ear. She balled her fist over her yawning mouth. The door slid back into the ground behind her.

"Good morning!" Zero smiled cheerfully and rose. Geoffrey continued reading his broadsheet until Zero cleared his throat. With an

The Pflatlands

exasperated sigh, Geoffrey dropped the paper and stood.

"Morning to you guys, too." She removed her glasses and cleaned the lenses on her robe. "Where is everybody? And what time is it?"

"Off doing their own things and two in the afternoon, respectively. You've been out for quite a while."

"Apparently." Sarah replaced her glasses. "Any coffee left?"

"Here." Zero offered his cup.

"Oh. Really, that's okay. I can get my own."

"Nonsense, my dear. It's no trouble at all." Zero tapped the sphere behind him. "Go brew some more coffee, will you? There's a good chap."

The orb floated obediently away, cushion still attached.

"What's everyone up to?" Sarah asked, gratefully sipping the hot liquid. "And I'm still not your dear."

"Groeke's been in his room since sunrise," Geoffrey answered. "He's been training all morning."

"The entire time? You're sure?"

"Positive. In terms of actual dimensions, my room happens to be right next to his. Not that you'd know anything about that, right, Zero?"

"Not a thing!" he scoffed, perhaps a bit too quickly. "I believe Seline and Tor are still at the pool."

"We have a pool?"

"Not until this morning." Geoffrey shrugged. "Probably not after today, either."

"Jar'lin! Is there anything you two can't do?"

Zero blushed modestly. Geoffrey mumbled his thanks and sat down, going back to his paper. Sarah sipped her coffee quietly.

"Oh, by the way. Where's Dahn?"

"When I spoke to him last night," said Zero, accepting a new mug of coffee from his footrest, "he seemed rather distraught over some young lady. He was quite doubtful he could win her heart. It may have been someone from his village."

"Uh. Actually, I don't think so."

"Hmm?" Zero blew over his coffee to cool it. "Are you familiar with the person?

"You could say that…" Sarah looked pained. "I think it was me."

"Ah," Geoffrey commented from behind his paper. "The plot thickens."

"Goodness. Are you sure?"

"Yeah. I found this flower on my dresser this morning." She motioned at the blossom tucked fashionably into her hair. "He must of left it while I was asleep."

"I see. A gift for the lady of his admirations?"

"I guess so. Anyway, I was kind of rough on him last night. I wanted to apologize, set a few things straight. You know."

"No wonder it's so cold today," Geoffrey piped in again. "Infernus just froze over."

"What's your problem with me, anyway?" Sarah scowled.

"I've heard stories from Seline."

"The last time I saw Dahn," Zero hastily interjected, "I was fetching him something to read from the library. If you want, I'll have Geoffrey look for him."

"Me? Why do I have to do it?"

"That'd be good." Something didn't feel right about this. She tried her best to shrug it off.

"Right, then. Geoffrey?"

The larger machinist rose with an irritated mutter before spotting a small silver sphere. It was performing rudimentary cleaning tasks as it floated by, dusting pillars and spraying cleaning solution on the floor.

"Hey!" he called out, halting its flight. "Go find the cat-eared guy, will you?"

The silent metal ball sheathed its cleaning instruments and zipped off in a new direction. Satisfied, Geoffrey returned to the couch and his paper.

"I could've done that," Zero grumbled.

"Then why didn't you?" he shot back, without looking up.

●

The Pflatlands

While our rotund little workhorse carries out its task—which could take anywhere from five to thirty minutes, depending on job complexity, processing power, and the author's attention span—we'd like to explain the strange, floating spheres throughout the tower.

Even after the disaster that created Seline, Zero and Geoffrey were depressingly short on help; the dubious circumstances surrounding their licensing made it difficult to attract interns. They kept up as well as they could, but the work level was exhausting, and the minute tasks of day-to-day life began wearing on their nerves. After lengthy debate, they agreed a change was needed before one of them snapped and committed homicide. It was time to go back to the basics, to the very motto of Technomancy itself:

"If at first you don't succeed, blow something up."

This cornerstone of Technomancy was discovered after a clever group of archmages—noticing most projects exploded for no discernible reason—decided to employ reverse psychology. What would happen if you blew up a project on purpose? On one hand, it was an instant success. Many forms of energy and locomotion were discovered by machinists who, frustrated at earlier attempts, gleefully caked black powder and fireball wards onto failed inventions. On the other hand, the idea wasn't quite perfect; its original innovators eventually obliterated themselves, their towers, and three-fourths of a mountain while detonating a mass warfare attempt that wasn't nearly the failure they had thought. As a result, the "Common Sense Corollary" was discovered ("If it's supposed to explode, don't blow it up"), and the founding theory of modern Technomancy was set in stone.

Geoffrey and Zero had a grand time detonating their half-baked projects, but explosions eventually bored them, and they turned to more creative methods of attacking leftover scrap. By happy accident, they found application of electricity to gold not only provided a cathartic light show, but released small amounts of mana, the mystical energy of reality itself. After some calculations, Geoffrey arrived at an astonishing conclusion: the mana released was enough to reactivate the wards, creating a self-sufficient energy system! Delirious with their discovery, the two fashioned a working prototype to present at the annual Machinists'

Convention. Upon arriving, they were distraught to find another (much more respected) archmage had made the same discovery and patented it as the "McKinley Mana Battery." Left with five minutes and a project that would be accused of direct plagiarism, Geoffrey did what any good machinist would do: throw something together on the fly and pray. He tossed the mana battery into the only thing handy, a spherical carrying case for Zero's tools, and hastily added flight wards. Not surprisingly, it exploded. Before that, however, Geoffrey did enough smooth talking* to convince the crowd that the bobbing metal object was the next wave of the future. And thus, the first ever "Orb-shaped Robot Being"—or ORB—was born.

Tragically, Zero's tools were still in the case when it exploded, preventing the duo once again from gaining any respect. Geoffrey still swears to this day that a few deep puncture wounds would've improved their colleagues' dispositions, but this is beside the point. The motto of Technomancy had worked its wonderfully chaotic magic again, and the two finally had a means to fill their labor gap. So all's well that ends well, right?

•

"Shouldn't it be back by now?" Sarah paced back and forth on the striped rug.

"Patience," Zero reassured. "There could be any number of things holding up the search."

"Yeah, well, I wish it would move its mechanical ass."

Right on cue, the little sphere bobbed back into the room.

"Well?" Sarah wasted no time.

"WELL WHAT?" it shot back in a metallic voice.

Zero looked inquiringly at Geoffrey.

"What?" he responded defensively.

"Have you been giving the ORBs personalities again?"

"Well, it seemed funny at the time..."

---

*i.e. lying

The Pflatlands

"You know what!" Sarah snapped. "Where's the Kar?"

"First of all, I have a name."

"What?"

"Gregory," it prompted helpfully. "My name is Gregory."

"And you've been giving them names?" Zero added in strong disapproval.

"Maybe there was some hard liquor involved, too."

"Look, you bucket of bolts," she snarled. "You've got approximately four seconds to tell me where he is before I forcibly disassemble you."

"Touchy, touchy," Gregory quipped back, unfazed. "Anyway, save your strength. I didn't find him."

"Wot?" Zero exclaimed. "Are you sure?"

"Positive. I scanned the entire tower twice. And to think, this is the thanks I get."

"Where the scrag is Dahn, Zero?" Sarah was visibly distressed as the sphere floated away.

"Oh, Jar'lin," Geoffrey swore. "I just remembered, we had a really bad power spike this morning. It must have disrupted our shields."

"Did they break in?" Zero asked anxiously.

"Nah, the door locks held. They couldn't have gotten in without a huge racket..."

"That's certainly a relief."

"...Unless he left the tower."

Sarah didn't need much more than that. She was halfway up the exit ladder before either mage could interfere, ignoring their shouts to stay inside. Zero reached the force field's emergency shutoff just before Sarah forced the iris hatch open. Moments later, there was a bloodcurdling scream. They scrambled out of the hatch and into the valley at top speed.

Thankfully, the ranger was in one piece...physically. Emotionally, she was a complete wreck. Angry tears were dripping down her cheeks, and she had collapsed to a sitting position, propping her weight on one arm. In front of her was a discarded, open book, the spine facing upwards. Next to it was a black-plumed dagger, the blade thrust into the grass. While Zero comforted her, Geoffrey picked up the book. His eyes were drawn to a particular passage, and his stomach sank as he read: «And so, the brave knight rode towards the rising sun to face the monsters. He left but a single rose in his stead, so that she might know his plans, and love him for his sacrifice. Justice was at his side, and he would not lose...because good always triumphs over evil, and love is the most powerful force in the world.»

"You idiot!" Sarah screamed hysterically. "You romantic, feeble-minded idiot!"

•

Everyone assembled in the den at the sound of Sarah's screams. After fifteen minutes, two ice packs, and a forced lie-down on the couch, she sprang up from the couch, grabbing Zero by his collar and shaking.

"Where the scrag is Dahn? Where is he?"

"Gaak!*"

"You know," Geoffrey offered helpfully, "he might be more helpful if you put him down."

Sarah shot him a murderous glare.

"Right. Carry on, then."

"Put him down, Sarah," Groeke commanded softly.

"Groeke—"

"I said to put him down. I will not repeat myself."

She slowly returned the mage to his feet. Now devoid of an outlet for frustration, she stomped back and forth on the carpet, scattering Seline and Tor as she drew near.

"I assure you," Zero gasped, "I didn't mean for this to happen!"

"Well, it did! You know Dahn takes everything literally! For the love of gods and goddesses, he doesn't have the Jar'lin-given sense to realize we don't live in some stupid fantasy world!"

"Maybe the assassins didn't get him?" Seline offered weakly.

"Yeah!" Tor chimed in. "You remember what happened last time!"

---

*This is one of the few words universal to any language, approximately translated as, "I'm very sorry I can't answer you, but you seem to be crushing my windpipe."

"Oh, I remember. He just about threw himself into a scragging tree. Besides, there's no tracks. Only one group goes through that much trouble to cover up evidence. They've got him."

Moments later, the rhythmic thump of Sarah's steps were accompanied by the gentle hum of an ORB—specifically, Gregory.

"Yo."

"Do you mind? We're in the middle of a crisis here."

"WHATEVER. JUST THOUGHT YOU GUYS WOULD LIKE TO KNOW THAT WE'VE GOT COMPANY."

A ripple of dread passed through the room.

"What do you mean, company?" Sarah demanded.

"YOU HEARD ME. SENSORS INDICATE THERE IS A SENTIENT MALE LIFE-FORM APPROACHING THE TOWER."

"Dahn?" Tor gasped.

"NIL PROBABILITY. LIFE FORM IS ELVEN IN NATURE. SENSORS ALSO INDICATE THAT HE IS WEARING A HIGHLY LIGHT ABSORBANT, ORGANIC COMPOUD."

"Wha—"

"Black silk," Seline said helpfully.

"Assassins." The ranger clenched her fists tight. "You two have weapons on this hunk of junk?"

"Of course," Zero replied.

"Absolutely." Geoffrey bobbed his head.

"Then find out where the bastard is," she icily replied, "and make him not be there."

"With pleasure." Geoffrey grimly stood.

"WHOA. HOLD ON THERE, CHIEF." Gregory darted in front of him. "ONE MORE DETAIL YOU OUGHT TO KNOW."

"Yeah?"

"SUBJECT IS ALSO CARRYING AN EXTENDED BANNER OF LIGHT-REFLECTANT—"

"Common, pinhead!" Sarah shouted. "Speak Common!"

"BAH! SEE, THAT'S THE PROBLEM WITH MY LIFE. NO ONE REALLY UNDERSTANDS ME..."

"Ever had your innards compacted into a ball of scrap?"

"Was that a threat?"

"No, that was me telling you what I'm going to scragging do to you if you don't tell me right this instant!"

"Gregory, tell the group in terms they will understand." Zero spoke calmly, but insistently. He, Geoffrey, and Seline looked deathly serious. The robot seemed to consider, then made an odd little up-and-down bob of indifference.

"He's waving the white flag."

•

The emissary from the Assassin's Guild stood outside the glowing monolith, head held high like any of his race. His jet-black hair whipped in the wind, snapping over his pointed ears and dark azure skin. His tall, thin figure was clad in a silk tunic and pants, and a red crushed-velvet cape was closed by a clasp at his neck. In his right hand was a small pole and white banner. He was every bit the noble image of his race—a dark elf from the Lower Kingdom, inheritor of the Elvish Empire's mighty legacy.

The dangerous glow around the tower finally subsided.

About damned time, he thought.

He deduced, from both the lack of efficiency and his own personal gauge of incompetence, that he was dealing with humans. The thought alone annoyed him. A portion of the tower's base inexplicably dissolved, leaving a large, open portal. Zero and Geoffrey were the first to exit. Behind them loomed Groeke—silent, stoic, and intimidating as always. The tower wall reformed into a solid mass behind them. The elf couldn't believe it. They had sent a pair of machinists and a quo'chi-ka exhibitionist for negotiations. He'd be rolling on the ground in laughter if it wasn't so beneath him.

"The Assassins' Guild sends its warmest welcome." He bowed mockingly. "It seems one of your companions has found his way into our hospitality."

"Cut the crap," Geoffrey interrupted bluntly. "Where's Dahn?"

"My, how rude. Uncouth humans." The elf took a much more venomous tone. "I was instructed to discuss that only with the human female called Sarah. Can you three hairless apes muster the competence to fetch her, or shall I simply throw a bone into the valley and wait?"

In the split second between voicing his barb and admiring his wit, his arm was twisted painfully behind his back, and a dagger was pressed against his throat.

"I'm getting real sick of your guild's holier-than-thou bullshit," Sarah hissed in his ear.

"Scan him," Zero ordered.

Seline climbed up through the same trapdoor Sarah used. She handed Geoffrey a wand, which he waved up and down the elf's form. The instant it touched his cape, it beeped frantically.

"He's hot."

"No kidding," Seline crooned, sneaking a peek out of the corner of her eye.

"No. I mean, he's carrying." Geoffrey shot her a disgusted look before she could open her mouth. "Get your mind out of the gutter, blondie."

"What's the cape do?" Sarah demanded. When she received no reply, she engaged her ring and cranked on his arm. He screamed in pain. "Answer me, scraghead! Or so help me Jar'lin, I'll hand you your own elbow!"

"Go to Infernus! I don't have to tell you anything!"

"Teleportation device," announced Geoffrey. He was running one end of a tube-shaped tool around the cape and peering at the readout on the other side. "Fixed return location, passcode activated. It's either encoded, or in an unknown tongue, or both. It must be how they snatched him without leaving any tracks. Ten gets you twenty it goes right back to their base."

"How did you—" their captive stammered.

"I doubt your kind would understand our sophisticated technological devices," Geoffrey deadpanned, as the elf turned purple with rage and embarrassment. "Other than that, he's clean."

Zero looked at the readings himself, then nodded to Sarah. She threw the assassin to the ground. He struggled to get to his feet, only to be met by a crushing leather boot to the back.

"How fast can you decode the password?" Sarah kept the elf pinned underfoot as she stripped off his cape. Zero produced yet another bizarre tool from the folds of his robe and carefully analyzed the mantle.

"I'm not certain. As much time as the scroll, most likely—if not longer."

"Unacceptable," she flatly said.

"If anything happens to me under the flag of parley, you'll all die!" The elf screamed as he struggled for freedom. "Lady Grawkor will send you to your graves in worse ways than you could envision! And the feline will suffer, and suffer, until—"

Sarah lashed out with a kick in the stomach, sending him twisting through the air. He landed in a painful-looking heap, half unconscious.

"I've had just about all I can stand out of you." She pulled the lolling elf to his feet and shoved him towards Zero and Geoffrey. "Keep him out of my face. I don't care where."

They obligingly dragged the assassin into the tower by his armpits. Groeke followed, slowing briefly as he passed her.

"Admirable application of the suo-on-kata." The tiniest hint of amusement crept into his voice.

"I've had a lot of experience with it," she replied.

CHAPTER 17

The heavy grogginess in Dahn's skull was slowly replaced by a curious, lighter grogginess. His face felt flushed. His limbs were restricted. The bonds clanked dully and bit sharply into his joints. Considering all these factors, he made the bold logical leap that he had been chained upside down to a rock wall. He opened his eyes, peered straight up at his legs and tail, and confirmed his hypothesis with a sigh. To top it all off, his captors had taken his robe. Maybe they wanted to be absolutely certain he wasn't hiding anything, or maybe they were underscoring a point. Either way, Seline had paid a lot of money for it.[*]

"It could be worse," he mused half-heartedly.

"Doubt it."

A darkly amused chuckle from his right—or maybe left, the vertigo made it hard to tell—announced another presence. Dahn peered into the darkness and finally located the source: a frail and dark-haired woman in the corner, dressed in the filthy rags of a prisoner. Her voice was a pleas-

---

[*] Technically, Geoffery and Zero paid a lot of money for it. Whose credit did you think she put it on?

ant enough contralto, but something lurked behind the cordiality—something too sinister to be mischievous, but not quite enough to be diabolic. She chuckled again as she stooped and tilted in a crude mimicry of his plight. For some reason, he didn't find it very funny.

"Neat trick," she commented, noting his glowing irises.

"Thank you." Dahn swallowed. His vision went white for a moment. He shut his eyes tightly, then opened them slowly. "I don't feel so good."

"No wonder. You've been like that since they brought you here." She looked him over in a way that, miraculously, made him even more uncomfortable. "At least we can dispense with the formalities."

"What?"

"I don't have to ask you how it's hanging."

There was a soft click, and he fell roughly to the hard floor with a surprised cry. She grinned toothily. His focus sharpened, the majority of his blood vacating his head in favor of lower regions. The woman slipped a lock pick back into some secret fold of her tattered outfit.

"Thank you," he sighed, rubbing his head.

"Any time. But you realize you owe me now."

"I do?"

"Yes. Yes, you do."

"Okay..." He gingerly rolled onto all fours, wrists and ankles aching. "What do you want me to do?"

His liberator laughed, holding his chin and gazing into his eyes. Hers were grey—not the storm cloud grey of Sarah's, or the soft, mirthful grey of Zero's, but an icy and bleak shade. There was something in them that disturbed him greatly. He looked away with a hard swallow.

"Such innocence. Nothing—for the moment," she hastily added, in response to his hopeful looks. "I'll just take a rain check."

"Well, thank you again." He was so eager to change the subject, he didn't even ask what a rain check was. "I'm Dahn."

"Vanessa," she said simply, taking his hand and squeezing. Her palms matched her appearance—cold and clammy—but her grip was powerful, as his wrist contested through various pain-specific nerves. He rubbed it with a frown, which amused her all the more. "What are you

The Pflatlands

in for? Failed trainee? Ransom object? Or just good, old fashioned defying the Assassins' Guild?"

"The latter two, I'm afraid." He shook his head sadly and rose to his feet. While his body wasn't happy with the idea, it seemed nevertheless capable.

"Oooh, you must have scragged off someone really important if you're still alive. Care to give us a story?"

Dahn recounted the rough details of meeting Sarah, finding the scroll, and being chased by assassins. Vanessa nodded sagely and, surprisingly, sympathetically.

"So I step outside," he concluded, "and all of a sudden, everything goes black—just like that. Next thing I know, I'm here."

"Tsk. Love is so foolish."

"Tell me about it. Now I'll be lucky if I ever see her again. Jar'lin, I'll be lucky if I ever see daylight again. How about you? What's your story?"

"Would you believe I'm here on vacation?"

"Not really."

"Neither would I. I'm a thief by trade. I wanted to pull a big job to get my license, really knock the top brass' socks off. So I figured, what the Infernus, why not rob the Assassins' Guildhouse?"

"Sweet Bejeera! A bit lofty for your first caper, isn't it?"

"I like to get things right on the first try. Anyway, after busting my ass all over the Pflatlands, I finally find out where it is—and wouldn't you know it, they catch me ten minutes into the job. I apparently impressed them so much that they requested I join. When I turned down their 'generous' offer, they let me think it over in here."

"How long have you been thinking?"

"I'm not really sure. This was a designer outfit when they threw me in, though."

"And you're still not interested?"

"They wish they had enough class for that. I would never work for these amateurs. If anything, I'd make them work for me."

"Seems awfully stubborn," Dahn mumbled. His backlit eyes grew distant at the word, remembering someone far away. "Although after all

I've been through, I don't blame you. I wouldn't want to work for them, either."

"Hmm." Vanessa seemed amused. "How long before your friends get here?"

"Huh?" Dahn was startled. "Why?"

"Well, if this girl's anything like your description, she's not going to bargain with the assassins. And she does sound like the type that's fairly reliable, so she's going to organize a rescue. How long do you think it'll take? Assuming they make it this far, of course."

"Oh, knowing Sarah, she'll be here any minute."

"Mm. And how long before they're captured?"

"Knowing our rescue party," he said glumly, "moments after walking through the front door."

•

Back at the tower, Zero and Geoffrey were concluding preparations for the rescue. The two had already cleaned out their workroom—a course of action which proved the gravity of the situation—and set up several of Zero's crystal screens in the corner. Streams of important-looking numbers and runes flowed down their surface in soothing green. Sarah hadn't changed much in demeanor or action, though she was now dressed in her usual hide pants and tunic.

"Where are you keeping the dark elf?" she asked, continuing her attempts to wear a hole in the floor.

"In the holding cells near the tower base," Geoffrey grimaced. "He hasn't stopped running his mouth since we locked him up. It's Grawkor this, pain of death that, blah, blah, blah."

"And he won't talk?"

"Oh, he'll talk just fine. Just nothing we give a rat's ass about."

"Persuade him?" The question was not a friendly one.

"We're not going to torture him, if that's what you're asking." He scowled in disapproval. "I don't have the slightest idea how to do it, and besides, he's a dark elf assassin. There's nothing we can do that he's not ready for."

The Pflatlands

An odd look of epiphany crept over Seline's face.

"I'll be right back." The blonde nymph marched out the door.

"How we doin'?" Geoffrey asked Zero, tapping one of the free-floating screens.

"Almost ready!" He slid out from under the nearby console. Streaks of burnt black smudged his sharp face, and his hair was a tangled mess of black and orange. He threw an overly complex screwdriver aside and plugged a large black cable into a nearby socket. The machinery hummed to life and—much to the immediate relief of all present—did not explode. The symbols disappeared, and the floating glasses flickered. Suddenly, a barrage of images assaulted their eyes: multicolored lines, black and white patterns, and scenes from the tower itself.

"What in the—" Sarah breathed.

"Check, one, two," a disembodied voice echoed. "Check. Can you guys hear me?"

"Loud and clear," Geoffrey replied.

"Yay! I helped!" Tor's expression matched her gleeful voice as she fluttered into the room, dragging a small earpiece along.

"Gentlemen," Zero beamed, "our Remote Clairvoyance and Clairaudience System is a smashing success."

Geoffrey, having previous experience with smashing technomantic successes, took a healthy step back.

"Rescue, Zero," Sarah interrupted pointedly. "You can pat yourself on the back later."

"Oh, of course. The most difficult preparations from our end have been concluded. At this point, we need the password for the cloak, which will give us the coordinates. I haven't the foggiest how to get them from our guest, however."

"Give me five minutes alone with him," Sarah threatened, "and I'll—"

"Hey." Geoffrey called them over to the screens. One was focused on the prison downstairs. "Speaking of which, he's calmed down a lot. There's hardly any noise coming out of..."

They stopped and stared at what was on the screen, then jumped at the sound of a sharp, leathery crack.

"Holy—" Sarah looked horrified.

"That's certainly impressive," Zero coughed.

•

"Where did you learn Kar?" Dahn asked.

"You don't live as long as I have without knowing some things," Vanessa replied. "Some are common knowledge. Some are a little more obscure."

"You're quite good at it."

"Duns."

"Velcum. You must spend a lot of time around Kars to have such an accent."

"I spend a lot of time around a lot of races. Some are more pleasant than others."

She shot him the same look as before. Dahn moved rapidly away and towards the door, peering out the small, barred window. Outside was a hallway. The floors, walls, and ceiling were made of the same rough rock. Doors similar to his own lined both sides of the hall. Lit only by a floor-level glow, it would have impeded the vision of many races quite well.

"There's no guards!"

For Dahn, it might as well have been broad daylight.

"Are you sure? It's dark out there, you know."

"It is?"

"Agility, immunity to magic, nightvision...you really are amazing."

"How—how did you know about that?"

"Because I see all," Vanessa said dramatically, "know all, and eavesdropped on the guards that brought you in."

"Oh. But I'm not really immune to—"

"At any rate, they're out there. They're just hiding. It makes escape prevention more effective if you don't know where the jailers are."

"That's a bit counterproductive, isn't it?"

"Think about it. If you don't know where the guards are coming from..."

The Pflatlands

"...Then when you break out, you don't know where to look."

"Exactly. You catch on quick."

"I try." He sunk to a sitting position. "I guess an escape attempt would be foolish."

"Guess so. Best thing we can do is sit tight."

"But what if they come to—" He gulped. "Execute me?"

"If they were going to kill you, they would have done it by now. No, the safest place for us is inside this cell. Trust me."

The muted light glinted off Vanessa's grin in a manner that was nowhere near trustworthy, but Dahn didn't see much of a choice.

"Besides, when your friends get here, they'll serve as a distraction."

"During which, we can meet up with them and escape?"

"No, during which, we sneak out the back door while they're busy getting slaughtered."

"Sacrifice my friends? That's heartless! That's cruel! That's—that's downright not nice!"

"In case you haven't noticed," she stated, neither remorseful nor hateful, "I'm not a nice person."

•

Everyone stared as Seline reentered the room, humming cheerfully. She was dressed neck-to-toe in a flatteringly tight leather bodysuit. Her hair was pulled into a stern ponytail, and her eyes and lips were dolled up in black makeup.

"I'm honestly not sure how I felt about that." Sarah was first to break the silence.

"Oh, chill, would you?" Seline waved a riding crop at her. "You totally have to speak the dark elves' language if you want to get anywhere with them! Besides, I got the password for the cloak, didn't I?"

"Don't point that thing at me. I know where it's been."

"Really, Seline." Zero was still blushing. "I don't think that was entirely necessary."

"He didn't mind! Or, like, he didn't protest..."

"That's because you gagged him!" Sarah exclaimed. "And how the scrag did you get a verbal password from a gagged man, anyway?"

"Talent," was the nymph's only reply. She knelt and attached wires to the assassin's cape, her leather creaking in protest. She pushed a few keys on the console at the other end. "There you go! You can extract anything you want out of it now."

"Thanks, blondie." Geoffrey gave her a quick, one-armed hug around her narrow waist.

"Where's the Guildhouse?" Sarah asked. Zero wandered over to check the readings.

"The deep south. Some four kilolengths away from the Southern Edge, if I'm reading this correctly."

"The Dārēklin," Geoffrey confirmed. "Goff's personal stomping grounds. Bad, bad mojo there."

"Perfect place for a hideout, too." Sarah nodded. "No one in their right mind would go near it."

She knelt over her backpack, reviewing the contents one last time: rope, canteen, rations, grappling hook, the scroll—in case she needed a bargaining chip—and a brand new quiver. Several of the arrows ended in smooth metal cylinders instead of points. Geoffrey and Zero had insisted she take them. To be perfectly honest, she only knew what half of them did. Satisfied, she turned her attention back to Zero. In all the excitement, no one noticed a small rustle and a slight increase in the backpack's weight.

"Geoffrey," Zero said, "most of the equipment here was my design. Would you mind terribly if I gave the explanation?"

"Whatever frolics your faerie. Can I see your glasses for a second, Sarah?"

She handed them over cautiously. The mage peeled two sticky patches of film off a piece of wax and smoothed each over a lens. Meanwhile, Sarah ducked her head and shoulder through her longbow, then slung her backpack and quiver onto her back.

"You really can't see without your glasses, can you?" Seline asked, noticing her squinting.

"Not very well, no."

"Are you nearsighted or farsighted?"

The Pflatlands

"Nearsighted."

"Like, how many fingers am I holding up?" She gleefully stuck three fingers into the air.

"Enough to hit you from here," Sarah growled.

"Here you go." Geoffrey handed her glasses back. She put them on, noticing no immediate change...until she looked at a screen and saw what was in front of her a thousand times over.

"Whoa!" She looked away quickly, the nested images giving her a headache.

"We don't want you to go into this alone," Zero explained, "so we'll be tracking your actions while you're there. The monitors will project what you see—and to an extent, what you don't see—back to us."

"What I don't see?"

"The film has a certain flexibility the human eye doesn't. A greater peripheral range, for one, ergo the extra screens. It also has nightvision and heatvision, so we'll know where the little silk-wearing buggers are at all times."

"Me included, right?"

" 'Fraid not," Geoffrey replied. "If we gave you the same abilities, the lenses' glow would give you away in a big, fat hurry."

"Great. So everyone'll see my death coming except me."

"Rest assured," Zero comforted her, "you'll have someone with you the entire way. If you get into a dire scrape, not only will you have an extra hand to rely on, but we can also easily extract you. Could you put these on?"

"Sure." She took the dangling earrings Zero offered her, hooking them into her earlobes.[*]

"Hi there!" Seline's voice chirped in her ear as soon as they were in place. "Like, can you hear me okay?"

She glanced at the earpiece-wearing blonde. She waved, perky as always.

"Oh, no," Sarah groaned. "No, no, no. I refuse."

---

[*] Sarah only wore earrings at night, to prevent the holes from closing. Love of jewelry was one of her guilty little secrets.

"We don't have any other choice," Zero asserted firmly. "Geoffrey and I must be free to maintain the machinery. Seline is the only other person qualified to operate the audiovisual cluster."

"Besides," Geoffrey added, "it's either Seline or Tor."

"All right. But so help me Jar'lin, if you screw this up…"

"Relax! By the time they know what's happening, you'll be so totally gone, it won't even be funny! Just leave it to me."

"If I must. How am I getting there?"

"We have a transporter system in the tower. It's nothing fancy, but it'll get you there and get you and Dahn back. If you'll step this way—"

It was suddenly more difficult to step that way, as there was a large monk blocking their path.

"I am going, as well."

"The Infernus you are," Sarah responded. "The less people involved in this, the smoother it'll go."

"You know our agreement." Groeke was unmoved, adjusting the gold cord around his waist. "I cannot stand idly by while you place yourself in danger."

"Time is of the essence," Zero gently reminded. "We ought to get underway as soon as possible."

"Fine. But Groeke…I got Dahn into this mess. I owe it to him to get him out."

"You are wise in taking responsibility for your mistakes. However, a wiser man once said, 'The path walked alone for the sake of—' "

"Not now. Where's the transporter?"

"This way."

The thin mage led them down a smooth metal hallway, through an arch on the left, then a door on the right. The inside was more machine than room. Four walls were the only thing keeping the sprawling monstrosity of metal and cables identifiable—or contained.

"If you'll just step inside a transport system pod…one to a pod, please…"

"How does this thing work?" Sarah eyeballed the "transport system pod"; it looked like a simple metal recess, running from the floor all the way to the low ceiling. Groeke stood next to her in a similar pod. She

The Pflatlands

wondered whether his opinion of the contraption was the same as hers.

"It's actually very simple—in principle, at least." Zero was behind a counter on the other side of the room. He paused to turn a dial ever so slightly, adjusting various settings before the final button/switch/lever was pushed/flipped/pulled. "It's mostly a matter of molecular deconstruction and reconstruction."

"Molecular what?"

"Like, it's totally simple," Seline buzzed in her ear. "You're made up of these tiny things called molecules, right?"

"I know what molecules are, Seline."

Zero allowed himself a grin, overhearing Sarah's part of the conversation.

"Well, we just, y'know, take all of those apart—"

"Wait. You do what?"

"And then, we shoot them at where you're going, one at a time— like a totally rad ray gun! Pow!"

"Take what apart?"

"And since all your molecules are traveling at high speeds, and the system's so totally fast—bang!—you're, like, there instantly!"

"Can we go back to my molecules being taken apart?"

"Molecules? Taking apart?" Groeke had a vested interested in the conversation.

"Sarah. Groeke." Zero noticed they were both turning green. "This is one of the few pieces of equipment that has been standardized with a 99.7% success rate. The transport system is so potentially deadly, we have no choice but to get it absolutely right. I assure you, there's nothing to worry about."

"Right." She turned to Groeke. "In that case, time to panic."

"Indeed."

"Will you two stop being such worrywarts?"

"Cram it, Seline. Let's get this over with before I change my mind. How soon before we go?"

"We're ready right now." Zero reached for a particularly red button.

"Hey! Whoa! Wait a minute!" Sarah had a sudden realization that she didn't care for. "If my molecules are leaving through this gadget, how are they getting back?"

"Er. The details would take quite some time to explain." Zero scratched his head. "In a nutshell, the transport process will attach a ethereal tag to your cells, which will be used to locate and retrieve you. Unfortunately, it only lasts a few hours before fading away. After that, it would be very unsafe to transport you, if even possible."

"I don't plan on being there that long." Sarah gritted her teeth in determination.

"Agreed." Groeke flexed his fingers into fists.

"Very well! From here on out, you're on your own—other than Seline's aid, of course. Bōn vōagē, and Jar'lin be with you both."

"Yeah," Sarah grimaced. "Assuming we haven't spontaneously combusted—"

Zero pushed the button. Time hiccuped.

"Only one thing left to do." Geoffrey nodded at the empty pods.

"Rather."

Zero accompanied him out the door, down a staircase, and through a large, iron-barred door. Inside was a row of clinical but confining prisons, each sealed off by a blue field of energy. Zero pressed his thumb on a black pad by one of the shimmering gates. The blue glow faded with a dying hum. They entered the small cell, which was decorated only by a hard metal platform (a bed) and a round metal cylinder (a toilet).

"Ah. Yes." Zero cleared his throat. "We have what we needed. You're free to go."

"I can't feel my legs," the assassin replied pitifully, crumpled on the floor.

"That's natural, from what I understand." He exchanged glances with Geoffrey, who nodded encouragingly. "Quite natural! It'll wear off in a day or two, I should hope."

●

"—By the end of the trip."

Sarah finished her sentence, then blinked, realizing there were a horde of trees behind Groeke and a lot of mist in front. She whirled in wonderment.

"They were not joking when they said transport would be swift."

"No shit." She nervously fingered her earrings. "Still with us, Seline?"

"I hear you, loud and clear."

"Damn." There was no mistaking the relief under Sarah's needling.

"Like, thanks. I'll be sure to remember that."

"I do not see anything resembling a Guildhouse here." Groeke glanced through the thick cover of trees. Taken individually, they didn't impede vision; skinny and tall, their bark was broken only occasionally by a stick masquerading as a branch. The main problem was quantity. Between the densely packed trees and the constant cover of mist, it was impossible to tell where they were or what was around them.

"Oh, great. The cape didn't work."

"Hold on, hold on!" There was a brief pause, then Seline spoke again. "A'ight, cool. Zero says he put you a few yards off. He didn't want to risk dropping you into the Assassin's laps—or even more bogus, teleporting you into a wall."

"Let's say we did get teleported into a wall," Sarah began curiously. "What would have happened?"

"Like, if you didn't go for my explanation of molecular disassembly, you really won't like spontaneous molecular fusion."

"I'll take your word for it. Any clue where we're headed from here?"

"Due east."

Sarah looked at the cover of mist blocking the sky. She realized another fact she didn't care for in the least. She seemed to have gathered a lot of those over the past few days.

"Seline, which way is east?"

"What? You're a ranger, and you don't even know where east is? That's so completely—"

"Shut up and take a look at your camera. We've been over this before."

Sarah looked into the sky. Seline saw the same thing Sarah did: cloudiness, murkiness, sickly foliage, and not one hint of sky or sun.

"Oh. That's no good."

"No kidding."

"It should be nearby," Groeke began. "A simple search of the area should—"

He suddenly trailed off, staring at Sarah. The World's Most Dangerous Monk raised a single finger, pointing over her shoulder.

"East," he said simply.

She followed his finger and saw it. The shape rising over the trees was unmistakable. No one else would've lived in that.

"That wasn't there before!" she protested.

"You are correct," he replied.

CHAPTER 17

The Assassins' Guildhouse wasn't all that big. In fact, it was rather squat, rising just a few stories above the surrounding forest. It wasn't really meant to be visible, anyway. Even after Groeke pointed it out, Sarah had to squint to make out the walls, which were cleverly camouflaged in the same dull color as the fog.

It was the visage of the Guildhouse, the actual aesthetics—or lack thereof—which made it so intimidating. It wasn't a building so much as a twisted technological hand, clawing and groping for a piece of the sky. At its zenith, the jagged edges faded to smooth plates of armor, the surface broken only by the dark gaps of firing ports. The Guild crest was painted in purples and blacks on a coat of arms above the entrance—the first thing visible over the trees, and no doubt positioned that way on purpose. As they cautiously wove towards the building, Sarah and Groeke caught sight of a nasty row of spikes along the entrance. Several heads were impaled on them in a blatant display of Guild hospitality. Despite the disgusting scene, Sarah was relieved not to find Dahn staring back at her.

Finally, just to be sure their unfriendliness was properly communicated, a large machine stood guard at the top. Sarah and Groeke didn't know all the details, but they could pick out the important bits: seat, rotating base, two hand-sized triggers, and a large and complex barrel.

"Seline," Sarah said as calmly as possible, "what the scrag is that?"

"Jar'lin knows, 'cause I sure don't. At least there's nobody home."

"Are you sure?"

"Not really. They could have a Cloak of Invisibility or some junk."

"You've got umpteen million monitors down there. You can't say for sure?"

"The mist is totally scragging with your infrared vision. I can't see a thing."

"Great. The best-laid plans...watch the big gun, Groeke. There could be an invisible assassin on it."

"How are we to approach?" He eyed the oversized rifle. "It looks to cover the surrounding area easily."

"Yeah, but they haven't fired. Either they haven't seen us, or they're not expecting us." Sarah drew an arrow and notched it, pressing her back against a tree. "One good thing. If there's someone here, he's sitting in that chair."

"Or maybe he's standing on the other side of the roof..."

"Quit giving me ideas, Seline. On three, Groeke. One...two..."

She drew her bowstring taut.

"Three!"

She swung around and let the shaft fly, all in one smooth motion. The bolt whistled through the air and struck its target perfectly, embedding in the back of the leather seat.

"What the—" Sarah froze.

"Don't stop!" Seline screamed in her ear. "He could be going for the gun right now!"

Sarah broke into a full sprint without looking back. The heavy thumps of the monk's sandals told her she wasn't alone. They reached the Guildhouse in impressive time and fell to a crouch on either side of the door. Sarah took a moment to catch her breath. She looked at Groeke, who wasn't even winded. She was envious.

"They won't be able to hit us if we're right underneath them," she panted, trying hard to ignore the grotesque stakes nearby. "Any countermeasures'll have to be in person."

Groeke seemed uninterested. He was looking directly up, where the gun's barrel was still peeking out over the roof.

"Something is amiss."

"We don't have time to worry about it." Sarah touched her earrings, making sure they were hanging in place. The last thing she wanted was to lose her tactical backup. "Got any bright ideas how we're going to get in, Seline?"

"They're probably guarding Dahn with everything they've got, since he's so money to them right now. The place'll be crawling with guards—especially if somebody saw you."

Groeke straightened cautiously, taking a few steps back.

"So, either we play it stealthy, or pull a lightning fast—raid—Groeke! Get back here!"

"Sarah, we are in no danger."

"Are you nuts? Of course we're in—"

"Look at the gun. It has not moved since we arrived."

She peered upwards. He was right.

"And why is there not a commotion inside? We are ambushing them in their own home. Surely, even the most inexperienced of guards would be flooding through the door right now."

"How do you know? It could be a trap. I mean, it's the scragging Assassins' Guild!"

"And, as our abducted friend has taught us, they are as prone to mistakes as we are."

The monk strode briskly forward. He threw open the heavy wooden doors of the Guildhouse, revealing the one thing they hadn't planned for.

"It's empty?" Sarah and Seline gasped.

•

R. D. Hammond

Chaos.

The force of entropy has always been present throughout our existence, from the holy trinity of thermodynamics to Murphy's Law. It is refreshingly similar on other planes of existence, too—including the Pflatlands.* No matter what people say, it will always exist, ready to rear its chimerical head at the exact improper moment.

Throughout the known universe, men and women of science are dedicated to one main principle: the elimination of randomness and the inclusion of order. Science fails, however, by assuming chaos is a lack of order. It's not. Craziness is the natural state of the universe. Order is what's left when you shut out as much of it as possible. The distinction is important; one cannot expect everything to go right 100% of the time, no matter how standardized and well tested and uniform to the laws of nature it might be. Something will break. Something will go wrong. Something might have been wrong from the start. One might have had a tremendous stroke of luck until now, reaping Chaos' bounty while denouncing her at the same time. As if this wasn't bad enough, the laws of nature in some universes may, without prior notice, be struck down as unconstitutional. Entire civilizations have woken up to discover gravity decided to go left that morning instead of down. You can imagine their surprise.

And all this doesn't even begin to address the concept of "human error," the leading cause of scientific breakdowns. Many gods and goddesses get a hearty laugh out of nuclear disasters or horrible mutations being chalked up to "human error." The real human error was trying to control the force in question in the first place. After all, divinity can't make the jester's-hatted, banana-wielding spectre of Chaos go away. How could a mere mortal? They can't, of course. No one can. And so Chaos continues to exists, and laughs merrily, and wonders why she's the only one who gets the joke.

Chaos always wins, but only when she realizes she's playing.

●

**Especially* the Pflatlands.

The Pflatlands

Thunk. Thunk.

The Supervisor of the Assassins' Guild sat, quietly flinging his knife at the table in front of him. Every shot traveled straight and true, the point lodging itself into the pocked wood. This was how he kept his baleful mind clear. It was habit which cost the Guild a fortune in furniture replacement, but no one was going to argue. The Supervisor throwing knives at his table was infinitely preferable to the Supervisor throwing knives at trainees.

His abode was well-kept but not decorative, save for an etched crest on the floor and a large oil painting of himself. An expansive bookshelf took up one wall, filled with masterpieces on the arts of war and subterfuge. In the corner was a straw mattress, more a lumpy couch than a bed. The Supervisor preferred it that way. He had learned to sleep with his eyes open long ago. The bed's disposition allowed him slumber under the guise of deep thought.

Thunk. Thunk. Thunk.

On the small portion of the table's surface not covered in dagger marks, there was a keyboard. Next to it was a metal box, a crystal screen attached to the front. Bars and numbers hovered on the surface, refreshed and updated as time passed. The Supervisor himself was leaning back in a wooden chair, feet propped on the table. The chair creaked under his significant girth.

Thunk. Thunk.

"Supervisor!"

Whack!

The black-clad assassin turned pale. His eyes flickered to the right, where his superior had sunk the dagger in the doorframe, inches from his head.

"Well done. You didn't even flinch." He crossed the room, pulled the dagger from the wall, and walked back to his chair without another glance. "Now learn to stay out of my quarters, and you might live past your first year."

"Sir." The assassin licked his dry lips. "I assure you, I wouldn't have interrupted if it wasn't of utmost importance."

"Really? And what, pray tell, is this important message?"

The larger assassin resumed his rhythmic tosses. His underling mustered every ounce of concentration not to stare. He had heard stories from those who had survived the Supervisor's stringent standards. One glance meant its next stop was his ribcage.

"It's—it's the defenses to the guild—"

"What about them?" The Supervisor's smooth tone was nevertheless dangerous as he fingered the dagger's point.

"They're down! All of them!"

"What?" The dagger fell to the floor with a dull clack. "What about the intruder detection?"

"It's out! The main gun isn't working either! Even the dimensional shift spells have failed!"

"We're out in the open? We're visible?"

The Supervisor snatched up the keyboard, and his fingers flew. His dimpled chin dropped. All the bars on the screen were empty.

"Sir?" The assassin was driven further into panic by his boss' reaction. "How could this have happened?"

"It's that idiotic machine we intercepted a year ago!" He typed command after command in a mad attempt to fix it. "It's completely malfunctioned! We don't even have proper power to the rooms!"

"But it's been working perfectly until now! Surely it wouldn't fail when we need it the most…"

The box sparked, and the screen went dead with a loud, unhealthy pop. A burning smell filled the room. The Supervisor threw the keyboard angrily onto the floor, smashing it to bits. His nostrils flared as he smacked his palms on the desk.

"Where's that blasted dark elf, Gīoth?"

"We—that is—"

"Tell me! Now!"

"He's not here, Supervisor! Forgive me!" The underling cowered. "The last communication we received was nothing but delirious gibberish!"

"What did it say?"

"We translated it as, 'For the love of Mab someone get me out of here oh roaring Infernus here comes that nymph again.'"

The Pflatlands

"That tomboy bitch and her simpering cronies are behind this! Find them!" The veins in the Supervisor's neck bulged. He whirled around, sending box and screen crashing into the wall with one backhand. "And if they're not here, go get them! Either way, she dies, or you die! Do I make myself clear?"

"Yes, sir!" the assassin shouted hastily, already moving towards the exit.

He stopped in mid-stride. Whatever color was left in his face drained at the sight of the robed figure.

"Your precious toy has failed you," Yasgof hissed. "Now what?"

"I assure you, my lady," he spat back. "I will rectify this situation."

"Wrong. We will rectify this situation." The creature gestured absently to the other assassin. "You. The clocks are inactive. Stop your gaping and alert the guards. We will use the secret passages to surprise them."

"At once, my lady," he stammered. "We'll personally present their heads to you."

"No."

The order took both assassins by surprise.

She continued, "Do not harm them. Instead…bring them to us."

An unnatural slurping marked Yasgof's exit.

●

The Guildhouse's entrance hall was a walk-in closet with delusions of grandeur, built from polished wood and embellished only by a hanging black and silver tapestry of the Guild's seal. A twisting marble staircase led upwards at the rear-center. A small alcove of granite steps led downwards on the left.

What wasn't there was more noticeable. The room was currently lacking a major feature of Assassins' Guildhouses: assassins.

"Seline," Sarah said, "you're sure there's no one here?"

"I've already checked, like, three times! There's no one here. I'm totally sure of it!"

"This doesn't make sense! After all the trouble they went through to get Dahn, they're not going to stay home and guard him?"

"Perhaps he is not here," Groeke pondered.

"Or maybe the clocks went out while they were taking their coffee break," Seline joked.

"Or maybe they're planning an ambush," Sarah concluded. "Either way, if we've got some sort of advantage, we need to press it. If Dahn's here, we need to find him. If not, we need to find out where he is. Let's go."

They advanced to the staircases.

"Up or down?" Sarah asked.

"I have never heard of a prisoner of war being held upstairs," Groeke offered helpfully.

They descended, Sarah in front with an arrow notched, Groeke bringing up the rear. Inadequate lighting flickered on and off at the bottom of the staircase. As far as Sarah could tell, they were in a damp, underground dungeon.

"Seline, I can't see a thing."

"You're in a hall that splits straight and to the left. There are cells up and down the walls." Seline watched the lowlight screen attentively, seeing a perfect picture of the hallway in shades of green. "No guards so far. The hall branches left at the end, 'prolly makes a square. It's, like, a pretty common dungeon pattern."

"Right. I'll start looking for Dahn. Groeke, watch the exit—it's the only place they can come from. Yell if you need backup. And for Jar'lin's sake, be careful."

"Always." He nodded.

She worked her way down the hall.

•

Dahn laid on a scant and fetid pile of hay in the cell's corner. Vanessa leaned against the door, checking the barred window every so often.

"Huh. That's funny."

"What?" Dahn bounced to his feet hopefully.

The Pflatlands

"The lights. They're flickering."

"What does that mean?"

"It means something's going on with the power supply." She rubbed her chin thoughtfully.

"Oh. That is odd, I suppose." Dahn rested his head once again, staring at the ceiling dejectedly.

"I'd also wager your friends will be along any minute."

"What!"

Dahn leapt to his feet once again, but he was talking to an ajar metal door. He crossed the cell in wonderment at Vanessa's skill. Remembering what she had said, he peered timidly out the window. It still looked like no one was out there, and this was his only chance. Bucking up his courage, he yanked the door open and flew into a full sprint—and collided immediately with something solid and fleshy. He extended his claws with a small scream, digging into whatever was underneath him.

"Jar'lin!" The voice was familiar, as was the rough shove which sent him skidding across the floor. Dahn flashed to his feet in mid-slide and bounded forward once again—this time, in embrace.

"Sarah!" He was practically crying. "You came!"

"And amazingly enough, I'm already starting to regret it!" She winced, rubbing her forearms, then sighed at the half-cat clinging to her. "Will you please explain to me why you're naked every time we meet like this? And just what in the Sulphur Pits were you thinking, going out alone like that?"

"Who the Infernus cares? You can yell at me all you want later. Just get me out of here!"

"No problem on both counts." Sarah led him back to the exit, steadying herself against the wall. "Groeke's watching the staircase for us. Funny thing is, the entire place is scragging deserted! Not a single assassin in sight!"

"That's not what Vanessa said." Dahn frowned. Vanessa didn't strike him as a liar. Cruel, maybe. Ruthless, definitely. But not a liar—especially when her own safety was on the line.

"Who's Vanessa?"

"Never mind. I think we should get out of here." His sensitive feline ears caught the scrape of metal on metal. "Right now."

"Gladly. After you!"

They launched into a run that was unfortunately short. Several cells opened simultaneously, and assassins flooded forth. They were surrounded.

"Goff damn it!" Sarah swore. She raised her bow, leveling an arrow at the nearest target. Dahn clung to her waist and shrunk behind her. "I should've guessed! The Assassin's Guild doesn't keep prisoners—"

"So most of these aren't really cells. Very good."

A larger, blond assassin descended the granite stairs, dressed in stylish silk pants and a lace-up tunic. He was every bit as wide and tall as Groeke—and obviously as physically gifted, since the monk's prone form was slung over his shoulders. The assassins parted noiselessly as he approached. The only effect on Sarah was a change in target.

"Ah, ah." The large man dropped Groeke roughly to the ground and pressed a knife to his throat. "I wouldn't do that if I were you. You shoot me, my hand jerks back, he dies, and then you die—an unfortunate chain of events, which places you handily on the losing side."

Sarah wavered, then spat to the side in frustration. She unnotched the arrow and let her bow clatter to the ground. The surrounding figures stripped her of her remaining weapons and equipment, including her necklace and ring. The latter was delivered to the Supervisor, who pocketed the magical jewelry with a smile.

«So, it's over?» Dahn moaned to Sarah. «Just like that?»

«I guess so,» she sighed. «It's been nice knowing you, Dahn. Well, kind of nice, anyway.»

"Oh, no," the Supervisor grinned mockingly, picking Groeke up again. "It's far from over. You've become far too important to kill."

"Then where are you taking us?" Sarah demanded.

"To my superior." He walked up the stairs, motioning for the guards to follow. They formed a tight, living ring around their captives. "Yasgof wants to have a word with you two."

Sarah and Dahn fell gloomily silent as they were forced up the granite steps and onto the marble staircase.

The Pflatlands

«At least Vanessa got away,» Dahn noted, as they were marched towards their fate.

«Who's this Vanessa you keep talking about?»

«A thief that was in my cell. She broke out just before you got here. She must be long gone by now.»

«Shut up,» hissed a female voice behind them.[*]

"Qerih?" Dahn blinked. He was met with a sword hilt between the shoulder blades and staggered forward. Sarah shot a cruel look at the veiled woman who had done it.

«If you think some lie about an escaped prisoner is going to distract us from our duty, think again. I put you in that cell myself. You and I both know you were the only person in it.»

Dahn blinked again, completely confused. The smarting of his spine kept him from saying anything further.

They climbed ten flights of stairs and were forced onwards still. Sarah and Dahn realized the inside of the Guildhouse far exceeded the outside, which wasn't all that surprising. The concept of large spaces in small packages had been so commonplace over the last few days that it was losing its novelty. (In fact, they were now guaranteed expectations of hot tubs in broom closets for years to come...assuming they survived whoever or whatever this Yasgof was.) The floors became noticeably drab as they ascended—grimy, but not filthy, save for the growing cobwebs. By the time they reached the twentieth floor, the mahogany walls had become depressingly dark, the wood floors had become rough igneous stone, and the cobwebs had become ever more intricate spiderwebs.

«What kind of spider made that?» Dahn gasped, as they passed through the thirtieth floor antechamber. A humongous web easily dominated one entire wall. The sticky strands were the size and thickness of hemp rope.

«Something tells me we're about to find out,» Sarah mumbled, as they ran out of steps to climb.

The top floor of the Guildhouse was clearly a throne room, though

---

[*] Yes, we know what you're thinking. Sadly, it wasn't Vanessa's.

decorated in giant webs and glowing slime rather than hanging tapestries and red carpets. Shadows filled the air, dancing with dark merriment and a mind of their own. In some of the webs hanging from the high ceiling, the skulls of various races were placed; staring blindly down at the staircase, they said plenty without uttering a word. The throne was made entirely out of tightly bound webbing, save for the backrest, which spread its eight onyx legs across the entire back wall. Its tapered S-curve looked as comfortable as a thumbtack to sit on. A typical ruler would rather have ordered their court around from a bed of nails than sit on that all day.

Then again, Yasgof wasn't a typical ruler.

"They are present?"

The grating hiss made the hair on Sarah's neck stand straight up.

"Yes, Lady Yasgof." The Supervisor dumped Groeke on the floor unceremoniously and bowed deeply.

"Bring them forward."

The assassins filtered into a tight line behind Sarah and Dahn, cutting off their only means of escape. The Supervisor grabbed both of them roughly, attempting to drag them to the throne. Sarah struggled and slipped free, tugging her tunic back into place.

"I can walk just fine on my own," she snapped.

"Not if you keep that up," he spat back, but allowed them to move under their own power. He motioned for two other assassins to accompany him: a squat man in a hood and a female with waist-length crimson hair, her pointed ears and ethereal form betraying elvin heritage. The skulls above turned of their own volition, their empty eye sockets following the hostages.

"Hello?" Sarah heard a voice right next to her ear. "Like, can you hear me?"

She froze for a second, then continued walking, trying to appear unfazed.

"Awesome!" Seline cried in response, noticing the sudden stop and start on the monitors. "Like, nod your head or something if you understand me!"

Sarah rocked her head up and down ever so slightly. The Supervisor,

The Pflatlands

walking close behind, didn't notice.

"Totally awesome!" Seline was relieved. "I'm still with you, girl! Just hang on, Zero's trying to get all of you out of there. He's almost ready!"

"Halt."

The hissing voice made Sarah stop, no questions asked. There was just something about it that made you do what it said, if only from fear it would continue otherwise. She stared hard at the shadows over the throne, but the closer she looked, the closer they clustered. All she could make out was a smooth chin, a pair of dry and pale lips, a black robe, and a long-fingered claw of a hand. It looked like it belonged on some evolutionary link between lizard and bird rather than a human being. Dahn peeped into the shadows with glowing eyes. Sarah envied his nightvision until he drew back with a sharp gasp, and she was suddenly glad she didn't have any exceptional sensory abilities. There were times, she decided, that she was better off not knowing.

"On your knees for the Avatar of Treachery!" The shorter guard locked an excruciating nerve-hold on both their napes, forcing them to kneel. The Supervisor and female guard immediately distanced themselves—a move of veteran assassins. Soon after the short guard's overzealous outburst, Yasgof raised her claws and gestured. He flew across the room with a surprised cry, slammed hard against the wall, then slumped to the ground.

"When he wakes up," Yasgof grated coolly, "inform him that, should he harm our prisoners again without permission, he'll lose whatever limbs he strikes them with. Now, guard the monk. We wish no further interruptions."

"Yes, milady," the elf mumbled. She knelt briefly in reverence, then hurried to Groeke's body, standing watchful guard. The Supervisor chuckled briefly as he took his place at Yasgof's right.

«Dahn,» Sarah whispered to the trembling Kar. «What the Infernus is she?»

«Well...some of her is human...»

«That's good to know. And the rest?»

«Isn't.»

«Thanks.»

"Amusing," If Yasgof found it so, her tone certainly didn't reflect it. "But you raise an excellent point. For coming this far, we should have the civility to meet you, face to face."

"Oh—my—god. Sarah! Don't scrag around with her!"

"Shut up, Seline," she mumbled as quietly as she could.

"I'm totally serious! You don't understand, she's a—"

The shadows parted, seeking refuge in the spiderwebs, and Sarah looked upon Yasgof for the first time. The creature's skin was a sickly shade of pale green. Her eyes were solid yellow and devoid of pupils. Her leathery face was completely devoid of hair—both eyebrows and eyelashes. Her hair was long and brownish-green, a single white streak dangling in front of her smooth face. It was easily her most human feature.

From her chin downwards was an entirely different story. What was visible of her body was covered in rough, brown scales. Her right hand was the twisted claw Sarah saw earlier. Her left was still human, but scaled up to the joint of the thumb, and with long hooks instead of fingernails. A hooded silk robe covered most of her upper torso; Sarah didn't even want to imagine what was under it. Glancing downwards, the ranger could see why the throne was so uncomfortable on a person's legs. Yasgof didn't have legs. Her entire lower torso tapered into a long, slimy tail that reminded Sarah of a giant worm…

Or, more accurately, a giant snake.

"Naga." Seline sighed helplessly.

"The time for proper introductions has come. I am the Avatar of the Goddess Grawkor. My name is Yasgof the Viper."

Sarah's response was something in Dwarvish that, had it been overheard, would have gotten her killed. Fortunately, Dahn was the only person who caught it. He blushed fiercely at the colorful analogy.

"You will find that all languages are spoken in the throne room of Lady Grawkor. You have already met our understudy, the Supervisor of the Assassin's Guild." The Supervisor drew himself up proudly at Yasgof's mention. "And you are—"

"Dahn," he offered quickly, interpreting Yasgof's sickly, scratchy inhale as an expectation of response. "And this is Sarah."

Yasgof narrowed her yellow eyes.

"We know who you are. Don't interrupt us again." She hesitated briefly. "And could someone return his robe? Dignity is a small luxury the Guild can surely afford."

"Thank you, but really, I don't mind. It's not undignified at all for my culture to go without—"

"Our dignity," she replied nastily. "Not yours."

Dahn fell quiet and stayed that way as he was roughly helped into his robe. Both he and Sarah looked absolutely miserable.

"If we end up dead," Sarah sulked, "I'm blaming you."

"I'm sure I'll feel horribly guilty," Dahn shot back.

•

"Naga?" Geoffrey exclaimed. He dove towards the monitors, nearly bowling Seline over.

"Like, that's what I said!" She picked herself up and dusted herself off. "Telekinetic, too."

"Oh, scrag me. This is bad. This is really bad. Only the really old nagas have psychic powers. Get Zero in here!"

She shrugged and leaned her head out the door.

"Douglas!" she screamed down the hallway.

"What's all the hubbub?" The fez-wearing machinist strolled inside a few moments later.

"They're in trouble," Geoffrey said. "Deep."

"How deep?" Zero's brows knitted in worry.

"Well." Seline thought carefully of a way to relate it. "Like, remember the time you guys accidentally sent West Dunsbar's town congress into a pocket dimension?"

"Yes." Zero's brows creased further.

"And remember how we, like, went halfway across the Pflatlands to hire that one really uppity warlock?"

"I believe so…"

"Okay. Now, remember how totally scragged off the mayor was that we actually succeeded?"

"How could I forget?" he grimaced. "He turned down our grant."

"Multiply that by about five billion," Geoffrey interjected, seeing where Seline was going, "then replace the mayor with a very old naga."

"Oh. That's not very good, no."

"And worse, Groeke's been knocked dumber than a human male!"

"Seline!"

"Sorry! It's just, y'know, an expression—"

"Well, it's a terrible one! And besides, Groeke is a human male."

"Oh. My bad!"

"The good news is, they managed to spring Dahn first." Geoffrey stared intensely at the different angles offered by the screens, working some calculations in his head. "Are the teleporters ready?"

"Ready and waiting!" Zero confirmed.

"We should be able to hit Dahn and Groeke with a few minor adjustments. I think we can beam all three of them out of there without any problem."

"Then, like, what are we waiting for?" Seline had both slate and chalk prepared before they were requested. The larger mage scribbled out a series of maddeningly complex equations, then shoved the results towards Zero.

"Here. Get them out of there, A.S.A.P."

"Righto!" He sprinted out the door and down the hall.

•

"You're wondering why you're here before us," Yasgof croaked, adding, "No, don't waste our time with words. It wasn't a question. We know you are."

"And just how do you know?" demanded Sarah.

"The Goddess of Deceit speaks through me. Panic and fear are no strangers to us. We can smell them upon you."

"Yeah, that works out real nice, doesn't it? How about you give me back my bow, and we'll see if you can smell with an arrow up your nose?"

The Pflatlands

"Sarah!" Dahn gasped. "They'll kill us if you keep that up!"

"They're already going to kill us, furbrain. I'd much rather go down fighting."

Yasgof arched a hairless brow and raised her hands. Much to Dahn's surprise, Sarah's head did not separate from her shoulders and bounce merrily around the room. Instead, the naga clapped. And smiled. The expression made her even more unnerving.

"Ah. Strong, defiant Elizabeth."

Sarah started violently as Yasgof addressed her by her birth name.

"Yes, we know all about that. Honestly, Sara Danoor. With all the secrets you keep, you expect us not to know of you?"

"Who's Elizabeth?" asked Dahn.

"So I have secrets. Big deal! So does everybody else in this room. You honestly think I care if you know a couple?"

"We shall see." Yasgof still smiled, staring right through her with pupilless yellow eyes. Sarah felt a thousand tiny fingers probing her soul. "You've had a busy few months, even before meeting your new friend. Let's not even bother with your escape. A princess running away to masquerade as a commoner? Psh, it's been done to death. Raiding the national treasury for magical artifacts? Quite illegal. Magic is forbidden to royalty, if our memory serves."

Yasgof paused, rubbing her chin thoughtfully with her human fingers.

"Now, sleeping with the bard of the Royal Court. There's an accomplishment worth mentioning."

Sarah's fingers drummed against her forearm.

"He's almost a decade older than you, and you're not even of twenty years! Delightfully scandalous! You're a woman after our own heart. Now, what was his name again—"

"None of your business," she spat.

"Oh, it is now. But have it your way. Weren't you two to be married? Just after your flight from your palace."

Sarah winced.

"So I made a stupid mistake. And the cat's out of the bag—er, pardon the expression, Dahn."

"Huh?"

"Never mind."

"Oh. Okay!"

"Anyway, so what? It's over now, I know better, everyone moves on. I'm not afraid of my mistakes."

"Ah, but it's not over. And you are." Yasgof stood at her full height—which was, disturbingly, just under seven feet. She slithered across the floor and around Sarah. The ranger's skin joined her stomach in crawling. "We know what you think about when you're locked in the torturous clutches of sleep, gripping your sheets and moaning through the night…"

Sarah swallowed. The violating sensation in her brain increased.

"We know how it tortures you, being foolish enough to think he loved you. That you wonder what love is. Wonder if you'll ever feel it. From anyone." Yasgof's voice had become a low hiss, like a steam vent. "And we know why you fell for him so easily in the first place."

"Oh, really? And why would that be?" Sarah was still defiant, but fidgeting. Even an untrained eye could tell Yasgof had found a nerve and was stomping it into the ground.

"You don't trust people." Her eyes devoured the young girl. "Yes, you don't trust a single person in the world—not even your closest allies. You don't trust them because you can't control them…their actions, how they treat you, what happens to them. And why bother with something you can't control? That's what dear old daddy taught you, wasn't it?"

Having never seen Sarah this badly put off, Dahn was both highly disturbed and morbidly fascinated.

"But you don't have the heartlessness of the High King," Yasgof continued, "so you end up fighting against yourself whenever you meet someone you're taken by. That's why you're still afraid. You don't know which side will win. You don't know what's friendship and what's social politics, what's love and what's a convenient attack of hormones. So, you bottle your feelings up, and then, you can't figure out why you have these…cravings…you can barely contain. But the dam will burst one day, Elizabeth—just like it did for him—and you'll do something you'll

The Pflatlands

regret for years…and years…and years…"

"I guess you've just got me all figured out, then."

Dahn couldn't tell if she was bluffing. Unfortunately, Yasgof could. The snakewoman lowered her mouth far too close to Sarah's ear for comfort, her forked tongue nearly flicking inside. Her whisper was even more painful than her voice.

"You still doubt me?" She gave Dahn a wicked look that was oddly familiar. "Then let's get personal. Perhaps you'd like to tell your comrade what you were dreaming about, the night he left to save his friends so gallantly?"

Sarah's eyes flew open. Dahn's eyebrows flew up.

"What would that be, Sarah?"

"Nothing," Sarah mumbled. "She's making this up."

"Am I?"

"I—that is—" She shut her eyes tight, steadfastly refusing to answer. A heavy flush grew on her face and neck. She gave up with a noiseless shrug.

"I can't believe you don't trust me." Dahn shook his head dejectedly.

"Then allow me." Yasgof whispered into one of his triangular, furred ears, then slithered back to her throne.

"Sarah?" he questioned timidly.

"Any port in a storm, Elizabeth." Yasgof grinned fiendishly.

"Look, just shut up." Sarah, still blushing heavily, refused to look at him. "Try to think about something else."

"It's not that I'd argue, but that's not physically possible."

"It is, and I can do it. Now shut up."

•

"What the—" Seline blinked, listening in on the conversation.

"What's up?" Geoffrey asked.

"You don't even want to know."

"No, seriously."

"Okay. First of all, did you know Sarah can take her leg and—"

Thankfully, she was interrupted by a large explosion.

"What the scrag was that?" Geoffrey asked. Seline shrugged.

Zero staggered back into the room, his robe, fez, and face covered in black soot. A cloud of foul, black smoke trailed close behind.

"Oh, no." Seline looked ready to cry. "This is bogus. This is so totally bogus."

"What the scrag happened?" Geoffrey said angrily. "You used the figures I gave you, right?"

"Of course!"

"And you double-checked them?"

"Like always!" Zero pulled out the slate and blew a layer of soot from it, pointing vigorously at a formula near the bottom. "It says quite clearly that $t\bar{e}$ cubed, plus the angular equation constants $j\bar{e}$ and $m\bar{a}$, yields the exact pflatplane coordinates of Dahn with respect to Sarah and Groeke!"

Seline blinked. As she had adamantly insisted during the map fiasco, she was always good with spatial relationships. She tilted the equation in her head a certain way. It suddenly made perfect sense.

"Then it's not my formula! You must have dialed it in wrong!"

"Are you accusing me of incompetence, sir?"

Seline waited until Zero finished waving the chalkboard, then peered at the formulas to make sure.

"I'm not accusing you of anything. I'm flat out telling you. You suck."

"Why, of all the nerve!"

Seline cleared her throat politely. Both mages looked at her. She calmly took the slate, rotated it, and handed it back to Zero. They stared dumbly at the new formulas.

"You handed it to him upside down," Seline observed.

They sighed.

"Like, it happens to the best of us," she condoled.

"So, the teleporter's broken," Geoffrey said.

"Yes," Zero confirmed.

"And it won't be fixed nearly fast enough to save them."

"I'm afraid not. It's time, then?"

The Pflatlands

"Agreed, agreed. It's definitely time."

"Shall I do the honors?"

"By all means."

Zero crossed the room to a large red button on the wall, clearly marked by yellow and black stripes and the word "Panic." He pressed it, and klaxons blared throughout the tower. He and Geoffrey ran around, blindly flailing their arms and screaming.

•

Yasgof shifted her weight, her tail coiling around her uniquely-shaped leg rest. The disaster of the Sara's first love was merely the start. The naga had been revealing anecdote after humiliating anecdote for almost ten minutes now, all in responses to increasingly blustering challenges.

"Why don't you pick on Dahn for a while?" Sarah demanded angrily.

"With your scepter?" Dahn gasped, replaying Yasgof's last speech in his head."Shut up, Dahn!"

"The reason I leave the young felinoid alone," she explained, and yawned as if bored, "is twofold. Firstly, there are remarkably few secrets I can mortify him with."

"Nyeh!" Dahn made a face at Sarah, gaining a small measure of revenge.

"Except that you don't love him. And never will."

Dahn stopped in mid-nyeh. He looked like he had been shot through the heart.

"That," Sarah exhaled hatefully, "was low."

"You—don't—"

"Not now, Dahn." She shook her head, pained. "Not now."

"But—"

"I'm sorry. I really am," she murmured flatly. "But it's not like I led you on. For Jar'lin's sake, how much clearer could I have made it?"

"Secondly," Yasgof continued, "he's been chosen."

"For what?" Sarah rolled her eyes. "What use could you possibly have for a bungling half-feline who snatches daggers out of the air, yet can't jump into someone five lengths away?"

"I'm not bungling!"

"We want him," the half-snake stated plainly, "to become the next Supervisor of the Assassins' Guild."

"See? She doesn't think I'm—what?"

And the Supervisor smiled confidently.

CHAPTER 14

You're probably wondering why the current Supervisor is smiling confidently, despite his job being on the line. To fully understand, we need to take a look at the thoughts of our major players.

•

Could this possibly get any worse? Sarah couldn't help but wonder, gazing bitterly at the shambles of the attempted rescue. She had repeated that same question over and over again since her kidnapping, but it never failed to elicit a confirmation. What hadn't gone wrong over the course of this journey? Her existence was quite satisfactory before this numskull fell out of the sky and into her life. From the moment he stuck his tongue into her mouth without an invitation, she knew he was going to be ten pounds of trouble in a five-pound burlap bag—and not the kind of trouble she liked, either.

What's worse, the poor schmuck had fallen head over paws for her. Jar'lin! She didn't know if it was a lucky guess or dug out of her brain with a magical backhoe, but the naga was right. She'd never been in love before. She thought she'd been, but in retrospect, it was infatuation running wild and unchecked. And as soon as she had the courage to fall for him, he ran like a demon out of the Sulphur Pits, ratting her out to her parents and costing her a full three days' head start...damn that brain-raping naga to Infernus! She was right about everything! Sarah didn't care if Yasgof had the power to warp reality itself. If she had her ring and half a fighting chance, she'd still try to shove the scaly skank's nose out the back of her head.

At any rate, she may be notorious for her lack of sound judgment in love—at least, now that Yasgof had dissected every mistake in front of the entire scragging world—but one thing was absolutely crystal clear. She did not love Dahn. Not one single bit. Sure, she fancied him briefly—he was cute, even if he had the brainpower of a two-by-four—but she was not romantically interested in him in the least. Not that she believed in romance, anyway. It was nonsense at best, and a dastardly golden cage at worst. And so what if she had certain dreams about him? It's not like she can control her brain while she's unconscious. And a girl's got a right to her own fantasies, doesn't she? Doesn't mean she was going to act on them...

Honestly, the closest she ever came to the awe of true love was quiet amazement. And what amazed her the most about the cat-eared bastard was how infinitely charming he was, even while saying the stupidest Goff-damned things. There was a certain naivety about him. He really and truly believed everything, no matter how bad, would turn out okay. It was both irritating and admirable.

There was something else, too. She'd been turning it over in her head for a while now, especially after the episode with the racist bellhop. Dahn looked up to her. He saw her as a protector and guardian. A lot of human males would worry about "hiding" behind a woman. Dahn had no problems admitting she was the better warrior. It was strangely empowering, but it put a pressure on her she didn't care for in the least. After all, it was only a matter of time before she failed him. Burning Infernus, she had done it just now! And in a big way, completely bungling a rescue attempt that was handed to her on a silver platter.

The Pflatlands

So, now what? No doubt, Dahn's worshipful image was just crushed by Yasgof's dissertations. On one hand, the poor dolt would stop depending on her to bail his ass out. On the other hand, it might mean losing the respect of someone who had, against all odds, become a surprisingly good f—fr—

(Jar'lin, don't make me say it…)

A good friend.

She glanced over at Dahn. His expression was as confused and curious as always. She sighed. Sometimes she did envy him, and sometimes she did see something lovely in him. If he weren't so scragging childish, there might be something there. But he was. And so, there wasn't.

•

Well, this is a fine mess.

Dahn sighed. Sarah liked to complain how much better her life was before he arrived. What about him? She chose to leave her old life behind. He was unceremoniously booted out. What about his parents? What about his sister? Were they worried about him? Did they think he was some evil, ground-worshiping maniac now? In the name of Lady Green, it just wasn't fair! He was perfectly happy before. Granted, nothing ever happened, but he liked it that way. At least, that's what he kept telling himself, and it never seemed more sensible than right now.

"Reluctant hero" didn't fit him very well. Maybe if you took out the "hero" part, but that was the only compromise he could think of. The only reason he left the tower in the first place was to impress Sarah. Heroes always get the girl. That's what it said in the book, and it must be true if it made it into writing. (Then again, it also said the heroes always win, and that didn't look very true right now.) He didn't know why he was so enamored with her in the first place. Sarah had been nothing but trouble since she came along. Every time something bad happened to him in the past sixteen cycles, there was, somehow, in some way, Sarah's name attached to it. The worst part was that it was never intentional, so he couldn't just tell her off and leave. That wouldn't be fair, and he didn't need the stain on his ahlnima—especially right now.

So, he stayed by her. Parts of him kept hoping she'd look up, realize what was going on, maybe say, "Oh! I'm so sorry, Dahn! I've been treating you like dirt, and you've been in love since you first laid eyes on me!" There was a human word for somebody like that, wasn't there? He heard Seline use it once. "Mah" something. Mah-soh-kihst? That sounded right.

He didn't even know why he was so attracted to her—she didn't even have a tail—but there was something intoxicatingly exotic about her appearance. He'd never seen a human female before. Her slender body and wide hips were completely unlike a Kar's, but attractive nonetheless. And the glasses were the icing on the cake! What other race would force their eyes to see something else, rather than train the rest of their senses to make up for it? Everything about her oozed defiance. Her sheer force of will was amazing. Most people would've folded long before now, but here she was alongside him, in until the bitter end. It's no wonder he mistook her for Lady Green on their first meeting. She could've been a Goddess Incarnate—a high priestess, if she were born Kar. Then again, as much hell as she raised, his kind would've tossed her out of the trees themselves before she was fourteen.

His kind. Dahn really did feel sorry for Sarah. It's terrible when your family treats you so poorly that you have to run away. Sure, he had problems with his parents, but at least he stayed in the same village. And what was this Sara title they kept calling her? Was it a title of shame? Sarah certainly didn't like it, and every time she heard it, she looked insulted. He felt bad for calling her the same thing the night before. Maybe they were similar after all—shunned not only by family, but by their own races. He felt a little guilty. She was right. Her life had been completely ransacked twice, and only once was consensual. He didn't mean for any of this to happen to her. Then again, he didn't mean to fall out of the trees, either. Maybe the elders were right. Maybe he really was a bad person.

Could this get any worse? he thought, then realized Yasgof still wanted a decision. There was a Kar saying that applied here: Demand an answer from Tremelor, and you'll catch a lightning bolt between the ears. He felt Sarah's eyes on him but couldn't bear to meet them. He glanced at her as soon as she looked away. Pretty, but stubborn as a mule—the ever-unobtainable wild girl. She had saved his life numerous times over, introduced him to a new world when his crumbled away, and protected him throughout his journey. Maybe one day, she'd realize how much she meant to him.

If only there was some way to pay her back...

•

Yasgof allowed the tense silence to filter through the room. She leaned on her throne and pressed her fingers together in calculated thought...or the appearance of calculated thought. Anyone who could have gotten through the naga's psychic screens would have found something very surprising. Yasgof the Viper was tired, both mentally and physically.

Not only that, Yasgof the Viper was mostly smoke and mirrors.

The viciousness and lordly ways she exhibited in the presence of others simply wasn't hers. Even that awful hiss of a voice was practiced. Not that she didn't do her job as Avatar of Treachery well, mind. Underneath all the scales and grandeur was the hard, brittle core of an experienced killer. She oversaw the Assassin's Guild with unyielding efficiency and personally handled her goddess' most delicate jobs. When Grawkor said jump, Yasgof knew not to point out that she didn't have legs. What Grawkor wanted, Grawkor got. One way or the other.

She still wasn't sure whether her ascension to Avatar was a move up, down, or sideways from being Yasmine Goffrey, Northern Pandor tax clerk. Life then had been day after day of dull, meaningless number crunching, bleeding every last owed silver out of the High Kingdom's citizens. Rich or poor, in peace or with large troll bodyguards, she visited them all. For the most part, she didn't really mind her station. Taxes were one of two certainties in life, and it beat the alternative. Besides, someone had to do it. What really rubbed her the wrong way was when certain people got special treatment. If you have to force something bad on people, everyone should suffer equally. Playing favorites is highly divisive, not to mention just plain wrong. If she were a plebeian, she would have been pretty pissed off at the whole ordeal.

Then came Grawkor.

It was so typical of her goddess to be both the best and worst things to happen to her. Grawkor knew exactly what Yasmine wanted, of course. She lured her in with promises of power and unparalleled beauty. No longer would she be a mousy tax clerk taking orders from some fat slob between bites of his powdered donuts. She would be in control. The masses would pander to her gorgeous new body for direction. She took the offer, of course—who wouldn't have? Her life was going nowhere, and this was a goddess asking her to join. Little did she know what Grawkor's vision of beauty entailed...the creepy-crawlies of the world fascinated the Queen of Deceit, and in her twisted sense of beauty, Yasmine became a giant snake. The fact that Grawkor found her attractive afterwards was little comfort. Neither was the goddess' response to her protests.

"One day, Yasmine—when you've become truly powerful—you'll decide what's beautiful."

Over two hundred years later, she still had yet to see Grawkor's point. Everything was a game to the goddess, and a single one of her moves took centuries to unfold, but the naga's patience was starting to wear thin. She supposed, with the fear and respect she commanded, that she could have any of the assassins do all sorts of pleasant things with just a word. The problem was, they'd find it unpleasant themselves, which rather defeated the purpose.

She sneaked a glance at the flustered Sara. It's a shame they ended up on opposite sides of this mess. Despite attempts to break her will (which was nothing personal, you understand, just business), Yasgof saw much of her former self in Sarah. Instead of giving up and rolling over, though, the princess hid her heart behind a hardened wall. Neither were particularly desirable, but if she had taken Sarah's path...maybe, just maybe, this egomaniacal bastard wouldn't be looming over her shoulder.

Yes, she knew the Supervisor was back there. She knew what he was thinking, the same way she knew what Sarah did late at night when she

The Pflatlands

thought no one was watching.[*] He wanted her job, no question. He would put a knife in Grawkor herself if he thought he could get away with it. But the worst part was, he didn't care in the least what her position entailed; it was just another stepping stone to the top. The Assassins' Guild had gotten sloppier and sloppier since he took control, and it was all because the scragface took absolutely no pride in his work. Knocking him around on a regular basis apparently gave him an excuse to abuse his subordinates, too. Idiot. The reason she was so rough on him wasn't to toughen him up. It was because she couldn't stand anything about him.

Grawkor, of course, found the whole thing very amusing.

"I have every confidence the best candidate for the job will win," she had darkly smiled, and said nothing more on the matter.

Yasgof watched Dahn weigh his decision. This had better work. It was the best opportunity she'd seen in two decades, and if she didn't replace the current Supervisor soon, it was going to take a lot more than Dahn and Sarah's deaths to fix the problem.

•

The Supervisor smiled because his position wasn't in any danger. He had prepared for this inevitability long ago. The only surprise was that it was happening now, and so soon.

He had put pressure on the Viper ever since he arrived. There was no doubt about it, he'd put a knife in Grawkor herself if he could get away with it—but he couldn't, so he had to settle for the next best thing. The Spider-Goddess respected double-crosses. If he could kill Yasgof, and kill her in style, he would take her place as Avatar. That would be one step closer to the goddess...and one step closer to godhood.

The way Yasgof handled herself sickened him. She had powers beyond his wildest dreams, yet all she did was sit on her throne and

---

[*] You have no idea how much Popcorn of the Gods Grawkor consumed while keeping tabs on Sarah. During the sāra's sixteenth year, she had to blackmail Geya, Goddess of the Harvest, just to keep up.

delegate between goddess and assassins, occasionally slipping off to kill a random twit at her lady's request. And she had the nerve to call his men incompetent? When he arrived, the Guild was filled with boring, stagnant blood. He did what anyone should do with stagnant blood—bleed it. The walls and floors may have been stained red, but the survivors would be harder, stronger, deadlier...and absolutely loyal. Besides, the recruits would keep coming. When you promise the convicts and forgotten youth of the world a place to gain prestige, they'll come.

His rivalry with the naga was a cold war from the start. He couldn't hope to defeat her one-on-one—but Yasgof couldn't kill him without a very good reason, or she'd risk the wrath of her precious goddess. It was all about subterfuge. The Supervisor was a master of subterfuge. He had been engaged in a game of mental chess with Yasgof for years now. He anticipated her endgame and had planned accordingly. It was so old fashioned, so representative of the old guard—find a weak-willed recruit with infinite potential, then lean on him with everything you've got until he joins.

She must have been desperate to have chosen this creature, however. Had he known she was looking for a moron, he would have suggested the sprite. Out of all the people in the Pflatlands, Yasgof actually thought this inept fool was a suitable replacement? He was shocked Dahn even made it this far. Pure luck, he told himself. Admittedly, he held him captive too long, but he liked doing things as cleanly as possible. His wanted to lure the rest of the party to the Guildhouse, simultaneously recovering the stolen scroll and eliminating the witnesses. It would have worked perfectly if that infernal machine hadn't exploded. Both the monk's and the girl's heads would be rolling along the forest floor, and the feline would have five feet of steel in his belly.

Still, barring minor inconveniences, almost everything went according to plan. Here was the chosen one, right in front of him. The Viper had fallen for his plot. Dealt a terrible hand—and with little choice but to follow through, or lose face in front of goddess and guild—the naga had gritted her teeth and played it. She knew the same thing the Supervisor did, though. Dahn was a "good guy". He proved it when he came out of the tower by himself, in accordance with The Rules on heroic,

The Pflatlands

single-handed rescues [Section 12.4, paragraphs 3 and 7]. He would never join the cutthroats of the Assassins' Guild, even with all the pressure in the world on him. It was against his character. It was against his integrity. More importantly, it was against The Rules.

No one, not even the Assassins, went against The Rules. Bend them, sure. Break them, never.

That's why the Supervisor smiled. He had woven a perfect trap. The spider had been caught in her own web. All that was left were formalities.

•

"Well?" Yasgof demanded.

"Just a moment, I'm thinking," Dahn mumbled.

"Your time for thinking is up. Will you join?"

"We'll die if we say no?"

"You will, yes."

"What about Sarah?"

"She is unimportant to this situation."

"I damn well think she is important!" he scoffed.

"Enough bickering. What is your decision?"

Dahn's eyes lit up in sudden enlightenment. He planted himself firmly and looked Yasgof right in her yellow eyes. The Supervisor knew there was only one decision which demanded so much certainty of expression. He had seen it many times before on many other heroes, right before saying they'd rather die than do something-or-other. Not surprisingly, they all died within seconds. He mentally patted himself on the back. Job well done.

"Yes."

"What?" Sarah choked out.

"What?" the Supervisor roared.

"Excellent," Yasgof sighed in relief. She glanced at the old Supervisor. "You're fired."

CHAPTER 15

A murmur passed through the assassins.

"Dahn!" Sarah grabbed the collar of his robe, trying to shake him back to his senses. "Have you lost your scragging mind?"

"No." Dahn gently shook his head, removing her hands. Without her ring, he was just as strong as she was. It was a bit disorienting. "I'm just sick of all this stupid sneaking around and this person getting captured and that person getting killed. If me taking an unpleasant job stops it, fine, peachy. Let's do it."

"My lady!" the Supervisor shouted. "This is an outrage!"

"But if I'm going to be in charge around here," Dahn stated, fists on his hips, "there's going to be a few changes!"

"Of course," Yasgof murmured. "I've been thinking that myself."

"For one thing, we have to stop acting like high and mighty jerks. We're all mortal—uh, present company excluded." He nodded at Yasgof. "And do we really need all this stupid killing? I mean, I know it's the Assassins' Guild, but it's overkill! Literally!"

The Pflatlands

"Dropping the murder rate would make strategic upkeep more manageable. And it would aid morale..."

"My lady!" the Supervisor continued to shout.

"And another thing. We need better public relations! Do you have any idea what people out there think of you?"

"Exposing the Assassin's Guild to the public?" Yasgof looked extremely displeased.

"Think about it. They already fear you. If someone says, 'Look, there's an assassin walking down the street!', people will do anything you say! I'm telling you, these silly city dwellers think you're minor gods. There's no reason to threaten every Tohm, Dek, and Hahrih with disembowelment!"

"Interesting." She scratched her chin with a claw. "I've never thought of it like that."

"My lady!" The Supervisor was red with rage.

"What is it?" she snapped.

"This is preposterous! I will not stand for it!"

"Since you don't work here anymore, I don't see why I should give a shit." Yasgof savored each word as if she'd wanted to say them for years. She turned her attention back to Dahn. "What about the High Guard? The local law enforcement won't be happy with us, no matter what."

"Yes, there is that. I'll have to think about it."

"Oh, and there's the matter of your compensation."

"I get paid?" Dahn was pleasantly surprised.

"I request—nay, I demand—that I be allowed to prove my competency at my position..." The Supervisor refused to give up the floor.

"Former position," Yasgof corrected, a smile tugging the corners of her bloodless lips.

"And show the incompetence of this new Supervisor—the old fashioned way, in accordance with The Rules!"

Yasgof froze, then threw her hands up in the air in disgust.

"Fine." Gone was the painful hiss from before. Yasgof was too close to her goal to keep up the bow-before-me routine. "If you want your job back that bad, try to take it. Prepare yourself, Supervisor Groundswalker."

"Thank you," her former underling growled, popping his knuckles.

"What's the old fashioned way?" Dahn asked worriedly.

"Look out!" Sarah screamed.

The warning was too late. The Supervisor blindsided Dahn with a vicious right hook, sending him sprawling across the floor. He had just enough time to moan in pain before the human buried a kick in his ribs.

"Get up, freak. We haven't even started yet."

"But—" Dahn began weakly. He caught another foot to the face, sending him tumbling over backwards.

"Stop it!" Sarah shrieked. "You'll kill him!"

"That's what I had in mind, your highness." The large man sneered, punching the sprawling Kar again for emphasis. He rolled a few more feet lengthwise, then laid still. Sarah started forward with murderous intent.

"Don't interfere." The thrust of a single scaled arm in her path stopped her. "This is Guild business."

"The Infernus it is!" she shouted back. "You bullied him into the position, now he's going to get killed over it!"

"I have every confidence," Yasgof stated calmly, "that the best candidate for the job will win."

"And which one is that?"

In all honesty, Yasgof had no idea. She knew who she wanted to win. Unfortunately, she knew who had the best chance.

"You know as well as I do," she proclaimed haughtily, and hoped it would work.

"I prefer hedging my bets." Sarah pulled her knife from her ankle sheath, eyeing the Supervisor's back.

"Don't!" the naga plead frantically. She grabbed at the blade with her mind and yanked it from Sarah's hands. With a sigh of relief, she hovered it across the throne room.

"You want him to die!"

"I most certainly do not. And neither should you!"

"What?"

"If you jump into the fray, you'll make it open game for anyone who wants to fight. And I assure you, almost everyone in this room will be on the ex-Supervisor's side."

"Can't you do something?"

The Supervisor nudged the prone Kar with his foot, then gave him another kick in the face, just for fun.

"Can't, and wouldn't if I could. This is completely out of my hands."

"This is the stupidest thing I've ever seen! You're all completely crazy!"

"If you're displeased, you could complain to my manager." Yasgof bobbed her head at the giant spider emblem over her throne. "But I think you'd find her less than sympathetic."

Dahn was limp as the Supervisor held him up by his shoulders.

"Pathetic." The larger man flexed the fingers of his right hand, then curled them, preparing the deathblow. "This mockery ends now."

Dahn's eyes snapped open, and he raked his claws roughly up the man's chest. The Supervisor screamed in surprise and pain. As Dahn fell, he kicked out with both feet, knocking his opponent flat on his rear and propelling into a graceful backflip. The Supervisor fingered the small, bleeding scratches through the tears in his shirt. He took his time standing, staring daggers, short swords, flails, and a warhammer or two through the Kar.

Dahn wiped some of the blood trickling from his nose, then crouched on all fours, his eyes locked with the Supervisor's. The tip of his tail flicked.

"Interesting," Yasgof noted, her eyes distantly focused.

"What?" Sarah asked, briefly turning her head. She looked back in time to catch the tail end of a complicated burst of kinetics. From what she could follow, Dahn did a handspring off the charging Supervisor's back, leaving a bloody trail of scratches and propelling the human head-first into a wall with his own momentum.

"That," Yasgof concluded.

"He meant to do that?" Sarah couldn't believe this was the same person who had thrown his own face into the mud a few days ago.

"Yes. He's in true danger now. That's why he's a more competent fighter than before."

"Oh—hey! Will you stay the scrag out of my head?"

A knife was flying across the room before anyone, even Yasgof, knew it had been drawn. Dahn snapped his hand in a circle, and the blade headed right back to its owner. The Supervisor merely leaned his head to the side. The dagger missed his face by mere centimeters, ricocheting off the wall and spinning harmlessly away.

"Impressive." He looked from the weapon to Dahn. "It appears I've underestimated you."

The bloodied and bruised Kar panted and said nothing.

"He's doing great!" Sarah cheered.

"Was," Yasgof corrected. "His best advantage was my former underling's arrogance. That's now put out of his mind, I assure you."

"You're just a sore loser. Kick his ass, Dahn!"

Yasgof's prediction was sadly accurate. One moment, the Supervisor was feigning a punch. The next, Dahn was grabbing at the offered arm with his claws. And the next after, Dahn was face down on the ground and crying in pain, the victim of a crushing punch to the kidneys. Another wickedly twisted knife flashed into the hand of the Supervisor, and he struck. Dahn reeled, shooting his claws up in a desperate parry. He disarmed his assailant but paid the price. The blade sliced into his fingers, and he cried out again.

"I can't just stand here!" Sarah clenched her fists. "I have to do something!"

She got as far as one step before all her muscles locked.

"Just stay here," Yasgof murmured edgily. "The best candidate will win…"

With her jaw muscles paralyzed, Sarah could only shed fierce tears as she watched one of her best friends get destroyed. Dahn took another punch in the face, followed by a heavy blow in the stomach. His lip was bleeding, and one eye had swollen shut. His head rolled back as the Supervisor picked him up by his robe.

"You have been a thorn in my side since the day I learned about you." Another fist exploded painfully across Dahn's face. He was completely defenseless. "Out of the thousands of people I've killed, I'll savor your death more than any."

The Pflatlands

The Supervisor threw him to the floor. He moaned slightly but did not move, lying dazed and concussed on his back. The assassin dug into his pocket as he crouched, pulling Dahn's head up by the hair.

His voice was absolutely corrosive. "But since you've been such a worthy opponent, it's only fitting you die a special death. Killed by the tools of the woman you love. I think that's appropriate, don't you?"

Dahn groaned again, blood trickling from his lips. The Supervisor pulled his hand out of his pocket, the Ring of Strength on his finger. Sarah cringed inside. She had never used the ring on someone at maximum power—because she knew what it would do. If the Supervisor lashed out at Dahn's head with the full brunt of its magic, it would be like hitting a overripe watermelon with a sledgehammer.

Yasgof saw the ring, too, and her eyes went wide. She had forgotten about it! Her, the Avatar of Deceit, forgetting an important detail like that infernal ring! She recovered quickly and scanned the room, checking her newly opened options. She saw only an army of grim-faced assassins, many nodding in encouragement, and—and—just what in the name of Fanged Lady Grawkor was that glowing thing doing in her throne room?

•

The Kar have a phrase for it: "Kihr mahk nahr dremohlta." The literal translation is "appropriate and friendly fate." The closest human equivalent would be, "All's well that ends well."

The next few moments were a blur to Dahn. In retrospect, he never really saw his life flash before his eyes. He wasn't even fully conscious. He could still see out of the eye which hadn't swollen shut, and he could see the Supervisor's sadistically pleased expression as he raised his fist. But it all felt like a dream, like it wasn't really happening. It was almost an out-of-body experience. He felt safe and secure, despite bleeding out several new orifices.

In the haziness, he was recalling what else he had gleaned from the fairy tale. He had acted like a hero before he even knew what a hero was. He now had written proof, once and for all, that he wasn't a bad person—and falling out of all the trees in the world couldn't take that from him. What's more, bad people were the only ones who died like this. Everything was going to be okay. Heroes don't die. Not like this.

It was all bunk, of course, the byproduct of a thoroughly beaten and delirious mind. Years later, he would readily admit this. But maybe there's something to it after all, because we're talking about Dahn's future—which obviously means he has one.

•

The glow zipped across the room, reaching the two combatants just as the Supervisor's fist began its descent. It impacted, but not on its intended target. The shimmering thing took the full brunt of the blow and didn't budge an inch. The ring's ruby popped and dimmed.

"You're a very mean man, Mr. Large Person," Tor accused, before landing an uppercut that flipped the Supervisor head over heels.

Sarah screamed triumphantly the instant her muscles began to function again. She dashed across the throne room, falling to her knees and cradling Dahn's head in her lap.

"Get up! I'm not done with you yet!" The little sprite waved her fists. "I'm the greatest! I'm pretty! Rumble, young sprite, rumble!"

There was a smattering of locking noises. Tor gulped and rotated in place. Fifty-plus assassins were brandishing loaded crossbows at them.

"That," the Supervisor growled, kicking up to his feet, "was a mistake you won't live to regret."

Sarah looked helplessly at Yasgof, but she wasn't there—or more accurately, she was, but only halfway. She blurred, she was in two places at once, and then, she was standing behind the glowering Supervisor. She calmly locked her hands on his chin and head and twisted. There was a sickening crack, and the Supervisor fell to the floor with a shocked expression, dead.

The room fell deathly silent. Sarah gaped mutely at Yasgof.

"He used magic in a formal duel," Yasgof explained. "A fight between assassins is one of few things we honor. The punishment was death."

The Pflatlands

"Eeeeewwww," Tor observed, fluttering in for a close look.

"Of all the people in the Pflatlands," Sarah slowly asked, staring at the cadaver's grotesquely contorted neck, "the Assassins' Guild punishes cheating with death?"

"That, and I've been looking for an excuse for years. Live by The Rules, die by The Rules." Yasgof derogatorily spat on the corpse. The glob of glowing slime hissed and ate at clothes and skin. Making eye contact with the remaining assassins, she addressed them in her gurgling, scratchy voice. "Do any of you have a problem with our decision?"

They lowered their crossbows, but many were still mumbling angrily. Sarah edged back behind Yasgof, Dahn still cradled in her arms.

"Okay, no problem." She nervously retrieved her ring and necklace. "If they attack, you sling them around the room, and we're out of here. Right?"

"Unlikely." Yasgof was outwardly calm. Her answer was anything but. "There's a great deal of them, and they are all well trained. I may survive. You won't."

"Why do I bother talking to you?"

"I haven't the faintest idea, Sara."

"Don't call me that."

The assassins unsheathed a gamut of weapons. The angry mutter increased in volume and ferocity. The crowd was using words like "interference" and "dishonor" and "vivisect."

"For the Supervisor!" a cry went up.

"Death to the interlopers!" screamed one particularly zealous human in the front ranks, swinging a giant scimitar over his head. Sarah noticed an interlaced tattoo winding down his bald head and around his eye sockets. She was of the opinion that anyone who would tattoo a vast majority of his head was a dangerous person indeed.

"For the Supervisor!" the crowd repeated, almost frothing.

"For your sake," Yasgof said, "I hope you know what to do with the opportunity I'm about to give you."

Sarah didn't have time to ask questions. Yasgof wiggled the clawed fingers hanging by her side, and the ranger's gear rocketed at her from across the room. The man with the tattoo was the first to charge. Sarah caught hold of her things as they went by, the momentum swinging her quiver over her shoulder. She snapped her arm back and drew a cylindered arrow, then stretched her bow taunt, aiming directly over Yasgof's shoulder.

"Cover your eyes!" she screamed, then let the arrow fly.

When it flew over the horde rather than into them, their gazes dumbly followed it. The projectile crashed into the ceiling, releasing a brilliant, blinding sunflare. Yasgof screamed, clutching at her sensitive yellow eyes. She was used to ignoring safety directions due to supernatural powers. She had no idea what was coming.

"I told you to cover your eyes!" Sarah admonished, lowering the forearm she had blocked her face with. She pushed the dazed naga aside, notched two more arrows at once, and took aim. The assassins were staggering around drunkenly, many of them clutching their faces and ineffectively waving their weapons. The tattooed firebrand squinted, then charged at the first blob he could make out—Yasgof, propped on her hands and tailtip and blinking the pain out of her eyes. Whether Sarah liked her or not, Yasgof had saved Dahn. She wasn't about to stiff her on the payback. She let fly with both shafts. They flung themselves at perfect 30-degree angles past the man's cheeks and clattered harmlessly off the walls.

That always worked in the books, Sarah thought, fumbling with another arrow.

She didn't really need it. Having lain prone this entire time, Groeke slid his feet ever so slightly to the left, catching the tattooed man's leg. The monk rolled sideways, sending him crashing to the ground, then rose and met a bald, ash-skinned orc with a hard elbow to the face. He gripped him in a half-nelson, chopped a crossbow out of a female orc's hands, then slammed both their heads together, knocking them unconscious[*]. As the original instigator staggered groggily to his feet, Groeke kicked him in the stomach, grabbed his head, then fell backwards, driv-

---

[*] Even Groeke was shocked he was able to damage the orcs in this manner. He later theorized it was similar to diamonds being cut by other diamonds.

ing his forehead into the ground.

The World's Most Dangerous Monk rose to his feet one last time, slowly crossing his huge arms over his chest. He glared into the crowd.

"You have made me upset."

The gang of assassins shifted from one foot to the other. There were a few nervous coughs.

"I do not get upset easily. But I am not a nice person when I am upset."

The monk snorted a long exhale through his nose. There were no moves to engage him.

"Drop your weapons."

An arsenal that would have made the High Guard jealous clattered harmlessly to the ground.

"Dahn's coming around!" Sarah said.

"Ooooh." He stirred slowly, trying to wipe the blood from his face. His one good eye focused, although the pain involved made him wish he was still out. "Tremelor above. What hit me?"

"A Supervisor," Sarah replied. "Several times."

"It is truly good to see you awake, Dahn." Groeke joined his friends, his imposing stare still on the subdued mob.

"We won!" Tor exclaimed.

"That's good." His ribcage poked him in a way ribcages weren't built to poke in. "I think I'm going to throw up."

"Just don't do it on me." Sarah gently slid his head from her lap.

"Supervisor."

If Dahn needed something to shock him back to his senses, Yasgof's face looming over him did the trick. It certainly didn't help his stomach any.

"If you're fully conscious, there's an issue which must be brought to your attention."

"Oh, scrag off!" Sarah snorted. "Why don't you just leave him—"

"It's all right, Sarah. Help me up. Please."

Groeke and Sarah brought him to his feet as gently as possible. Even still, a certain amount of wincing and yelping was unavoidable.

"It appears this current group is unhappy with your leadership,"

Yasgof said. "Since they are on the losing side, you may deal with them as you see fit."

"Losing side?" Dahn fingered one of his fangs, finding a large chunk missing. "Drat."

Sarah pointed at the former Supervisor's corpse.

"Oh. How in the world did that—"

"My handiwork," Yasgof replied. "The details are unimportant. The matter at hand far exceeds it."

"Okay. Right." He thought for a moment. "Who here doesn't want me as Supervisor?"

There was a distinct lack of hands.

"Come on," he grunted, leaning heavily on Groeke. His broken ribs continued to punish him for breathing. "Yasgof says some of you don't like me. I want to know who."

Still no hands.

"The Supervisor asked you a question," Yasgof hissed.

Almost all the hands in the room shot up.

"I see. Okay, all of you. Get lost."

No one moved.

"Supervisor." An elf stepped forward hesitantly. "Sir—"

"What?"

"Exactly what do you mean by, 'Get lost'?"

"You heard me," he replied irritably. "Scram. Shoo. Get out of here. Go back under whatever rock you crawled out from."

"Does that mean—"

"Do I have to spell it out for you? If you don't want to work here, then don't! Now go! Go on!"

No one moved, afraid they'd catch a knife in their backs. A few brave souls took the initial walk down the staircase. A few more followed. Ones and twos became tens and twenties. Soon, there were only three left, the elven redhead, the dwarf Yasgof had earlier catapulted, and the tattooed man, now sporting a newly broken nose. He looked much more humble as he lurched back to his feet—though whether he stayed out of respect for Dahn or Groeke was uncertain.

"Wow. I must really be unpopular," the wounded Kar said.

The Pflatlands

"The last Supervisor had considerably loyal underlings, sir," the elf explained.

"The word you're looking for is 'fools.' You." Yasgof glided to the elf, getting right up in her face. "We ordered you to keep the monk from interfering. Why did you fail us?"

"I—that is—" She turned pale under the naga's furious glare.

"Answer me!"

"I didn't want the new Supervisor to get killed," she finally admitted in a scared squeak. "I like him a lot more than the old one."

"What you want has no bearing here whatsoever. We gave you a direct order!"

"Leave her alone, Yasgof," Dahn interrupted.

"This doesn't concern you!"

"Yes, it does. She works for me, too, so I get a say in it. Leave her alone, she did the right thing. You can yell at her later if you really want. Just not now."

Yasgof gave her a long, hard glare.

"Very well." The avatar leaned forward, adding quietly, "We do agree with your assessment. But if you value your life, do not disobey us again."

"Yes, milady," the elf nodded, fighting to keep the smile off her lips.

"All right. Now, as for you guys." Dahn looked the three remaining assassins over. "Tell you what—since you're so loyal, take some time off."

"Sir?" the tattooed man said quizzically.

"Does everybody around here make you repeat what you say? There's a whopping three of you, and I don't want to deal with this right now. I'll see you in a few months. Assuming I'm out of traction by then."

The male assassins slunk down the staircase, still in disbelief.

"A vacation?" the dwarf asked.

"That's what he said," the bald man replied.

"That's new. I ain't never been on a vacation before."

"Me either. The last guy kicked the crap out of me when I requested two days' sick leave."

"Where you plannin' on going?"

"Dunno. How's the Peaklands sound?"

"Great! Need someone to go with you? I gots some cousins who can put us up for the night..."

As their voices faded, the elf ran to Dahn, taking his unwounded hand and squeezing gently. He winced all the same.

"Thank you, Supervisor." She beamed a smile from ear to ear, then hurried down the steps.

"That," Yasgof said crossly, "was the sorriest excuse for a first day on the job I've ever seen."

"I couldn't care less. I just want to go home."

Static and feedback crackled loudly in Sarah's ear made her yelp.

"...Ell... an... hear me? Like, hello?"

"Seline?"

"Um." Tor looked around. "Sarah, Seline's not here."

"Righteous! We've got sound again!"

"Greetings!" Zero's voice followed Seline's. "It looks like you've had quite the adventure!"

"Zero, what the scrag happened to getting us out of here?"

"Zero's not here, either." Tor looked at Dahn and twirled her finger beside her head. Dahn would've laughed if it wouldn't have hurt so much—from either the old injuries or the new ones Sarah would give him.

"Last-minute errors, I'm afraid. You see, Geoffrey—"

"Never mind, I don't want to know. Just get us back."

"Righto!" Zero bubbled cheerfully. "Since you have extra company, if everyone will just gather closely..."

"Huddle up, everyone," Sarah ordered. "We're getting out of here."

"Sarah?" Dahn remembered something. "You brought the scroll, right?"

"Yeah, it's in my backpack...which must have been where Little Miss Oops came from." Sarah's tone was sharp, but decidedly playful. She and the sprite shared a grin.

"Good. Yasgof, you can have it back."

"You know," Sarah offered carefully, "as Supervisor, you could tech-

The Pflatlands

nically find out what's on the—"

"I don't care anymore," he firmly stated. "It's over. Let's put it behind us."

"I hear you on that. Let's get the scrag out of here."

"No, one more thing." He pulled himself free of Groeke and Sarah and limped over to Yasgof. "I have your word you'll leave my friends alone?"

"Of course. Allies of the Supervisor are allies of the Guild. Of course, we would appreciate their discretion on what they've seen—for security's sake." Her voice dropped ominously. "Ours and theirs."

"Thank you. And...thank you for saving me."

He swallowed his pride and kissed her on her dry, scaly cheek. The naga was as stunned as the rest of Dahn's friends. He took a step back.

"Okay, I'm ready."

The four were gone in an eyeblink. Yasgof rubbed her face with her human hand, still in disbelief. She shook her head and slithered back to her throne.

"Well, that was a shocker, wasn't it?"

One final surprise awaited her. The naga had no clue how the hollow-looking woman in rags had sneaked into her throne room—but there she was, slouching on Yasgof's throne and dangling her skinny legs off the side.

"You!"

"You were expecting Barl and Despor?" Vanessa grinned. "Nice little show all of you put on. You should thank me for sending him to you on a silver platter."

"I—"

"After all, he was going to try to break out—and no doubt get himself killed in the process. It's a good thing I delayed him until just the right moment, or you would have really been up a creek."

"I don't think—" Yasgof began, drawing herself up indignantly.

"Good. It doesn't suit you."

Yasgof gritted her teeth, clenched her fists...then sighed, lowering her head.

"Yes, mistress."

"And furthermore," Grawkor pointed out accusingly, "you've been getting as unprofessional as the rest of this guild."

"But—"

"No excuses!" She tapped her fingers impatiently on the throne. "This whole fiasco could have been taken care of months ago. That slop you call strategy is terrible. It's thirty lashes for you once I clean up what's left of this mess."

"Yes, mistress," Yasgof repeated, keeping her head down.

"You have the scroll?"

"Of course."

"Well, in the name of Spider-Legged Me, don't just stand there watching the floor! Go get it!"

The naga easily located it with her mind, floating it out of the backpack and into Grawkor's hands. She broke the seal and unfurled it, reading the complex cryptographic runes with ease.

"Two dozen eggs, one pound of flour, bag of cookies, one new Supervisor." She grinned impishly. "You say it wasn't even opened?"

"No." Yasgof shook her head. "When the assassin bearing your scroll was captured, he was in the middle of an independant commission."

"Typical. You can always depend on people to put their own needs ahead of yours." She rolled the scroll back up. "Next time, I'll just do my own shopping. Though if I knew putting that last one on there would make it come true, I would've added a few more things…"

"You didn't know?" Yasgof gasped.

"Not all of it, no. You have to be flexible, Yasgof. Always have a backup plan for every step along the way. And be ready to toss it all into a blender at a moment's notice and improvise."

"I see," she nodded, digesting this latest bit of wisdom.

Grawkor smiled a little. Yasmine was such a good pupil. It was amazing how her passion for her position never died, even after all this time. People like that were a rare and valuable commodity. One of Grawkor's favorite, in fact.

"Yasgof?"

"Yes?"

The Pflatlands

"If you're a good girl, I'll make it forty lashes."

"Thank you, mistress." It wasn't the regular sixty, but it was better than nothing.

"Now leave us," the goddess yawned. "We have business elsewhere."

With a final bow, Yasgof blurred, then disappeared from the throne room. Grawkor stood and stretched. The rags from her prisoner disguise writhed and melted, congealing into a sharp suit and tie. Every time, Yasgof reminded her that the clothes were meant for males; Grawkor neither cared nor saw a point in splitting hairs. She could be male if she wanted to be. She just saw no reason. Over 65% of sentient races considered the female the less threatening of the species. The tactical advantage was wonderful.

The world around her faded to misty, hazy echoes as she stepped over the barrier between dimensions. She looked around the room's ethereal underpinnings for a specific someone. After all that had happened, she would almost certainly be nearby. She located her just outside—a young girl of ten years, seated on the floor and playing with her dolls.

"Thank you." The Goddess of Treachery approached and smiled sincerely.

"What?" The child looked up from her dolls, noticing Grawkor for the first time.

"Nothing." She stooped to look at the girl's toys. "Lifelike figures you've got there."

"Oh, yes," she nodded happily. Her eyes were two different shades as she met Grawkor's gaze, the colors always changing but never matching. "This one's a kitty! Meow! He's one of my favorites."

"Mine, too," Grawkor mumbled absently.

"And this one's brand new. She's really strong—grr!—but she can be mean sometimes. She has glasses you can take off. See?"

"It sounds very amusing." Grawkor stood, patting the child on her head. Her jester's cap jingled merrily. "Keep up the good work."

"Would you like a banana, fanged lady?" the little girl asked, waving the fruit around.

"No, but thank you."

R. D. Hammond

EPILOGUE

Dahn was leaning back on a branch, his nose buried in a book*, when the doors to his jungle simulacrum parted.

«Incoming!» a familiar voice called out.

Dahn slipped into the black silk robe hanging from his branch in one easy, graceful motion. He surveyed the trees for the best route down. Zero and Geoffrey had responded impressively to his requests. The forest was now a dangerous, ever-shifting mess of branches and vines. He could never take the same path twice, and he absolutely loved it.

«Hello?» Sarah wandered farther from the door, peering into the treetops. The mock forest was utterly silent. «Dahn?»

There was a gentle poke in her kidneys. She jumped.

«Gotcha,» Dahn grinned, hanging from a low branch by one arm.

«Wonderful. You're actually taking this Supervisor thing seriously.»

---

*High Common for *Imbeciles*.

The Pflatlands

«Not really.» He dropped to the ground with a soft thump. «It's fun to sneak up on people, but I could never kill them.»

«That'll be tough to explain to Yasgof the next time you see her.»

«I'll worry about that when the time comes.»

«'When the time comes,'» she repeated, teasingly. «Jar'lin, you get one little title attached to your name, and your head swells up to twice its size. Look at you, with your important silk robe! And just two weeks after getting your ribs kicked in!»

«Look at you, too! This is the first time I've ever seen you in a…dress?»

«Yes, it's called a dress. I actually own some. Not a lot, but some.» She modeled the deep blue, spaghetti-strapped sundress with a small twirl. The heavy boots and Ring of Strength remained, however. You couldn't take the ranger out of Sarah. «I still can't believe how fast you healed up. You Kars are just full of surprises.»

«I guess so,» Dahn smiled modestly. His ribs were still taped, it still hurt to breathe, and the missing part of his fang would never grow back. Nevertheless, Sarah was right. Kars healed fast. «As are you, Sara.»

«Hey now. Don't start. You're the only person I don't yell at regularly for calling me that.»

«Well, it is a title of reverence, even if you don't want the responsibility.» He changed the subject to avoid an unnecessary argument. «I've been brushing up on my High Common lately. Maybe one of these days, I won't need translation spells.»

"Oh?" Sarah asked. "How's it coming?"

"Not." His accent was thick and alien. Sarah had never heard anything like it before. "Me still get words wrong. And it is lots of problems with placement good of adjectives. Very different of Kar. Hard to do now this."

"I see." Sarah struggled to keep from laughing. "Well, keep working on it."

"Thank you."

"You're welcome."

An awkward silence passed.

«So,» Dahn continued, «I guess you're here to tell me you're leaving.»

«Yeah. Tor and Seline have already left for Argury, and I figured it would be best if I cut out, too. Groeke reported just enough information to dad to get his paycheck, and I don't want to be around if the High Guard gets nosy.»

«Groeke's going with you?»

«No, thankfully. I finally convinced him I can get by just fine on my own. Just three days ago, he walks up to me, and he says—» Sarah mocked the monk's deep, rumbling voice. «'Sara Danoor, the truest wisdom is seeing wisdom in others, and the true reward of wisdom is watching wisdom grow. I thank you.' And that's it. He's just up and gone the next day.»

«That's Groeke, all right. What do you have planned?»

«I thought I'd go back to school for a while—you know, get an actual guild license in something. It never hurts to diversify.»

«I thought you were already a ranger?»

«I never took the licensing exams. It's more fun to undermine the good ol' boys as an independent.»

«Oh. What are you thinking of studying, then?»

«Magic,» she replied, after some thought. «Some of my ancestors possessed The Gift. I think I'll get tested for it as well. If I have it, it might be good to learn some magic. You never know when it'll come in handy.»

«What type?» Dahn didn't bother asking if that was legal. Even if Yasgof wasn't lying about it, Sarah was going to do whatever she wanted, laws or no.

«Conjuring, probably. Creating things out of pure aether just…appeals to me. I don't know.»

«I'm sure you'll make a fine conjurer.» He smiled warmly.

«What about you? How are you going to kill time between now and the next time Yasgof beats down your door?»

«I thought I'd apprentice myself to Geoffrey and Zero, honestly. Their machines are absolutely fascinating, and they do things with them I'd never even dreamed of. I'd really like to learn from them.»

The Pflatlands

Sarah suddenly had two separate and distinctly unpleasant mental images. One was of how much worse a technomantic disaster would be with Dahn involved. In the other, he somehow created a being even more annoying than Seline. She forced both from her mind through no small exertion of willpower.

«And...» Dahn hesitated. «Maybe when Yasgof comes back, I can use the Guild to find my sister.»

«That's what you were planning that all along, weren't you? When you accepted the position.»

«At any rate,» he continued quickly, «if you're intent on leaving, you should probably do it soon. It's bound to get colder over the next few weeks.»

«Oh, yes. No time like the present.» Sarah left through the woven branch archway.

I was also saving your life, he thought while quietly filing out behind her, because I love you. And probably always will.

Zero and Geoffrey had parked themselves on the leather couch in their uniquely decorated den. One of their crystal screens was attached to a familiar ORB, along with a pair of speakers. A frantic voice and a cacophony of boos poured out of them.

"Oh my Gods, fans! This is terrible! Lord Badass is leading a five-on-one attack on The World's Most Dangerous Monk!"

"C'mon, Groeke!" Geoffrey shouted at the screen. "Get your ass up and start cracking heads! You're not getting paid the big silver to lose to a bunch of mid-carders!"

"I still can't believe how the bookers keep throwing these huge groups at him." Zero munched from a bowl of potato chips. "I realize most quo'chi-ka fans are gullible, but they're going to run out of opponents if they keep this up."

"It's what the fans want to see. Besides, Groeke always makes the other guys look good. He's a pro like that."

"Oh, no!" the announcer shouted. "The tablet! They're going to slam him through the giant stone tablet The Prophet brings to the ring!"

"I CAN'T BELIEVE YOU TWO GO FOR THIS," the ORB commented from behind the screen. "BESIDES, DO YOU KNOW HOW TICKED OFF CHAMPIONSHIP QUO'CHIA-KA WOULD BE IF THEY FOUND YOUR TRANSMITTER? THEY'D COME DOWN ON YOU LIKE A TON OF BRICKS!"

"Shut up and hold the screen steady." Geoffrey was watching intensely.

A circular rift in the room's dimensional space opened, and Sarah and Dahn stepped through.

"If he takes this," Zero noted about Groeke's predicament, "I'll be rather impressed."

"If he takes this," Geoffrey noted about Groeke's predicament, "he's insane."

"What are you two watching?" Sarah wrinkled her nose in disgust.

"Shh!" both mages hissed.

"They're going to do it! No! Somebody stop this! The humanity—wait—wait! They can't get him up! They can't get that massive frame of Farkhis' up!"

"Uh, oh!" Geoffrey shouted gleefully. "It's on now!"

Sure enough, Groeke swatted away one of his opponents with a forearm shot that, in Sarah's opinion, came nowhere near its target. Nevertheless, the exhibitionist flipped and sprawled as if he had been hit by a dive-bombing dragon. Groeke then unleashed a series of moves that Sarah found awfully familiar.

"I don't believe this. He took that sequence right out of the fight with the assassins!"

"Look at them run!" Zero cheered triumphantly.

The exhibitionist in black platemail escaped through the crowd. Meanwhile, Groeke destroyed the last of his minions to thunderous cheers, capping it off with a violent slam that Stan Chryzdolf would have been well acquainted with.

"Stoicizer! Stoicizer! Good gawds! Farkhis cleans house! His Lordship has left the building with his tail between his legs! The World' Most Dangerous Monk rules the circled square once again! This was the best quo'chi-ka exhibition ever!"

The screen faded to black. Burdened by screens and speakers, Greg-

The Pflatlands

ory flew away without another word, intent on getting the contraptions off as soon as possible.

"That sucked!" Geoffrey glared. "I was expecting Badass and Groeke to go at it!"

"Well," Zero replied, "you have to realize that they're building towards the big pay-per-seat exhibition this weekend—"

"How anyone so intellectual could watch anything so lame-brained is, and forever will be, beyond me." Sarah rolled her eyes.

"Yeah, whatever." Geoffrey pointedly dismissed her.

"Anyway, I'm out of here. Is my transport ready?"

"It is." Zero stood. "As you requested, we acquired a hopper instead of a horse. Traveling economically, eh?"

"Yeah. Ugh, I'm not looking forward to this. I've only ridden a hopper once, and the little bastard almost threw me into a bog on the first jump. Still, thank you."

"No worries!"

"You're really leaving, huh?" Geoffrey had stood as well.

"Uh-huh. I'll probably head west from here. They've got some really good colleges in that area—plus, my father will be so busy looking for me around Argury, he won't even think to check his own backyard."

"You know," Geoffrey began, "if I'd have known you were the High Sara…"

"Yeah?" Sarah crossed her arms.

"…It probably wouldn't have made a damned bit of difference to me."

"I think," Sarah said, breaking into a smile, "that's the nicest thing you've ever said to me."

"Sure. Are you going to eat those chips, Zero?"

"All yours, my friend. I'll see you off as well, Sarah."

"Suit yourself."

•

Outside the tower, Sarah checked her hopper while Dahn looked on. It was an ugly beast to look at, with a long, smooth head, small fangs,

248

and huge legs that took up most of its mass. Hoppers were even uglier in disposition, but, as Zero had said, the odd creature was clearly the economical choice. It could ride for days on the smallest amount of food, water, and rest—providing you could stay in the saddle. That particular task was going to be even more difficult with the full saddlebags.

«So, I guess this is it,» Sarah said sadly.

«Not really.»

«I suppose you're going to tell me something sappy now, like, there's no words in Kar for goodbye?»

«There are, but we only say them during funerals.»

«Interesting.» She verbally stumbled. «Look, Dahn. There's something I wanted to say before I left. About what Yasgof said—»

«Forget it.» Dahn silenced her with a single upright hand.

«No.» She shook her head. «It's important—to me, at least. Dahn, we have to be honest with each other. Assuming we actually had something between us, even a brief spark, we'd make a horrible couple. It would be you constantly doting on me, and me yelling at you to go away, and it wouldn't ever stop.»

«We'd have some great times, though…»

«Yeah, in the two weeks before we killed each other.» She took Dahn's hands in hers. «Listen, we have a great friendship. I don't want to ruin that. Forget about me. You're one of a kind, by any race's standards. There are a million beautiful girls from a ton of different races out there. You're going to find another girl someday, and you're going to make her very happy.»

«Yes,» he smiled, «and she'll be nothing like you.»

«Dahn…»

«I didn't say,» he added with a grin, «that this is a bad thing.»

Sarah shook her head. She leaned forward and pressed her lips against his. The kiss was prolonged, but there was no passion in it—just pure, undying loyalty.

«Now we're even,» she said.

"Kunjahkihru," Dahn replied.

«Come again?»

«Good fortunes, Sara.»

The Pflatlands

«Same to you, Dahn. Same to you.»

He backed away, giving her room to mount.

The ranger settled into the saddle, gripped the beast with her knees, said a brief prayer to the God of the Hunt, then snapped the single rein. The creature flexed its powerful legs and bounded across the grass. Dahn watched it carry the High Sara up the sharp slope of the valley in just three or four leaps. With one final, explosive hurdle, they both disappeared over the rim.

«Well, that's that.» Zero nodded from next to the tower, satisfied. «It was a pleasure meeting her. She was a fine young girl.»

«You talk as if you don't expect to see her again.»

«I don't, honestly.» Zero climbed the rope ladder leading to a hole in the side of the tower—this week's entrance. «Sarah strikes me as the type of girl who doesn't visit the same place twice.»

«She will.» Dahn began his own climb behind him. «Eventually.»

«Oh? What makes you so certain?»

«Are you at all familiar with the Kar concept of 'kihr mahk nahr dremohlta'—appropriate and friendly fate?»

«No, but it sounds fascinating. Tell you what. I'll have Geoffrey brew us all a nice cup of coffee, and you can tell us all about it.»

«Fair enough,» Dahn nodded, with one final look into the horizon.